THROUGH STORM AND NIGHT

LAUREN JANKOWSKI

Crimson Fox
PUBLISHING

TURNER, OREGON

THROUGH STORM AND NIGHT: Book Two of the Shape Shifter Chronicles

Published by Crimson Fox Publishing
www.crimsonfoxpublishing.com

Cover art by Najla Qamber Designs.

This is a work of fiction. Names, characters, places, and incidents either are the product of the author's imagination or are used fictitiously. Any resemblance to actual events, locales, organizations, or persons, living or dead, is entirely coincidental and beyond the intent of either the author or the publisher.

ISBN: 978-1-946202-45-1

Second Edition.

DEDICATION

For anyone who has ever gone after an impossible dream

Lauren Jankowski

CHAPTER ONE

In the week before Christmas, the mall was packed with people frantically seeking out last minute gifts. Clothes flew off the shelves — as did games, books, jewelry, and of course, toys. The shoppers had bundled up in their warmest clothes, mostly dull in color, and appeared to be nothing more than dots of gray and muted red moving about on the polished tile floor. In the center of the mall, an artificial pine tree stretched from the floor to the ceiling. Cheap ornaments, garishly colored with sparkling paints and glues, hung on the green plastic branches. The base of the tree was covered in fake snow and a small train had been set up for children, offering their parents a few moments of peace. Christmas carols blared over the speaker system, occasionally interrupted for news of a sale in one of the many stores.

On the second level, a woman leaned against the imitation chrome cylinder that served as a railing, looking below her with disinterest. She glanced at the brown leather watch on her right wrist. He was late. Typical. Onyx straightened up, running her large hands over the smooth railing. She was waiting for Blackjack and she had a feeling he was late just to piss her off.

It had been about five months since the change in leadership among the assassins, culminating in the brutal deaths of Adara and Gia. Neither Onyx nor Blackjack had lost much sleep over it, both having bigger things to be concerned about. Loyalty was never the most important thing to assassins. Money, however, was vital, and that was exactly what Adara's biggest client offered the two assassins, the man who helped Blackjack take the position Adara had held for many years. They didn't know much about the man. He was powerful — more powerful than anyone they had ever encountered before. He had made contact the night after the debacle with the Four, but would only communicate with Blackjack and had no interest in speaking with Onyx. As long as he paid, she couldn't care less.

Onyx glanced to the right and blinked a few times, not believing her eyes. Blackjack was approaching, but he looked different. He no longer wore his brown trench coat, or any of his usual apparel. Instead, he wore a powder blue shirt and tan slacks, which made him look like an CEO on vacation.

"What the *hell*?" Onyx said the first thing that popped into her mind. Blackjack just glanced to the lower level, ignoring her.

"The sun rose red today," he mentioned, resting his weight against the railing, not looking at Onyx. His eyes stayed focused on the people below them. People rushed around on the second level as well. A few men glanced in Onyx's direction, taking in her toned body with suggestive eyes. It took every ounce of will power Onyx had not to throw punches. Humans were a plague and she would not miss them when they inevitably died out.

"Been at the vodka again, Blackjack?" she asked. What remained of her patience was long gone. Blackjack met her yellow eyes.

"I suppose it's lucky we're not at sea," he replied in a bored tone.

"Do we have a job or did you just want to watch the fascinating spectacle of parasites losing their minds over yet another holiday?"

Blackjack smirked as he continued watching the stressed out humans below them. Onyx shook her head and looked out over the mall, knowing she could be a smartass to him because he owed her. Only a few months prior, the legendary assassin had narrowly escaped capture by the Four. Onyx had helped him get away unseen.

"He's sending out a team," Blackjack replied evenly. "Which means we must act as gracious hosts and make some changes to accommodate them."

Onyx frowned. "Changes?"

Blackjack grinned, a gleeful spark in his eye. The two assassins glanced below them when they heard the sound of a child screaming. A young boy dressed mostly in blue was clinging onto the small train, refusing to leave. "Rudolph the Red Nosed Reindeer" started playing on the mall's sound system, masking the sounds of the young human's tantrum.

"Funny how humans think of color. If an animal in a song aimed at children has a red nose, it's considered adorable. Yet red is also the color of danger, sex, and of course, blood," Blackjack continued thinking aloud.

"Yeah, it's a mad world," Onyx retorted with a roll of her eyes. "What kind of changes?"

"Mr. Carding, the Corporation's liaison, requires that we dress in proper attire and follow a few other . . . small rules of his," Blackjack responded as he looked at her clothing. Onyx's yellow eyes narrowed as she crossed her toned arms. She was wearing a contemporary look with subtle western touches, nothing that made her stand out.

"What do you mean proper attire?" she growled. She knew Blackjack thought he was above her and that was why he enjoyed tormenting her. He wanted her to recognize his status as a better assassin and it was annoying as hell.

"He's quite strict about the way subordinates dress and behave around him and his associates," he replied, enjoying how infuriated she was. "They abhor the color black, so under no circumstances are we to have anything black on us, weapons included. You are not allowed to carry a weapon in their presence. You must wear a modest business suit, neutral in color. No pants or slacks, you have to wear a skirt that goes down to at least your knees. Your hair has to be tied back, tightly—"

"You have *got* to be kidding me," Onyx grumbled, interrupting Blackjack. She ran a hand through her long dark hair.

"I never kid. Should you break any of his rules, the team will not hesitate to eliminate you," Blackjack finished. Onyx glared at him, not believing her ears.

"So basically I'm to act as a pet the entire time the team is here," she summarized, scowling when Blackjack nodded. "What about you?"

"What about me?" Blackjack asked. Onyx pointedly looked him up and down.

"According to you, they don't like black. What about your name? Should I just call you Jack?" she asked, obviously baiting him. Blackjack shook his head.

"They have no problem with my name. We already discussed it. I will also have to wear neutral colors for the duration of their stay, but it will be worth it to see you wearing a skirt," he responded coolly.

"Blackjack, if you wanted to see my legs, you only had to ask," Onyx replied with a teasing smile.

"You are also expected to conduct yourself *modestly*, which means no wanton flirtation or cussing." Blackjack berated her as if Onyx were a misbehaving child. "And remember, it has to be a modest business suit. Don't dress like a common rodeo prostitute for once."

Onyx clenched her jaw so tight it felt like it would snap. She was beginning to tire of the cloak-and-dagger routine. She didn't understand why they couldn't just kill the hybrid bastard in the old-fashioned way. Clenching her fists a few times, Onyx finally nodded in acquiescence.

"There's a good girl," Blackjack praised, turning to look back at the shoppers below them. "If all goes well, soon we'll no longer have to share space with these parasites."

"When will the Corporation's people arrive?" Onyx asked.

"End of the week," Blackjack answered. "You're to pick the team up at the train station and drop them off wherever they want. You are not to speak to them unless you're spoken to. You won't be."

"I thought they'd be staying with us."

"You thought wrong. They don't share quarters with subordinates." Blackjack glanced over to Onyx. "And you are not to interfere with their business. We're to be their servants for however long they stay, meaning we do what we're told and don't ask questions."

Onyx rolled her eyes. "You're sure we need them?"

"The Grenich Corporation is more powerful than any client we've had before. You want to be on the right side of a war, or you'll end up another nameless casualty," Blackjack responded in a tone that clearly told her the matter was closed. She shrugged, not concerned with anything other than being paid. Grenich was paying a good sum to her and Blackjack to stay the hell out of the way for the most part. They were to act as inside informants, city guides, and nothing more. It was a strange request, but the Corporation paid enough for their silence. Somewhere below them, the high-pitched scream of another child's tantrum echoed throughout the mall.

"We both have things to do. You need a new wardrobe and I have business to attend to," Blackjack said, pushing off the railing he had been leaning on.

"Still looking for the Key?" Onyx asked, cocking an eyebrow at the legendary assassin. She knew how angry he was about his failure to retrieve the Key months ago. It had practically been in his hands and he still managed to lose it.

"No," he grumbled. Onyx snorted and shook her head. She loved it when Blackjack failed. It reminded him he was nothing special.

"Face it, Blackjack. You're losing your touch. Best to just let the team do their job," Onyx comforted with mock sympathy. Blackjack turned away from her and she knew it was because he didn't want to give her the satisfaction of seeing him angry. She just smirked as she looked across the mall again. They were both lower than official Grenich operatives, but in the world of assassins, Blackjack still assumed he was top dog. It amused Onyx to no end the few times he was proven wrong.

"I'm going to make sure everything is in order for the team's arrival. Go get a skirt, and try to behave," he called over his shoulder, disappearing around a corner.

Onyx turned to leave the opposite way. She knew if she wanted to live to see another day, she'd have to follow Carding's ridiculous demands. She didn't like it, but she would do it. No assassin knew much about Carding or Grenich. Few had even heard of the powerful organization. The only thing they knew about Grenich was if someone crossed or disobeyed the organization or its operatives, that unfortunate individual would vanish, never to be seen or heard from again.

Onyx walked back into the crowd of frantic human shoppers. Something big was coming, and she wanted to make sure she was on the right side of whatever it was.

~~*~*~*

In the Meadows, Isis sat in the meeting room of the guardian women. Four individuals sat across from her. Aneurin, head of the guardian men, sat to the right, near the end of the table, studying the parchment in front of him. Jet and Lilly, head of the faction of shape shifters called protectors, sat to the left — Jet looking less than pleased. Lilly had a neutral expression, with her hands crossed in front of her on the table. Adonia, queen of the guardian women, sat between Jet and Aneurin. She looked calm and gracious as ever. Isis bit the inside of her cheek in pure annoyance. Almost five months had passed since the whole debacle with Coop and the Key and Aneurin still insisted on holding "meetings," which Isis was convinced were held to make her feel like a criminal.

Her arms were crossed over her chest, her fingers rhythmically drumming against her bicep. The long wooden table in front of her was bare save for the parchment that sat in front of the two guardians and the leaders of the protectors. She assumed it was a record of offenses she had committed. Isis continued to sit still, just staring straight ahead, and biting her tongue. After a moment, she started fidgeting with her clothing. She was wearing one of her favorite black backless tops with grayish-tan pants and black boots that went above her ankle. She had planned to go shopping downtown with Shae, until Jet sprang the news of the meeting on her. Isis had been about to protest, but saw how angry he was and chose to keep her complaints to herself.

Isis looked at the individuals across from her again, studying them. Her eyes fell on Adonia, her biological great-grandmother. She wore a soft lilac dress made of a shimmering material Isis recognized as guardian silk. It added to the grace Adonia always exuded. She glanced up and her soft green eyes met Isis' — which were also green today — and she smiled at her. Isis smiled politely back before looking over at Jet.

Jet wore a dark blue shirt and black jeans, which made him stand out in the Meadows. He didn't seem to care. Isis chalked it up to the fact that Jet had practically been raised in the Meadows. He was more at ease around the guardians than any other shape shifter Isis had met in the short time since discovering her heritage. He sat tilted back in his ornate wooden chair, arms folded across his chest. It was hard to say who was more fed up with the frequent meetings: Isis or Jet.

Beside him sat his lovely wife, Lilly. She held herself with a regal air, clothed in a dress of bright green velvet, which made her sapphire blue eyes stand out. Lilly also seemed comfortable in the Meadows, but Isis knew it was likely because she had originally been a guardian before she had become a leader of the protectors. Lilly was a wise and levelheaded leader, someone who Isis had grown to respect since she came to live at the mansion. Lilly studied the parchment before her, her slender fingers drifting over the gold lily charm she wore at her throat.

Isis next looked to the final man, who was sitting at the opposite end of the table. Aneurin sat on Adonia's right side. He wore a dark blue tunic with gold trim, something similar to how Isis always pictured the ancient Greeks dressing. He had dark brown hair and light blue eyes. He drummed his fingers on the table. Pursing his lips as he studied the parchment, his eyes drifted back and forth over the print, but Isis doubted he was actually reading whatever was written on there. Aneurin finally dropped the parchment and folded his hands on it, smiling at Isis. It was a smile that made her want to smack him.

"Well, I can hardly remember our last meeting. It feels like it has been half an eternity," Aneurin said, chuckling at his own joke.

"It was last week," Jet grumbled, his eyes remaining on the ceiling. Lilly whispered his name and shook her head when he glanced over at her. Isis tried not to smile at the leader's retort, which proved near impossible. Though she would never outright admit it, Isis truly admired Jet. He knew when to make a stand and when to back down. In the short time she had known him, Isis could always count on him to have her back.

"I'm sorry, Jet. Not all of us live among mortals," Aneurin sighed. His tone, though congenial, indicated that was a barb at Jet. Jet put the legs of the chair back on the floor, clenching his jaw. Isis continued to fidget with the sleeve of her shirt, boredom beginning to get the better of her.

"Aneurin, perhaps you could just tell us the purpose of this meeting," Adonia suggested evenly. Jet looked in Isis' direction, though not directly at her, and shook his head. Lilly kept her attention on the two guardians.

"All right. Isis," Aneurin turned back to her with the same infuriating smile. "Where is Coop?"

"Not again," Jet muttered, running his hand over his hair and even Lilly sat back. Isis knew they were sick and tired of going over the damn incident repeatedly. She could tell Jet was angry with her for the possible part she played in Coop's escape, but he was even angrier with Aneurin for making it seem like she had caused the entire event.

"Jet," Adonia warned, looking to the exasperated shape shifter. Jet shook his head and straightened his posture. Isis kept her eyes on Aneurin's, her gaze unwavering.

"I don't know," she answered truthfully.

"Mm," he nodded as he looked back to the parchment in front of him. "Please refresh my memory. You met him in a bar, correct?"

"A dance club, to be specific," Isis responded. Jet, Lilly, and Adonia remained silent, allowing Aneurin to continue his questioning.

"That's right. Tell me, what were you doing there?" Aneurin continued, sitting back in the ornate chair. Isis remembered her sister telling her that most of the furniture in the Meadows had been hand-carved by the messengers of the forest realm. Everything in the Meadows had been handmade by guardians or messengers.

"Rebelling," she responded. Even though Isis was being a smartass, she was telling the truth. She was curious about where Aneurin was going with his vague line of questioning. Lilly glanced at her, but remained quiet.

"Was there any kind of," Aneurin tilted his head from

side to side as if searching for the right word, "attraction between the two of you?"

Jet, Lilly, and Adonia all twisted in their chairs, staring at him. They obviously had no idea where his questions were going.

"Aneurin, perhaps you could tell us what you're looking for?" Adonia asked. Isis could tell Jet wanted to say something as well, but was holding his tongue. Lilly had a quizzical expression but remained quiet.

"It's a simple question, Isis," Aneurin addressed her, not looking at the others at the table. "Please answer it."

"Aneurin, are you questioning her loyalty?" Lilly asked, her dark blue eyes not moving from the guardian. Aneurin turned to face Jet and Lilly, obviously fed up with what he saw as blatant disrespect.

"It's a legitimate question, especially considering the environment she's currently living in," he replied.

"The *environment* she's living in? It's going to be about my wife and me this time? There's a change," Jet snapped. Lilly laid a hand over his, saying his name again. Isis was surprised by the sudden hostility from the protector leader. She had heard Jet get annoyed at guardians before, but never outright angry. Then again, she had never heard a guardian blatantly insult his family the way Aneurin did.

"I think we're forgetting what she did—"

"What's this really about, Aneurin? This particular incident or how my family, not to mention Passion's, doesn't fit into your idea of an ideal world?" Jet demanded.

"Jet, that's not fair," Adonia attempted to interrupt the argument. Isis crossed her right leg over her left, waiting for Adonia and Lilly to break up the two men.

"I know this is hard for you to understand, but we have rules. You may not like all of them, but they keep things in order here," Aneurin answered, ignoring Adonia. Isis let out a soft sigh and rubbed her eyes, irritated with the old argument.

One of the guardian's sacred laws stated no shape

shifter could have a romantic relationship with a guardian. The relationship between the two races was to be strictly platonic — a business association. They could have friendships, but that was incredibly rare because the shape shifters remained on Earth and the guardians in the Meadows. The consequences of a guardian pursuing a relationship with a shape shifter, or any other being besides a guardian, were that the guardian would be stripped of their title and banished from the Meadows. It was a law that had been strictly enforced for millennia, longer than most of the current guardians had been alive. According to her twin sister, Electra, three guardians had broken that sacred law but only two were stripped of their title. One of the two guardians happened to be Lilly, who was allowed to visit the Meadows because she was one of the leaders of the protectors.

The third guardian, Isis and Electra's mother, Passion, was allowed to remain in the Meadows and keep her title. However, there had been consequences for her actions, one of which included giving up Isis to be raised as a human. Her right to marry was also stripped, as was her right to have more children. Isis and Electra were to be her only heirs and even though they were part guardian and part shape shifter, they were classified as guardians. Though Isis lived with protectors and was even part of the Four, she was still considered a guardian. This fact was beginning to grate on her nerves.

"No, no! This is completely ridiculous!" Jet's angry voice interrupted Isis' thoughts, bringing her back to the present. Isis had to do something. She slammed her hands flat on the table. The loud bang successfully drew the attention of the four people in front of her and she looked at them for a moment before speaking.

"Okay, now that I have your attention," she began, "I think we are wasting too much time concerned about Coop. He seems to be unimportant compared to the Key. Yes, I realize he punched through unbreakable glass and yes, I know he healed at a rate that can only be described as unnaturally fast, but these seem to be trivial matters. Why don't we try to focus on more pressing issues? If Coop is connected to the Key, which seems likely, then he's bound to turn up in our investigation eventually."

"You're awfully quick to defend him," Aneurin commented, casually. Isis narrowed her eyes at him.

"He didn't try to kill me. Onyx, on the other hand, did. I choose to pick my battles," she replied. "Now, can I please go and salvage whatever is left of my evening?"

Adonia glanced between Jet, Lilly, and Aneurin before turning back to Isis, nodding once. "You, Jet, and Lilly are dismissed. Furthermore, I'm closing this matter for the time being. We have reviewed the information enough and Isis is right. There are more pressing matters that we need to focus on."

Isis nodded gratefully. She stood up and disappeared in a flash of brilliant silver light.

~~*~*~*

Isis opened her eyes when the familiar scent of Jet's study filled her nose. She always closed her eyes when Appearing since the bright silver light was blinding.

It had been a little more than a year, to her estimate, since she had left behind her "normal" life to fulfill her destiny as part of the Four. Since then, Isis had become more adept at keeping her cool. Before, the meetings with Aneurin would likely have sent her into a fit of rage. Now, they were a mere annoyance that was quickly forgotten. Even though she was more levelheaded, her personality remained her own.

Aside from becoming more composed, Isis had also learned quite a few skills, including fighting. She was proficient in hand-to-hand combat and a skilled warrior, better than she could have ever imagined. She could even toss Jade around a bit, despite the centuries of experience the older shape shifter had on her. Remington, the Four's trainer, was very pleased with her progress.

Isis glanced over her shoulder when she spotted light out of the corner of her eye. Jet and Lilly soon appeared in a flash of blue light. *Oh goody, here it comes,* she thought as she put her hands on her hips, awaiting the inevitable scolding. Jet, however, simply stepped around her and exited the study. Isis frowned and glanced at Lilly, who shrugged her shoulders in response. Isis rubbed the side of her nose, knowing both protector leaders were upset with her — Jet in particular. She followed him out into the hall. The mansion was silent around them. It was still early in the evening and the other shape shifters were out enjoying life or sleeping.

"Jet?" Isis called when he didn't acknowledge her presence.

"I'm not going to talk about this anymore, Isis," was his reply. He didn't even glance over his shoulder at her. Isis continued to follow him, recognizing the disappointment in his tone.

"Look, I really believe Coop is on our side. He said there were others who needed his help," Isis insisted. Jet snorted humorlessly as he continued on his way to the kitchen.

"Of course, because our enemies would never think to lie. That would just be crazy," Jet said as he entered the large kitchen. It was dark, most of the staff having retired for the evening. A quiet hum suggested a couple dishwashers were still on. Jet reached over to the wall, switching on the lights over the counters.

"Fair enough, but what if he was telling the truth, Jet?" Isis responded as she leaned her weight against the counter. "What if there are a lot of people or shape shifters who do need his help and you kept him in the dungeons?"

Jet gave her a skeptical look, to which she shrugged and spread her hands. She watched as he opened the stainless steel fridge and grabbed a large red and gold apple. He pulled a knife from the large block on the counter near the fridge and sliced into the apple.

"If that's the case, hopefully Sly can find him and we can offer our assistance," he responded, focusing on slicing the apple. Isis bit her lower lip, unsure of how to feel about that.

"Are you still mad at me?" she asked, changing the subject.

"I'm always mad at you, but why should you start caring now?" Jet asked with a small half-smile. Isis grinned and shook her head as she turned and left the kitchen. Things were okay with Jet, and that was enough for now.

She left the kitchen and made her way down the long hall to the stairs, jogging up to the second floor. The art on the walls became a blur as she made her way to her room.

When she reached her door, Isis pushed down on the gold handle and opened it. She closed it behind her and locked it; crossing the room to her nightstand and switching on the lamp. Isis made her way over to the bed and reached in between the mattress and the box-spring. Her fingers closed around a thin spiral, which she pulled out from its hiding place. Flipping it open, Isis glanced at the scribbled notes she had written. It chronicled everything she knew about Coop and some theories she had drawn from her few encounters with him.

Isis turned to a clean page and sketched the symbol she had seen on the wall of the warehouse the night she had photographed the murder scene. The one that had disappeared. She carefully drew the long backwards "P" and the odd crossed patterns that Steve told her resembled cuneiform. A strange assortment of stripes and arrows was on the right. The left side consisted of simpler lines with ninety-degree angles. It was a symbol she would never forget; one that was forever burned in her memory. Isis chewed on the end of the pen, looking at the page. That had been before she had found out about shape shifters and guardians, which seemed like a lifetime ago.

Isis rubbed her forehead, thinking about the mysterious Coop. Even though she believed the protectors truly wanted to help him, Isis didn't think they could. Jet and Lilly, though more flexible than the guardians, were still in a position of authority. Being leaders of the protectors meant they had a responsibility to follow rules and uphold their laws. If they captured Coop, he would undoubtedly spend some time in the dungeons. Even if he didn't, Jet and Lilly would still need to ask him a number of questions and then figure out the best strategy. There was no telling how much time they would waste doing that. If there were shape shifters in danger, time seemed to be of the essence. Coop didn't strike Isis as someone who had a lot of time to waste, especially considering how quickly he disappeared after the fight at the Obsidian Manor.

Isis sighed and glanced towards the window, studying the dark sky. Her night was definitely unsalvageable. Even if it wasn't, Isis was no longer in the mood to go out. She put the spiral in the nightstand drawer and moved over to the wardrobe, pulling out her nightclothes. After she had changed, Isis pulled back the covers on the bed, climbing underneath before reaching up and switching off the lamp.

CHAPTER TWO

Phil finished closing up Dionysia, the arrival of dawn signaling business was done until the next evening. He enjoyed his job; bartending came naturally to him. Sure, the music was awful and the occasional rowdy drunk was a bother, but it paid well.

He flipped the last switch and grabbed his coat from where it rested on the back of one of the chairs. It had been a slow night, typical for winter. The club filled late and emptied early. The crowd was noticeably thin due to people going home for the holidays. Christmas just wasn't the season for club goers. He bundled up and made his way to the front door, stepping out into the frigid day and shutting the door behind him. Twisting the key and sliding the deadbolt into place, Phil turned to face the icy winter morning.

"Yah!" he let out a startled yell at the sight of a woman standing to his left. He hadn't heard her approach. She was wearing a long charcoal-gray coat and her hands were hidden in the deep pockets. Sunglasses with clear lavender lenses covered her eyes. She was wearing black boots with a small heel.

"I'm sorry, I didn't mean to scare you," the woman said

with an apologetic smile.

"You didn't," Phil replied, a little defensively. She raised an eyebrow, obviously not buying his response. *She could at least pretend and let me salvage what remaining dignity I have left,* Phil thought as he moved away from the door.

"Club's closed," he said. She was quick to follow him toward the employee parking lot around back.

"That's all right. I actually came to ask you a few questions, if you wouldn't mind," she replied. Phil turned to look at her, frowning.

"Questions? You a cop?"

"Fuck no!" She laughed with a shake of her head. "You don't recognize me, do you?"

"Uh, lady, I see a lot of people. Not a lot of them stand out," Phil replied. "Should I recognize you?"

"Probably not. I came to the club a long while back," she said. "I was with three of my friends, one of whom knew you, which I'm sure a lot of women do."

"Thank you," Phil interrupted, enjoying the ego stroke. The woman studied him for a moment, squinting a little, before shaking her head.

"Anyway, my name is Isis. I'm Shae Miller's cousin," she continued, her breath fogging in front of her when she spoke. "I'm looking for someone I met that night."

"I see. Does this mystery person have a name?" Phil asked, walking into the cold parking garage. At dawn, it looked a lot grungier and the graffiti was more noticeable.

"I came to the club last night to ask about him. No one seems to have heard of him or remembered anyone fitting his description. I figured that I might have a better chance asking the bartender, since I know you saw him when I came here the first time. He said his name was Mark Cooper, but he went by Coop," Isis replied, matching Phil's long pace as they continued down the rows of cars.

Phil frowned, vaguely recalling Coop. The man had stood out, though he seemed to be trying to do the opposite. He never drank, but spent most nights at the bar, like he was waiting for someone. The odd man always had a haunted look in his eyes, which was apparent the few times he had taken off his dark-tinted sunglasses. That was probably the one of the more unusual things about him: he usually wore sunglasses that concealed his eyes, even in the dark club. Phil had tried to ask him about it a few times, but Coop wasn't much of a conversationalist. The way he moved was eerie, with an ease and grace Phil had never seen before. It was as though the man had no bones. Coop was like a flesh and blood ghost, appearing and disappearing into thin air. Phil glanced at Isis again, vaguely remembering her coming into the club with her cousin and two other women. *Come to think of it, that was the last time I saw Coop*, he thought, remembering the way Coop had perked up when he spotted Isis. It was the first time Phil had seen him display anything remotely resembling emotion.

"Clean shaven guy, brown hair, about so high?" Phil asked as he gestured with his hand. "Always wearing sunglasses?"

"That's him," Isis confirmed, nodding. "And there was another man, black hair and a tan baseball cap. He spilled his drink all over Coop when we first met. He had a very similar manner."

"Ah, Dane," Phil said with a smile that was more like a grimace. He knew that guy a little better, which wasn't saying much. He was almost as mysterious as Coop, but he blended in a little better. Dane could often seamlessly blend into a group of people. Phil suspected him of being a pickpocket, but he never caught Dane in the act, so there was nothing he could do about it. Dane was charismatic with a capital "C." Phil always thought the man would make a great politician due to his silver tongue. It was impossible not to find the man appealing. There was just something about him that drew people in and captivated them.

"Dane?"

"Yeah, he occasionally comes into the club. I haven't seen Coop in a long while. I just assumed he moved or something," Phil answered as he came to his dark blue sedan.

Isis thought for a moment. "Have you seen Dane recently?"

Phil shrugged, pulling his keys out of his pocket and unlocking his door. "He might have been in here a few nights back, but I can't be sure. I caught a glimpse of someone who looked a lot like him, but their back was to me, so I can't be sure."

"Is he a regular?"

Phil shook his head. "Nah, he's pretty sporadic. If there's a pattern to his comings and goings, I haven't noticed it."

"Do you have any way to reach him? An address or a phone number?" Isis asked hopefully.

Phil laughed. "Yeah, I have addresses for all the patrons of the club."

Isis shrugged. "You seem to have a rapport with him. I just assumed you two were friends."

"I don't think anyone is friends with Dane. He always leaves alone, despite the fact that most of the patrons are usually fawning all over him. The guy's alluring, probably because no one knows anything about him," Phil replied. Isis nodded, looking a little troubled.

"Ever seen any other patrons like them?" Isis asked.

Phil shook his head. "Can't say that I have. Those two were both one of a kind, which is really the only reason I remember them. I've really got to be getting home, so if you don't mind . . . ?"

"Thank you for your time," Isis said as she turned to leave.

"No problem. Give your cousin my best," he said as he dropped into the driver's seat of his car. He started the engine and glanced up at the rearview mirror, watching as Isis disappeared around a corner. He found himself wondering about the two mysterious men as he pulled out of the parking space. However, once he was on the road, he had forgotten about them and instead thought about what he would do over the holidays.

~~*~*~*

Sly had never been patient by nature. Standing in a large, quiet library, she was reminded of that fact while she waited for some high school jock in a letterman jacket to check out a book he'd never understand for a class he'd probably skip or sleep through anyway. It was night and Sly had hoped that would be enough to keep the slackers at bay. Sadly, it had not been the case, judging by the idiot in front of her. Sly glanced up at the clock behind her. The library was going to close in another hour.

"So the cliff notes are like in the book?" the jock asked the ancient librarian.

"Guardians have mercy," Sly muttered under her breath, pinching the bridge of her nose. *Jet, if you think I'm going to let this one slide, think again,* she thought. Jet and Lilly had requested her help in locating Coop while the Four looked for the Key. Sly had agreed, only because it was in her own best interest to figure out what the hell was going on. In her experience, unanswered questions led to unpleasantness. Unpleasantness was something she didn't like and wanted to avoid. Sly could take care of herself. She had never declared her loyalty to any particular group of shape shifters, preferring to borrow from each group, while also not needing to bow to any leader. Sly was ruthless when she needed to be and never hesitated to use lethal force if a situation warranted it. Not many shape shifters would even think to mess with her. Even assassins and separatists left her alone based on her reputation, and Sly wanted to keep it that way.

"So like the notes are printed right in?"

"Hey, librarian," Sly spoke loudly from behind the guy, causing them both to look at her. "Since you're busy with the Rhodes Scholar here, can you just point me in the general direction of where I'd find your old newspapers?"

"Right down that way," the ancient librarian said, pointing a gnarled finger down one of the silent halls.

"Thank you," Sly said icily, her patience long gone. She stormed down the hall, her soft black shoes not making a sound on the dark green carpet. Since it was incredibly cold outside, she had chosen to wear a long sleeved mauve sweater. Over it, she had on a long black winter coat complete with matching scarf and driving gloves. The coat was mainly to hide the sleek battle knives she kept hidden in her sleeves, ready to slide out at a moment's notice. The coat's length also helped hide the Beretta in her thigh holster.

When Sly reached the archive room, she looked around, observing the few people sporadically seated about the large open area. There was an older man flipping through a newspaper, a tall thin woman reading a thick book at another table off to the side, and a teenager in front of her with paper cluttering the table he was sitting at. He was writing frantically on a sheet of loose-leaf paper, his index finger placed on the opened textbook in front of him. Sly could feel him stare at her when he looked up, but ignored him. *Men, so easy, so boring,* she thought as she moved along the aisles. She had decided to try the library first, planning to research a few years of missing persons using old newspapers. *I'm going to have the stench of humans on me for weeks,* she thought irritably as she headed towards the microfilm readers, intending to go through a few ancient papers first. On her way, she spotted the computers on her right, most of which were empty. She mentally kicked herself for not thinking of that sooner. Sly moved to one of the more isolated machines and sat down, clicking on the browser icon. She typed a web address into the URL bar.

Sly had seen pictures of Coop from the pools in the Meadows. The guardians didn't have much in the way of modern electronics, but Adonia had allowed her to look into one of the seeing pools. It was a pond that revealed clear images through ancient guardian magic. Sly was granted permission to look in it since she was going to be the one looking for Coop. It was difficult to search for someone when you had no idea what the person looked like.

Coop had seemed familiar, but Sly had no idea when or where she had seen him before. Lilly mentioned that Coop indicated he knew her and that bothered Sly to no end. She had decided to research disappearances from the past twenty or so years, figuring that was as good a place as any to start. Sly glanced over her shoulder, making sure she was still alone, before turning back to the screen. She found a link to the public records database and clicked on "Missing Persons." She scrolled down first to the last names starting with "C" although she knew it was a long shot. Sure enough, there were no Coopers matching the description she was looking for. She next skimmed through the unnamed section. It turned out to be another dead end, something Jet and Lilly had warned her about. Searching for Coop would mean encountering numerous dead ends and leads that went absolutely nowhere.

Sly next clicked on a link that had missing person flyers. She had just about given up any hope of finding anything when one description caught her eye. Clean shaven, dark brown hair, blue eyes, correct height and weight. Sly's interest was piqued, even though she knew it was unlikely to be anything useful. The vague description could be a number of men. Still, she clicked on the link to an image that went with the description.

"Hello there," Sly murmured to herself with a grin as she stared at the image. The man in the picture looked remarkably like Coop. He was older, a few gray hairs peppered his dark brown hair, and he had lighter blue eyes.

Sly tapped her lip, thinking. Shape shifters under constant stress, be it grief or any other strong emotion, had been known to show subtle signs of their true age such as lightly graying hair. It was possible that this man, a Mr. Mark Waterson, might have some kind of familial connection to Coop. The same first name had not escaped Sly's sharp eyes.

She printed out the image and information about the missing man, and possible shape shifter, and deleted her search history. Sly smiled as she grabbed the two pages of information complete with picture. Things were starting to look up in her hunt for the mysterious Coop.

~~*~*~*

"You could've just left it to me. I don't need a goddamn chauffer."

Jet stared ahead at the small suburban house, tuning out Sly. She had done nothing but complain ever since he told her he was coming with her to question the daughter of the man who looked like Coop — the only person who was looking for him. *Or had been,* Jet thought grimly.

"Honestly Jet, I'm hurt that you don't trust me," Sly continued from the passenger side.

"I'm sure," Jet said dryly.

"You don't think I can interrogate a possible lead?"

"The fact that you used the word 'interrogate' tells me you can't," Jet replied as he spun his car keys around his index finger.

"What's wrong with interrogate?" Sly asked, looking out her window. Being winter, the streets were mostly empty. A tall, athletic man with his large black German Shepherd jogged down the street past the car. There were some kids screaming and running around in the snow in the front yard of the house on the corner behind them.

"She's not a suspect in any crime we're investigating.

She's an innocent woman who is, or was, looking for her missing father," Jet responded, looking at Sly. As he expected, she snorted in amusement.

"Innocent? Jet, nobody is innocent. When are you going to get that?"

Jet let out a long sigh and rubbed his forehead. Sly rolled her eyes over to him, smiling in mock pleasantness as she bit her tongue. Jet found Sly's pessimism was exasperating, though she insisted she was actually a realist. Sly once explained that she recognized the world for what it was, not what she wished it was. His thoughts were interrupted when Sly opened her door and got out of the car. Jet mirrored her actions on the other side. They both glanced back to the house on the corner when one of the playing kids let out an ear-piercing shriek.

"Aren't you supposed to keep those things on a leash after dark?" Sly grumbled as they moved towards the house where the man's daughter lived with her husband and infant daughter. They walked up the steps to the front door. Jet rang the doorbell and stepped back.

"Please let me do the talking," Jet whispered to Sly without looking at her. Sly shrugged and gestured for him to go ahead. If he wanted to deal with humans, or shape shifters pretending to be human, then more power to him as far as she was concerned. They had researched the man's daughter and wife earlier that day. There wasn't much information at all on Waterson's wife.

The door soon opened and a petite woman stood there, an infant balanced on her hip. Her dark brown hair was done up in a loose bun. Some strands drifted about her face, framing it. The baby stared at the two strangers with bright blue eyes. The smell of a meal drifted out from the warm house — some kind of pasta, as near as Jet and Sly could tell.

"Yes?" the woman asked in a soft voice. She looked between the two of them, her eyes fixing briefly on Jet. Jet was now certain the woman was a shape shifter. He had already suspected as much from the research he and Sly had done.

"Are you Mrs. Cara Rodriguez?" Jet asked. The infant stuck her hand in her mouth, drooling all over an orange-stained fist, staring at Sly curiously. The two could feel the warmth from inside drift out into the frigid winter night.

"Yes. Can I help you?"

"Cara, do you recognize me?" Jet asked. He was in a bit of a hurry and he could almost hear Sly's ire rising next to him.

"No, I'm sorry, I don't," she replied. Sly snickered and leaned against the wall to her right, crossing her arms over her chest.

"All right," Jet said, nodding. He understood some shape shifters just wanted to blend into the "normal" world with the rest of the humans. He didn't think it was the healthiest or wisest decision, but it was their choice, not his. Jet certainly wasn't going to judge them for it.

"If you're looking for Will, he'll be home this weekend," Cara stated.

"Unbelievable," Sly muttered under her breath and Jet struggled not to roll his eyes. He knew how much she disliked being around humans, particularly in the suburbs. Being surrounded by humans for extended amounts of time put Sly on edge. Groups of humans could be unpredictable at times.

"Actually, we're here to ask you a few questions," Jet replied, "about your father's disappearance."

"That was more than twenty years ago," Cara said, her blue eyes widening. "I already told the police everything I could remember."

"I know, but we have some follow-up questions," Jet responded gently.

Cara swallowed, looking hesitant, before nodding and holding the door open for them. Jet glanced at Sly as he moved into the house. She shrugged and followed him inside.

"Please, have a seat," Cara said, gesturing to the worn couch that sat against the wall in the main room. She put the infant in a playpen that sat off to the side before sitting in a nearby rocking chair. She smiled affectionately as her daughter began playing with one of the soft, brightly colored toys.

"She looks just like you," Jet commented with a smile as he watched the young girl bite down on her toy. He remembered when his children were that young and small.

"If you start speaking in babytalk, I'm leaving," Sly warned, drawing him out of his musing. Jet looked over at her, irritated. She smiled as she crossed one long leg over the other and rested her head against her thumb and index finger, her eyes daring him to reply. Her eyes wandered over to the Christmas tree near the TV, as well as the stockings above the small fireplace and she shook her head. Unlike Jet, Sly felt perfectly within her rights to be judgmental about such ridiculousness.

"Thank you," Cara said to Jet, casting a nervous glance at Sly. "You said you had questions about my father. Are you detectives?"

"Cara, please, it's just us. I've been around long enough to recognize another shape shifter. You obviously recognized me on the porch, otherwise you never would have let me in your house," Jet pointed out. The woman bit her lower lip and glanced at the windows.

"Look, I'm just trying to lead a normal life, just like everyone else," she finally relented. "I don't want to have anything to do with the world of shape shifters."

"That's your choice, but can we please drop the charade for the time being? It will make things much easier," Jet answered, his voice becoming a little firmer. Even Sly was impressed with Jet's sudden turn. He knew when to use the leader card.

Cara nodded and folded her hands in her lap. "Why the sudden interest in my father's disappearance?"

"We're actually trying to locate another shape shifter. A

man who goes by the name of Coop," Jet responded.

Cara frowned in confusion. "What does that have to do with my father?"

"Your father looks very similar to Coop. It's an uncanny resemblance," Jet said, leaning forward. "Cara, do you have a brother or a cousin or any other relative who went by that name?"

Cara shook her head. "My parents were both only children and so was I."

Jet and Sly exchanged a look. That was strange, but not entirely unheard of. Most shape shifters came from large families, due to their normal practice of living with multiple partners, usually in open relationships. They viewed marriage as an outdated human tradition and preferred living with multiple lovers and friends. However, Jet lived in a similar situation to Cara. He was one of the very few shape shifters who preferred monogamy, which many shape shifters found incredibly peculiar. Even his siblings and parents had found his choice to be odd.

"Can we talk to your mother?" Sly asked, her eyes traveling back to the woman. Both Cara and Jet stared at her. Cara looked suspicious.

"Look, we know she's trying to hide and I respect that. I just need to ask her a few questions," Jet explained, attempting to be reassuring.

"I don't think she would want to talk to you," Cara said with a shake of her head.

Sly smiled pleasantly. "Can we just try? It's very, *very* important that we find this man. Who knows? Our search might turn up some answers about your father."

"I really don't think—"

"Look, Cara," Sly began, an edge creeping into her voice as she leaned forward. "We just want to talk to her. However, if you keep acting evasive, I'm going to lose my patience. If I lose my patience . . . well, there's no telling what I might do. How do you think your little Stepford community would react to learning there is a mythical creature living right under their very noses? Might bring about a new era of flaming torches and pitchforks. So run along and fetch Mommy's number for us or watch your little community descend into a modern interpretation of the Salem Witch Trials."

Jet stared at her, his mouth falling open. If she thought she could get away with that, she had lost her mind. Cara looked to Jet, unnerved by Sly's threat.

"You wouldn't let her do that. You wouldn't dare," Cara stated, sounding very unsure. Sly snorted, causing Jet to whip around again and glare at her.

"You think *he* could stop me?"

Cara was quiet for another few moments, thinking. "You just want to talk to her?"

Sly nodded, running a finger over the arm of the couch. "Just a pleasant chat, I promise. Jet can go by himself if you prefer."

Cara stood up and moved toward the small kitchen at the back of the house. They could hear her shuffling through drawers. Jet turned his body so he fully faced Sly, who smiled at him, unbothered.

"Don't get your panties in a twist, Jet. You know I'd never expose myself like that in public," Sly reassured him as she looked at her nails with indifference. "I'm not suicidal."

"You're sadistic, Sly," Jet growled from behind gritted teeth. "That was cruel. You didn't have to scare her like that."

"And what was your brilliant plan? Sit here yapping about tea cozies and doilies? Sorry, Jet, I have better things to do than play house with June Cleaver."

Jet opened his mouth to reply when Cara came back from the kitchen. He turned and smiled politely again, accepting the small scrap of paper with her mother's phone number on it.

"I'd appreciate it if you'd both leave now," Cara said, crossing her arms over her chest. Jet nodded and stood up, as did Sly. They both made their way to the door, showing themselves out. They weren't surprised to hear the deadbolt slide into place once the door shut.

Sly was quiet until they got in the car. Jet turned the key in the ignition and the engine purred to life. He reached forward and switched on the heat, cranking it up.

"Jet, I have a really bad feeling about this," Sly mentioned, gazing out the window to the snow-covered landscape.

Jet frowned as he pulled out into the empty street. "About what?"

"Coop, the Key, this whole situation," Sly responded. "A lot of things just seem . . . off. Why is Cara's mother hiding? There's some bigger picture here and I feel like we're missing it."

Jet sighed as he made a left turn. He shared Sly's uneasiness and had ever since first learning about the Key years ago when it had first been referenced in the guardians' book of Oracle. It was supposed to be a tool of immense destruction, capable of severing the tie between the Meadows and Earth, something that would be disastrous and possibly even apocalyptic. The prophecy was maddeningly vague and the evidence Jet had been able to glean from it pointed to a flashdrive, which contained a virus capable of overriding any computer programming. Recently, he had come to suspect the flashdrive was being used to direct the protectors' actions. By whom or what, he still didn't know.

"That's why we're investigating," Jet answered as he switched on his turn signal. "We need to find the Key. And if Coop is tied to it somehow, we need to know. There are just too many unanswered questions right now. If we don't find answers soon . . . well, that could be very bad for us."

"Yeah," Sly murmured quietly, but Jet could tell that something was still bothering her. There was silence between the two for the rest of the drive.

CHAPTER THREE

As Christmas drew nearer, the surge in crime officially ended. It not only ended, the rate dropped significantly and things stabilized among the assassins in a way that had never been seen before. The man in possession of the flashdrive that some thought to be the Key knew something was wrong. He had lived long enough to recognize when things were too quiet. He tapped the unnaturally cold flashdrive against his upper lip as he stared at the screen of his laptop. His small home/office was a plain windowless room hidden in the back of an old hotel. He rented from the owner, one of his few allies. She agreed to keep his secrets, no questions asked. Like him, she recognized when things were off and knew of the danger lurking in plain sight.

"You rang?"

The man looked up from the screen, not surprised to see his brother leaning against the wall by the door. His green eyes were tired and defeated, which didn't surprise the man. He knew he had put that look in the once vibrant pools of green, but he really couldn't care less. In his book, his brother deserved whatever misery he felt.

He tossed the Key to his younger brother, who caught

it and looked at it, confused. "And you're giving this to me because . . . ?"

The man smiled. He had been waiting for this for a long time. "It's time for you to turn yourself in."

His brother raised his eyes to him, staring at him for a moment. "Has anyone ever told you that you're incredibly cruel when you want to be?"

"You calling someone cruel? Now *that* is entertaining," the man answered as he leaned back in the old creaky chair behind the ancient desk. The small dwelling was cool in temperature, mainly because the man never turned on the heat. He had no real use for it.

His brother was quiet for a long while as he examined the small flashdrive in his hand. "It's so cold."

"I know. Most things attached to the Corporation are," the man agreed.

"We're certain this isn't the real thing?"

"You're smarter than I give you credit for," the man replied before shaking his head. "It was made to gather the Four. If it had been that easy to find, Grenich would already have it. No, the Key is definitely a living being and the Corporation is still actively searching for whomever it is. I take it you've seen this."

The man turned his laptop around so his brother could see the screen. His brother squinted as he skimmed the story.

"The Grenich Bank?" He straightened up again. "I passed by it late last night. Opened a couple months ago, right?"

The man nodded. "He's getting bolder. Unfortunately, he can be. He's got enough power and sway and he knows it."

His brother tucked the flashdrive away in one of the pockets of his jacket. "You do know that once I go there, you won't have any way to contact me."

"I consider that a blessing," the man responded. "I trust you remember what to do."

"Yes." His brother looked to the ground, rubbing his forehead. "They're not going to believe a word I say. You do realize that, right?"

"Well then, you'll have to figure out a way to convince them that you're trustworthy," the man said and scoffed. "Good luck with that."

His brother gave him a look of annoyance and turned to leave, pausing at the door. He put a long hand on the frame.

"Swear to me that you know what you're doing," he muttered. "Tell me this plan is foolproof and it will work."

The man hesitated, feeling a certain amount of sympathy toward his brother for the first time in ages. Truth be told, he didn't know if what he had planned would work. Nothing was foolproof, especially when dealing with the monster they were fighting. However, looking at his brother, the man could tell he just wanted some kind of reassurance, even if it was false. Therefore, he granted his brother's request.

"It will work," he stated with conviction. Working in the Corporation as long as he had, the man knew how to lie and lie well. The Grenich Corporation was built on lies, and in order to survive, one had to become a master deceiver.

His brother nodded. "Thank you."

And then he was gone, vanishing from the man's life for the first time in a long while. The man looked back to his laptop, clicking on a link. He had work to do.

~~*~*~*

Isis walked into the mansion's enormous kitchen, noticing Shae sitting at the small table, staring at her tablet screen. She glanced up at Isis' entrance.

"Well if it isn't Miss Scandalous," she greeted, beaming from ear to ear. She looked completely surprised when Isis snickered softly. "Somebody's in a pleasant mood and on

Christmas Eve no less. Usually I have to talk you down from opening fire in the clock tower."

"Shape shifters don't celebrate Christmas," Isis said, grinning as she sat across from her cousin. She lifted the Arts section of the paper that was on the table, folded it in half, and held it up so she could read it. She looked pointedly at Shae's tablet.

"Give me a physical paper any day," Isis commented.

"Update to this century, ice queen. I have access to almost every paper in the world on this modern marvel," Shae responded as she tapped another link and Isis snickered.

"So where are the others?" Isis asked, turning a page in the paper.

"Alex is out having dinner with Remington and Jade's off with her lover, so it looks like it's going to be a quiet night again."

"And the good news keeps coming," Isis remarked with a larger smile. Shae switched off her tablet and laid it to the side.

"Hey, what's been up with you lately?" she asked. Isis looked up from the paper.

"What do you mean?"

"You've been kind of . . . distracted," Shae observed. "When we're not out looking for the Key, you're locked in your room. Do you have a secret lover scaling the walls or something?"

Isis smiled and shook her head. "No secret lovers scaling the walls, still Gray-A. Sorry to disappoint."

"Then what is it?"

Isis looked back to her paper. "Just had a lot going on. Aneurin's been calling meetings practically every other week. We're still looking for the Key. It's a lot on my plate and I relish in whatever little me-time I can manage."

Isis tried to focus on a review of a play, which wasn't terribly interesting. She had been rather closed off in the past few months, mostly because she was trying to lay low in order to avoid Aneurin's attention. Her three teammates were able to have both social and professional lives but Isis had temporarily tabled her extracurricular activities, preferring instead to continue researching Coop. Once she had found the answers to a few mysteries, she fully intended on returning to a normal social life.

"Oh!" Shae snapped her fingers, briefly closing her eyes as she remembered something she almost forgot. "Did you know that Steve has a new partner?"

"That's a bit out of nowhere. Wait, he met someone else?" Isis couldn't help but be intrigued by this new bit of news. Shae smiled and nodded, taking out her smartphone.

"Yep, sometime last week when he was on shift," she said.

"He didn't tell me," Isis said, her eyes sliding to the side for a minute. "Who is this mystery person? Is he good enough for our Stevie?"

Shae snickered and pulled out her cell phone, flipping through it. "*Her* name is Tracy Rose. Steve met her at the ER while on duty. He was getting a victim's statement, some kind of domestic disturbance, and Tracy was visiting a friend. Apparently, he literally bumped into her. She works at that new bank in town. Oh, what's it called?"

"Grenich," Isis offered, frowning at Shae's words. "Her? I thought Steve was more interested in men. I can't even recall the last time he had a girlfriend."

Shae shrugged as she continued flipping through pictures. "You know Steve, sometimes his tastes change. He has had a couple girlfriends in the past."

"What does Justin think of this?" Isis asked, sipping her coffee. She had only met her best friend's boyfriend a few times. They got along rather well, surprisingly.

"I imagine he's fine with it. He and Steve have never been exclusive. Justin's still overseas at the moment, investigating something or other for Jet and Lilly, saving the world in his own way," Shae said, tapping on a picture on the phone to enlarge it. She handed the phone over to

Isis, who looked at the screen. She chuckled and shook her head. Shae had obviously taken the photo while passing by the building.

"You are such a voyeur," Isis teased as she flipped to the next picture. Steve and Tracy were aware of the picture being taken. Steve looked mildly annoyed but Tracy was grinning happily, enjoying being photographed. Tracy had cropped blonde hair, bleached from what Isis could tell. Her eyes were dark, but Isis couldn't tell the exact shade due to the quality of the picture. Based on the picture, she looked friendly enough.

"She's nice. I think even *you* will like her," Shae commented. Isis gave her a look that said *Gee thanks.* Shae merely shrugged.

"He's out with her right now. If you hang around, maybe you'll get to meet her."

"He's going to bring her to this mad house?" Isis asked, pausing to think that over. "She's a shape shifter, isn't she?"

Shae nodded. "That she is. Shape shifters don't often date humans. I have my own theories about why."

Isis arched an eyebrow. "Such as?"

Shae grinned devilishly. "Our stamina. We'd ride the poor person to death."

Isis shook her head, smiling. "You and that dirty mind of yours."

The two turned when someone entered the kitchen. One of the Monroes' sons entered the kitchen, Devlin or Declan. Isis was still trying to figure out how to tell the two apart. He smiled at them and made his way to the fridge.

"What's going on?" he asked, opening the door.

"Same old, same old. Just having a pleasant chat with my cousin," Shae replied. Isis turned her attention back to the Arts section of the paper.

Eventually, Shae and Isis wandered into the main entertainment room where they continued to enjoy the quiet evening.

"I think you should get laid."

Isis looked up from her book to where Shae sat on the windowsill. Her cousin was searching for any sign of Steve and his date. Isis sat on the opposite end of the room in a large chair next to a lamp, her legs folded underneath her. The comforting glow lit the book that she had been engrossed in. The mansion was pleasantly warm and it was a peaceful night. Jet was in his study with Lilly. Since she had come to live at the mansion, Isis rarely saw Jet without Lilly. Their children had gone out for the night, likely to a dance club. Hunter had dropped in earlier in the evening to ask if Isis or Shae were interested in going with them. They had both declined.

"Excuse me?" Isis asked, looking back to her book.

"You need to get laid, Isis," Shae replied with a nonchalant shrug. "You are part shape shifter. That libido needs to be fed."

"Okay, first off, Gray-A. I don't have the same sort of libido shape shifters typically have. Secondly, in case you hadn't noticed, I've been a little busy this past year. I promise you, once we solve the mystery of this Key, I will immediately go out and find a date or whatever," Isis mumbled dryly, turning a page in her book.

Shae snorted. "That's your excuse for everything: too busy or too ace. The three of us have just as many responsibilities as you and we still find time. Oh look, Jade's back."

Isis glanced over her shoulder when she heard the door to the garage open and footsteps enter the mansion. Jade strolled into the entertainment room. Her clothing was in slight disarray and her coat was draped over her arm.

"Were you in a fight?" Isis asked.

"Not exactly," Jade responded with a suggestive smile.

"Seriously? In the freezing cold?"

Jade leaned over Isis' chair. "Give me some credit. I went to the club my partner stays at during the cold months. Not that making love in the snow isn't exhilarating, but only very occasionally. Making love outdoors comes with more than a few issues."

Isis turned back to her book. "I'll take your word for it."

"Jade, doesn't Isis need to get laid?" Shae asked without taking her eyes from the window. Jade glanced over at her other teammate.

"Isis can't get laid. She's technically a guardian," Jade replied. That got Isis to look up from her book.

"Come again?" she asked. Jade smiled sympathetically, leaned down, and kissed her cheek.

"Why do you think I never hit on you before?" she teased, flopping down on the rocking chair near Isis, tossing her coat over to the couch. She pulled the tie out of her hair, allowing her dark hair to cascade down, and laid her hands over her toned stomach.

"Okay, I'm still a bit unclear on this whole 'technically a guardian' business," Isis said. "I'm not even a full guardian. I don't live in the Meadows and I'm one of four prophesized *shape shifters*."

"Doesn't matter, your mother is a full guardian and of the royal line. Plus you were born in the Meadows, which makes you a daughter of the Meadows," Jade countered with a shake of her head.

"Secondly, could the guardians possibly be more archaic? Telling others whom they can and can't have a relationship with. *Humans* are more lenient," Isis continued. Jade laughed and even Shae chuckled a bit.

"Their rules aren't perfect, but honestly, what cultures are? Hey, at least you're on the ace spectrum. That should take the sting out of it a bit," Jade responded. Isis turned back to the book. She was too distracted to get into it. Her thoughts frequently strayed to what the bartender, Phil, had told her about Coop and Dane. She was debating whether to try sneaking out in a week's time to try to find the mysterious men. She wanted answers, and it seemed like this search would only yield more questions. Isis glanced over at Jade and considered asking for her advice. She didn't want to be in the same hot water that she had found herself in after letting Coop go.

Shae's cell phone ringing brought Jade's and Isis' attention to her. She answered it and moved out into the hall. The two remaining women sat in silence.

"So are we ever going to meet your girlfriend? Properly meet her, I mean," Isis asked.

"Perhaps," Jade replied. "I don't think she'll be making an appearance this winter."

"Any reason why?" Isis asked, curiously. Jade looked over at her.

"Let's just say she's not overly pleased with some of the errands she's been sent on recently. Are you trying to live vicariously through me or something?" she asked, smiling.

"Might as well, since I apparently have to live a life of celibacy," Isis grumbled.

"Not celibacy, discretion. None of us is going to turn you in. Aneurin isn't going to spy on you. Take as many lovers as you like, whenever you like, just make sure it doesn't get back to him," Jade explained. "It's what your sister and mother have been doing for years."

"Good to know." Isis glanced up when Shae stepped back into the room.

"Steve's staying at her place tonight, but he does want to have dinner with us tomorrow," she said.

Isis looked over at Jade again. "Are there any missions or outings I could possibly volunteer to do tomorrow? Any duties of the Four that need attention?"

"No you don't," Shae quickly interjected. "Steve really likes this woman, Isis. You owe it to him to at least make an effort."

"I know this is hard for you to believe, but I do know how to behave," Isis replied. She did owe Steve quite a lot. Not only had he been protecting her since they were children, back when she had no idea of her heritage, but he had always been an extremely loyal friend. At different times in her life, he had sometimes been her only one.

"Good," Shae said before turning to Jade. "Are we expecting anything tomorrow night?"

"Nothing expected, you two have fun. Alex and I will cover for you, but keep your phones on. Just in case," Jade answered.

"Are things always this quiet during the winter time? Do our adversaries go into hibernation or something?"

Jade shrugged. "Don't look a gift horse in the mouth. Enjoy the quiet. It'll be over before you know it."

~~*~*~*

Holidays weren't celebrated in the Meadows. They were just regular days for almost all the guardians. They rushed around doing what they did best: keeping the world in order and on schedule.

Adonia passed Passion's quarters and saw her door was opened, revealing an empty room. She knew exactly where her granddaughter would be. The wise leader of the guardian women continued down the hall, soon spotting Passion on the large balcony overlooking the entrance hall of the Pearl Castle. The first queen of the guardian women, Betha, used to stand on the balcony and watch the goings on in the castle. Adonia herself sometimes enjoyed standing there, watching the messengers and other guardians go about their business. It was a very peaceful place.

Passion was sitting with her back resting against one of the large balusters. She wasn't watching the grand hall and the activity below. Instead, she looked toward the entrance of the balcony. Her eyes were blue, as they usually were during the colder seasons. One of her legs was folded under her while the other was folded at the knee and brought up to her chest so that she could rest her chin on it.

Adonia watched her granddaughter as she sat still as stone. Passion was often depressed come winter. It was the anniversary of Roan's disappearance. It was when everything in her life had completely fallen apart.

Adonia approached the younger guardian, pausing when she stood next to her. "Would you mind if I joined you?"

Passion, without looking up at Adonia, just shook her head. Adonia sat down, resting her shoulder against one of the large balusters, her legs folded under her. She studied her granddaughter's face, which remained expressionless. Her sun-colored hair was tied back loosely; a few stray strands framed her lovely face. Only yesterday, Passion had threatened to shave her head during an argument with her mother, Artemis. It was an empty threat thrown during an equally empty argument. It was anyone's guess what the fight had been about on the surface, but Adonia knew deep down it was about Passion's past. It had been one of their more volatile fights — setting an old portrait ablaze before Adonia was able to split it up. Electra had been standing dangerously near it and narrowly escaped being burned.

"Sorry about the painting," Passion murmured, her eyes never leaving the wall. The glisten of her skin was noticeably dimmer.

"That's all right. I never liked it anyway," Adonia reassured her. Passion smiled slightly, but it didn't reach her haunted eyes.

"Might I inquire what you're thinking about?" Adonia asked.

Passion sighed heavily and rubbed her forehead. "Mainly about how I would give anything for even a little bit of closure."

"Roan?"

Passion nodded once. "Where did his body go? The protectors never found a trace of him. People don't just disappear into thin air."

"No, they don't," Adonia agreed.

"So where did he go?"

Adonia shrugged. It was anyone's guess as to what had happened to Roan.

"Have you considered that maybe his past caught up with him? Roan was high up in the world of assassins, the leader of an important territory. There is no way of knowing exactly how many enemies he made," she offered.

Passion shrugged. "That seems likely." She was quiet for a moment, thinking. "But why take his body? And how would someone get it out of the apartment without leaving a trace?"

"There are some things that we may never have—"

Passion looked over at her grandmother when Adonia trailed off. Her eyes were wide as she stared at something in the entrance hall of the castle. It was one of the first times Passion had seen Adonia genuinely surprised.

An unnatural silence fell over the castle, as if the whole world stopped for just an instant. The heavier the silence became, the less Passion wanted to turn around and see what had brought it on. Some part of her heart already knew what she would see.

Passion swallowed and closed her eyes, suddenly wanting to run as fast as she could. She didn't know where nor did she care. Pushing herself up to a standing position, she kept her eyes on the entrance in front of her. Passion felt as though she were immune to the normally calming presence felt throughout the Pearl Castle. She took a couple of deep breaths, trying her best to remain calm. Then, she slowly turned around.

A lone figure stood in the middle of the entrance hall. The messengers all stood a fair distance away. She recognized him immediately. Roan.

He looked exactly as he had the night he went missing. He wore a dark jacket, unzipped to reveal a dark shirt, and black jeans with sneakers on his feet. His long hands were tucked in the pockets of the jacket. Roan's reddish blond hair shone in the light that illuminated the castle. Long legs made up the majority of his height, giving him a lanky appearance. He still had a very pale complexion, the same one Passion saw in her daughters. The only difference Passion could see in him was his eyes. They were still green but they were no longer bright and lively. Rather they were dull and almost defeated, even as they fixed on her. Yet, as he held her gaze, Passion felt those eyes captivate her, as they always had. Long ago, those eyes used to make her feel as though she were the only woman in the world. They had sparkled with love and admiration.

Only now she knew of his deceit, his darkness. He was a murderer, an assassin, someone who killed people simply because the price was right. The man before her had killed one of his own brothers and numerous other innocent people. He was a boogeyman among shape shifters and few even dared speak his name aloud. Because of him, her daughters had a stigma attached to them. His treachery had cost her everything, and she wanted to hate him. She wanted to hate him more than anything and it should have been easy. But it wasn't.

Passion did the only thing she could think to do. She sent an icy glare in his direction and stormed off, hoping she would never see him again.

Adonia watched as her granddaughter disappeared down the hall leading to her room. When she first saw Roan, Adonia didn't know what to do. She was even less sure of what to do when Passion became locked in a stare-down with the presumed dead shape shifter. He had turned her entire life upside down and Adonia couldn't help but wonder how her granddaughter would react to his sudden and unexpected reappearance. She had seen the conflict on Passion's face. The younger guardian had loved the man. He had given her two daughters, both of whom she loved more than life itself.

Adonia hadn't expected the relatively calm reaction of

her granddaughter. She had expected her to knock Roan down using telekinesis at the very least. However, Passion just walked away, down the hall toward her room. Adonia glanced at Roan again and saw remorse in his tired green eyes. He looked up at her and then dropped his head, unable to hold her gaze. He slowly removed his left hand from the pocket it was hidden in. Adonia's eyes widened even more when she saw what he brought out of the pocket: a thin gray flashdrive.

"I believe you're looking for this," his smoky voice traveled up to her. Her gaze moved from the flashdrive back to him. Roan stood out in the sea of pastel that surrounded him. Messengers stood around, unsure what to do. Some messengers looked up at Adonia expectantly, awaiting orders. Many others simply looked terrified, especially the younger ones. Roan's ruthless reputation was still widely known throughout the Meadows, though he hadn't been seen in more than twenty years.

"It's not what—"

"Quiet, Roan," Adonia ordered. He closed his mouth. Adonia motioned for one of the messengers to take the flashdrive from Roan. The messenger — dressed in pale blue indicating she was from the water lands — approached him very hesitantly, with the same caution she would a feral beast.

"Two of you take him to the dungeons, solitary confinement," Adonia commanded. "I need to speak with Jet and Lilly."

At that moment, Electra strode into the entrance hall from the wing off to the left. She froze mid-step when she saw who was in the middle of the main area of the castle. She stared at him, her expression gradually becoming furious. Roan glanced toward her and stared, horrified. He looked back at Adonia and then Electra.

"Get him out of here!" Adonia yelled, making her way toward the stairs. Her shout snapped everyone into action and two messengers escorted a compliant Roan toward the dungeons. The messenger from the water lands brought the flashdrive to Adonia, who was halfway down the stairs. Adonia nodded her thanks, dismissing the messenger to go on her way, glancing at the flashdrive she held. It was freezing cold, which struck her as a little odd. Electra still stood in the entrance of the wing she had come from.

Electra's fists clenched and unclenched a couple times as she closed her eyes and let out a long breath. She opened her bright green eyes and looked to Adonia.

"Is that who I think it was?"

Adonia nodded. "I'm afraid so. That was Roan."

"Impossible, he's dead," Electra stated strongly.

"I thought the same," Adonia said, glancing toward where Roan had been standing only moments ago. "Apparently we were mistaken."

"Where's Mom?" Electra asked.

"I believe she went to her room," Adonia replied. Electra moved toward the stairs, hurrying up them.

"Electra?"

Adonia's voice halted Electra at the top of the stairs. She looked back at her great grandmother. Adonia turned to face her.

"Passion saw him when he first Appeared. She's understandably upset."

Electra nodded and continued to her mother's quarters. Adonia sighed and looked back at the flashdrive in her hand before moving in the direction of the stairs. She headed for her office, thinking about how to tell Jet and Lilly.

~~*~*~*

Electra reached the door to her mother's quarters, pausing for a moment before hesitantly knocking. When she received no response, she tried the handle and found it open.

"Mom?" Electra called out as she stepped into her room. The bed was made and everything was tidy. The curtains were drawn, letting the warm sunlight stream into the room. Both windows were fully open to let in the pleasant breeze. Electra looked over to where her mother sat at her desk, writing with a fountain pen. Her hand supported her head as the pen scratched hurriedly across the paper. Electra closed the door behind her before moving over to where her mother was.

"Mom, are you okay?" she asked. Passion looked up from the paper for a moment, studying her daughter. It was the first time Electra was unable to read what her mother was feeling. Normally, Passion's emotions were raw and naked, easy for anyone to read. Seeing her mother guarded unnerved Electra.

"You know?" Passion asked. It was more of a statement than a question. Electra nodded, leaning against the desk.

"I saw him, right before a couple messengers took him to the dungeons," she said.

"Electra, I am so sorry," Passion began apologetically.

"Why? You didn't know he was still alive," Electra replied.

"No. No, I did not," Passion agreed, turning her eyes back to the paper she was writing on. The pen resumed its neurotic scratching.

"Who are you writing to?"

"Donovan," Passion answered, laying the pen down and folding the paper. She grabbed a stick of red wax and a candle she had lit when she had first entered her room. Holding the stick over the candle, she melted the wax over the folded paper.

"I have to warn him, Electra. If the High Council finds out what really happened . . ." Passion stopped, not needing to say anything more. Electra looked down briefly, knowing her mother could be in a great deal of trouble if the truth became known. Passion and Donovan had been on Earth without protector escorts, which was against guardian law. The fact that they had been there to cover up Passion's role in trying to help Roan carried an even greater penalty.

Passion opened a desk drawer, pulling out her seal. She pressed it into the drying wax, leaving an impression of their family crest. The red color of the wax would tell Donovan it was from her. She stood up, holding the paper. Electra took the letter from her, raising a hand when Passion started to protest.

"I'll take it to Lucky. He's Donovan's apprentice and I happen to know that he's in the library today," Electra said, tapping a corner of the paper against her hand. "You and I both know Donovan has a habit of ignoring messengers. The High Council has been on his case about it forever. He can't turn away his apprentice though. Lucky likes you and me. He won't be nosy. Your letter will get to Donovan faster and you'll know that he got it."

Passion leaned back in the chair, balancing the pen between her fingers as she looked at her daughter.

"Thank you," she said after a moment, putting the pen on the desk. She ran a hand through her soft hair.

"We should tell Isis," Passion mentioned, leaning against the desk.

Electra nodded, standing up again. "I'll go to her after I see Lucky."

"That's probably best. She's more comfortable with you," Passion agreed, unable to hide the melancholy in her voice.

"Only just," Electra replied with a shrug. "Isis isn't really comfortable with anyone other than the shape shifters. She's lived on Earth all her life, so it's only natural that she would be more comfortable with them."

"Perhaps," Passion said, sitting up again. "Lucky is Donovan's apprentice?"

"Apparently so. Phoenix told me a while ago," Electra said, smiling a little. "The High Council has finally found a way to punish him. I don't know who to feel sorrier for: Donovan or Lucky."

Passion gave a watery half-smile. Electra straightened up and started walking back toward the door. She opened it and turned back.

"You sure you're all right?" she asked.

Passion shrugged. "I will be once I have a chance to process everything."

Electra nodded and closed the door behind her as she left.

CHAPTER FOUR

Isis sat in her bed, her back against the headboard. She was paging through her spiral on the mysterious Coop. It was late afternoon and she still had to get ready for the dinner she had promised to attend with Shae. Truthfully, she was looking forward to seeing Steve again. Isis hadn't seen much of him since the whole debacle with Coop. She missed him enough to stomach getting to know another person. Normally getting her to leave the comfort of a heated house in the middle of winter was a near impossible task, especially if it involved meeting a new person. As it was, Isis wasn't looking forward to venturing out in the cold weather. She glanced over to the window. Even with the curtains drawn, the harsh glare of the sun on the snow was almost headache inducing.

A knock on her room door brought Isis out of her ruminations. She leaned over to the table by her bed, pulling open the drawer and sliding the spiral inside. She closed the drawer again and stood up, crossing the room to the door. Isis wondered who it could be. It was much too early for Shae to fetch her for the dinner at Steve's. Jade and Alex were working out. Jet and Lilly were at a meeting, along with Remington. The mansion was mostly empty.

Isis opened her door, unable to hide her surprise at who was there. "Electra?"

Electra was dressed in her plainclothes; jeans and a cream-colored sweater, her hair tied back in a simple ponytail. She looked about as unsure as Isis had ever seen her look.

"Hey, Isis," she began, glancing down the hall. "I need to talk to you about something. Would you mind if I came in?"

Isis shook her head, opening the door even wider to allow her sister to enter the room. She closed the door and turned to face Electra. Her twin walked over to her bed, lightly sitting on the edge.

"Is something wrong?" Isis asked.

"No. Well, yes in a way," Electra paused and frowned. "Actually, I'm not really sure."

"Uh oh," Isis said, crossing the room and leaning against one of the bedposts. "That doesn't sound good. Is Aneurin holding another one of his inquisitions?"

Electra smiled at the jest, but it didn't reach her green eyes. "Hopefully not."

She ran her hands over her face, leaning over her knees. Isis tilted her head, trying to see her sister's expression.

"Electra, what happened?"

Electra straightened up again, biting her lower lip and drumming her fingers. Isis could tell she was thinking over what to say, choosing her words. Isis crossed her arms over her chest, furrowing her brow. She was nervous about her sister's hesitance and prepared herself for whatever kind of bombshell Electra would drop.

"Earlier this morning, around dawn, someone Appeared in the Meadows. Someone who had long been thought dead," Electra paused and looked up at her sister. "Roan — he's back."

Isis' squinted at Electra, confused by the news. It

certainly hadn't been what she was expecting — not that she really knew what to expect.

"Roan? Our biological father?" she finally asked. "Are you sure?"

Electra nodded and Isis sat on the bed next to her. She had been told very little of her biological father. She really only knew of his reputation as the most feared shape shifter assassin. Assassins tended to stay relatively anonymous and tried to remain as discreet as possible, but Roan had somehow been able to kill openly without being caught. Whoever backed him had enough power and sway to keep him out of prison and away from the protectors. He moved and killed without being seen, but he made sure protectors knew about his kills. Hell, Isis had heard some shape shifters wouldn't even speak his name aloud, as if the simple act could somehow conjure him.

"So he wasn't dead? Where has he been?" Isis questioned, looking over at Electra. Electra shook her head and shrugged.

"We don't know. He's been gone more than twenty years," she said.

"And he just Appeared in the Pearl Castle this morning? Did he try to kill anybody?" Isis asked. Electra leaned back.

"No, he didn't. He Appeared and gave Adonia the Key, or what we think is the Key," she replied. Isis tilted her head, feeling a faint sense of disappointment. The Four had been looking for any trace of the Key since Coop's disappearance. *We've been searching for that damn thing for months and then it just drops in our lap. So much wasted time,* she thought, somewhat annoyed. *Well, maybe we won't have to deal with so many dead-ends.*

"Where is he now?"

"In the dungeons, in solitary," Electra said. "Where he'll hopefully stay for eternity."

Isis looked at her sister, surprised by her bitterness. Electra had been a little stand-offish when they first met, but eventually warmed up to her sister. Since then, Isis had seen her twin's natural extroverted and friendly personality. To hear her sound so cold was a little off-putting. Then again, Jade had told her that guardians grew up with a very black and white view of good and evil. They sometimes didn't understand the gray areas of issues. Isis imagined Electra was also quite protective of her mother. After all the grief Passion had gone through because of Roan, Isis could understand her sister's resentment toward the man.

"He willingly turned himself in?" Isis asked, putting her hands on her hips.

"Yes."

"And gave Adonia the Key? Why?"

Electra shrugged. "I don't know. Who knows why assassins do anything?"

"Maybe he has changed," Isis suggested. "He was able to Appear in the Pearl Castle."

Electra let out a cynical laugh. "Men like Roan don't change. Once a murderer, always a murderer. The only reason he can Appear is because he's a Deverell."

Isis leaned back against the bedpost, folding one leg under her. "So what does this mean? What happens now?"

"I don't know. I wish I did. I just came down to tell you, Jet, and Lilly. What happens next is entirely up to the High Council and the protectors," Electra said, looking over at her sister. "Speaking of which, where are Jet and Lilly?"

"They went out to a meeting. They should be back soon," Isis replied. "I guess I should cancel my evening plans."

"Probably a wise idea," Electra responded, lying back on the bed and closing her eyes. "The Four are likely going to be incredibly busy for quite some time."

Shae's going to be annoyed, Isis thought, sad that she wouldn't be able to see Steve. She realized the Key had fallen too easily into their laps and it would likely lead to more questions about where it had come from and what it was exactly — questions she and her three teammates would have to investigate. She looked over at Electra, who had laid the back of her hands on her brow. Her twin was the very portrait of relaxed.

"How's Passion handling this?" Isis asked.

"Surprisingly well," Electra answered, opening her eyes and looking up at the canopy high above her. The room was pleasantly warm and smelled of lavender; one of Isis' favorite scents. She had worked hard to make her room relaxing, especially since she didn't spend much time in it. Isis relished whatever little time she could spend in the spacious room.

"Is she going to get in trouble?" Isis knew her biological mother had broken quite a few rules back when Roan had supposedly died. Passion had told her and Electra everything that had happened that night, along with the possible repercussions if the full story ever came out.

"I don't think so. If Roan talks, there might be some trouble," Electra stated. "But I doubt the High Council will believe a word he says."

"What about the other guardian that Passion mentioned? The one who helped her?"

"Donovan? No, he would never put Mom in that position," Electra said. Isis wondered how much weirder her life could get. *Biological father is an assassin and apparently came back from the dead. Add that twisted branch onto the ol' family tree,* she thought as she looked back to her sister.

"Can I ask you a somewhat personal question?" Isis began, feeling a little unsure. Electra turned her body toward her sister, propping herself up on her elbow. Her eyes reflected curiosity as she studied her twin.

"Sure," she said. Isis shifted uncomfortably, regretting broaching the topic. She was still getting used to how open the shape shifters were compared to typically conservative suburbanite humans who made repression an art form.

The guardians sometimes seemed to be even more reticent than humans were. Her twin sister lived as a guardian her entire life and seemed to have been able to skirt their code, so Isis figured she would be the best person to ask.

"You've told me about the strict courting rules of guardians," Isis continued, rubbing the back of her neck. "Have you ever been in a relationship?"

Electra gave a half-smile, clearly amused by the question. "Isis, are you asking me if I've ever had sex?"

"No! No! God, no," Isis stammered. "It's just . . . Jade mentioned that I'm technically not allowed to date or anything else, but said I just needed to be discreet. I'm not entirely sure what that means, aside from the common sense definition of keeping my private life private. I was just wondering if you had any advice about being discreet should I ever want to get involved with someone in the future."

Electra chuckled, looking at her twin. "You've had relationships in the past, right?"

"Not very many. Aside from being ace, I apparently have a reputation for being difficult to get along with," Isis responded with a half-smile. "I haven't had any since finding out about all this madness. Truthfully, I haven't even really thought of it."

Madness didn't even begin to describe it. After Jade told Isis about her being a guardian, Isis had gone into the mansion's library to try to figure out exactly what that meant. She had needed Alex's help to clear up the complex traditions of guardians, which required a ridiculous amount of mental gymnastics. Together, they had figured out that Isis being considered a daughter of the Meadows prohibited her from having romantic relationships with any of the supernatural races, including shape shifters. However, since she was a half-breed who lived on Earth, many guardians wouldn't want her marrying into their family lines.

"So the High Council forbids you from dating shape

shifters. Though you are officially allowed to participate in guardian courtship, almost no guardian is going to want a half-breed sullying their family line," Alex had summarized with a sympathetic smile. "Basically, you're screwed. Just not in the good way."

"I've had a number of lovers," Electra's voice brought Isis out of her thoughts. "Mom taught me first to respect myself and my body. She also taught me to ignore what others thought of me. Most of the old-fashioned guardians already think we're promiscuous simply because of our mother and therefore should be ashamed. The trick is to not let it get to you. They'll think that no matter what you do. If you meet someone you're attracted to and who respects you for who you are, then do what you like. If you want to sleep with them, sleep with them."

"It can't be that easy," Isis said, skeptical of the simple answer.

"Believe it or not, it is. Just make sure you know whom you can trust and whom you can confide in. The only way Aneurin can find out about your personal life is if you tell him or someone else does. He doesn't have a magic mirror and he doesn't know nearly as much as he thinks he does. If he implies that you're sleeping around, that's just his way of saying 'like mother, like daughter.'"

"Well that's a relief," Isis replied. "I thought I was going to have to cast some sort of cloaking spell every time I wanted to have sex."

Electra laughed. "That would be positively *awful*."

Isis stood from the bed and moved over to the window, glancing out at the snowy landscape. Electra rolled onto her stomach, watching Isis. She folded her hands and rested her chin on them.

"Has anyone in particular caught your eye?" she asked, kicking her legs up. Isis gave her a look.

"No. I just wanted to know for future reference. Like I said before, Jade brought it up and I wanted to know exactly how the whole covert sex life worked."

"Ah," Electra said. She rolled back over and stood up. "I'm going to go down and wait for Jet and Lilly. Chances are they'll be calling a meeting with the Four."

"I should probably go and tell Shae," Isis mentioned, letting out a sigh. "She is *not* going to be happy."

Electra shrugged and offered her a sympathetic smile. "Such is life when you're part of a guardian prophecy."

~~*~*~*

Roan sat in his comfortable cell in the dungeons. It seemed like an eternity since he had been brought down, but it had only been a few hours. His jacket was lying on the bed beside him. He sat on the chair next to the small desk in the cell. The chair was facing the back wall of the cell and Roan had propped his feet up on the bed, large hands casually laced over his flat stomach. Almost everything in the cell was dark gray. The majority of the wall, the floor, and even the ceiling were dark. There were rectangles of light near the ceiling illuminating the space. Behind him was a transparent wall of guardian glass. The entire dungeon was clean and brightly lit, the polar opposite of what dungeons were perceived to be.

Roan's thoughts were mostly of Passion. He knew she hated him and he deserved no less. His past mistakes probably had more than a few negative repercussions on her. He knew of at least one.

Roan glanced over his shoulder when he heard a couple pairs of footsteps coming down the hall. After a moment, Adonia stepped into view, followed by one of the head guards, Astrea. The guard was wearing the typical guardian leather armor of the dungeon guards. Her black hair was tied back from her face and her deep brown eyes betrayed nothing. Standing stiffly in the background, Astrea kept her eyes forward.

Adonia stood in front of the glass, staring at him with her normally compassionate green eyes. Her expression was unreadable. Roan looked back to the wall before swinging his long legs off the bed and standing up. He turned and approached the clean glass, holding Adonia's gaze. They stood in silence for a long while, just watching each other.

"I imagine if I were to ask why you're here, I wouldn't get a straight answer," Adonia stated. It was no secret Roan was naturally cagey. Even before he had become an assassin, he had been a closed book to everyone, including his family. It was this trait that had helped him survive for so many years.

"I imagine any answer I give would be written off as a lie," Roan countered.

"Try me," Adonia responded, crossing her arms over her chest.

Roan leaned his shoulder against the glass, running a finger down the clean surface. "I can and will answer any question the protectors ask me, and I will answer truthfully. All except for one: where I've been. It's completely irrelevant."

"Why are you here, Roan?"

"I'm hoping to atone for my past," Roan answered, his gaze never wavering from Adonia's. "There's something you need to know about the Key. First off, that flashdrive is a diversion, meant to distract Jet and Lilly, while also forcing them to gather the Four. The real Key — the one that is supposedly capable of severing the ties between Earth and the Meadows, essentially destroying both — is a living person. And I know where to find him or her. At least, I think I do."

Adonia looked skeptical as she glanced back to Astrea before turning her attention back to Roan. "Where?"

"Wouldn't Jet and Lilly like to sit in? This does concern them as well," Roan pointed out. "They're not the only ones looking for it, which I'm sure you already know. I'd prefer they get it before other . . . interested parties."

"They'll question you once they get permission from

the High Council," Adonia responded. Roan stared at her, not believing his ears.

"Seriously? How long is that going to take?"

"I do not know. Hopefully just a week or two."

"That's too long," Roan growled, turning away from the glass and pacing the cell for a moment. He needed to talk to Jet and Lilly immediately and he had to make sure it didn't get back to Passion. At least not right away. *If she knew all that I know . . . guardians only know what she would do,* he thought as he steepled his hands and placed his fingertips against his lips.

"We have a process that we must adhere to. You know that." Adonia paused. "Is there anything you wish to tell me before I leave?"

Roan turned his eyes back to the glass, dropping his arms. "May I request something?"

"You can request, but I cannot promise I can grant whatever it is."

"I need a book. A shape shifter account or telling of the War of the Meadows."

Adonia blinked a few times. Of all the things she expected Roan to request, that was not one of them.

"There isn't much to do and since I won't have visitors for a while yet, I need some way to pass the time," he explained with a small tired smile. Adonia once again looked back to Astrea, who looked similarly puzzled.

"Is there any particular account you desire?" Adonia finally asked.

"Oh no. Any protector account will do," Roan answered.

"Very well. I shall have a messenger bring it to you shortly," Adonia stated before turning to leave.

"I suppose it would be too much to ask if she is all right?" Roan spoke again, not looking at the departing guardians but rather at the wall.

"Yes. It is too much to ask," Adonia replied before leaving him alone again. He glanced over his shoulder when she was out of sight before returning to the chair that sat alongside the bed. Roan returned to his casual position and waited for a messenger to arrive with the book.

~~*~*~*

Sly ran a hand through her short black hair as she waited for the light to change. The streets were calm, as they usually were at night. Snow glistened under the few streetlamps. She was pursuing a lead concerning Coop's whereabouts. She had decided to inquire at the Lair, a popular rebel shape shifter club. It was run by one of Sly's partners, Alpha, the leader of the rebels and a non-conformist if ever there was one. She was also very well-connected. If anyone would know of a strange shape shifter's whereabouts, it would probably be Alpha. If nothing else, she might have an idea where to continue looking.

The Lair . . . Sly smiled when she thought of the rebels' base, one of the rare places where she felt safe. It was an old hotel the rebels had acquired ages ago and renovated into a club catering to different desires. Aside from the dance club on the first floor, the rooms of the hotel each had a different theme. Whatever someone wanted, it could be found in the Lair.

The rebels were a group of shape shifters, mainly from protector lineages, who wanted to live by their own rules. They didn't want anything to do with protectors or guardians and didn't conform to the rules of other shape shifter sub-cultures. They were a colorful bunch, believing life was about desire, dancing, and freedom from rigid norms. Their club was hidden, but not so hidden that humans couldn't find it. Every species was welcome in the Lair: supernatural and mortal alike. It was always an interesting blend and one of the only places where humans regularly encountered what they would label supernatural. Many old-fashioned shape shifters, as well as the other supernatural races, frowned on the daily contact with mortals, believing it to be dangerous. The continued existence of the Lair seemed to prove this belief wrong. The rebels lived by their own rules and wouldn't back down if challenged. Sly frequently referred to it as *organized anarchy*.

While the rebel leader was indifferent to Lilly, Alpha disliked Jet. She felt he inspired conformity, the ultimate evil in the rebel book. The rebels refused to talk to the protector leaders, so Jet and Lilly asked Sly to drop by the club and ask a few questions. Since Alpha was her lover, Sly was on good enough terms to be an occasional liaison. With her attitude, she fit right in with them when she needed to. She would never live among them, though. Firstly, most rebels enjoyed dying their hair neon colors — bright shades that made one dizzy if looked at for too long. Then there were the piercings, which never held any appeal to Sly. And of course the daily contact with humans, just the thought of which turned Sly's stomach.

Sly glanced in the convertible's rearview mirror when a pair of headlights illuminated the inside of her car. Noticing a large SUV riding her tail, Sly rolled her eyes. Goddamn humans and their ridiculous vehicles. How they continued to survive and thrive, Sly would never know. She turned her attention back to the road, trying to ignore the blinding lights behind her.

The truck rammed into the back of her car. Sly fought for control of the steering wheel as the car swerved about. She glanced behind her, just in time to see the truck slam into her again. Her car was miniature in comparison to the monster behind her. She was on a practically deserted road and had no idea about what was on either side of her, so she glanced to both sides. It looked like a ditch or field of some kind to her left and a wooded area to her right.

The SUV came alongside her and Sly ripped up the

handbrake while spinning the wheel, hoping to wind up facing the opposite direction before the truck could recover. The enormous vehicle sped right past her as she spun about. Sly floored the accelerator again and took off in the opposite direction, glancing in the rearview mirror to check how far the truck was behind her. She narrowly missed a sedan that pulled out in front of her from a side road. Sly gritted her teeth and stomped on the brakes again, swearing loudly. Her car screeched to a halt just a few inches from the side of the sedan. The SUV stopped a few feet behind her, effectively blocking her in. *Great,* Sly thought, hitting the steering wheel and glaring at the sedan.

The driver's door of the sedan opened and a shadowy figure stepped out. Sly squinted as she looked at the approaching figure, who was possibly the most non-descript man she had ever seen in her life. He had a pale face, was average height and weight, and wore a well-tailored brown suit. His thinning hair was light brown and he had an unreadable expression. She glanced behind her at the truck, cursing when the doors to that vehicle opened as well. *Well, this might get ugly,* Sly thought, drumming her fingers on the wheel. Her mind was racing through possible options of dealing with the situation.

The plain man continued his trek toward Sly's window, her headlights illuminating his brown pants. An expensive-looking ring rapped on her window. Noticing his gold cufflinks, Sly spotted the mysterious symbol Isis had told the protectors about and sketched for them. *Uh oh,* Sly thought as she reached down, acting as if she was rolling down the window. In actuality, she was reaching for the gun in her thigh holster, subtly popping open the snap that held it securely in place.

She glanced in her side mirror, checking the actions of the truck's occupants. They were just standing there in the winter night, near her bumper. She noticed none of them were wearing coats. Sly rolled down her window and was greeted by the sight of the plain man's face. Cold blue eyes bore into hers and a deceptively pleasant smile danced across his thin lips. He didn't smell human or shape shifter. He didn't have any kind of scent at all, which she had never encountered before. Sly kept her hand hovering just above the Beretta, waiting for the right moment to spring into action.

"The infamous Sly, at last we meet." His rich voice caressed her ear. Something about the pleasant voice was off. There was venom hiding just beneath the polite exterior. She carefully took the gun out of its holster, hiding it in the shadows coating her lap.

"Well, you appear to have me at a bit of a disadvantage," she stated, smiling up at him. "You know my name and I don't know yours."

"Sly, our employer knows you are an informant for Jet and Lilly. He has a message for them," the man continued, his own hand going behind his back, most likely to retrieve some kind of weapon.

"Well, hate to break it to you, but I'm not a goddamn secretary," Sly replied, switching the safety off. "I'd recommend using the email or the telephone and delivering your message yourself."

"He just wants to say hello," the man replied, ignoring Sly. His arm started to come around from behind his back. Sly pointed her Beretta out the window and fired, ignoring the curse the man shouted as the bullet embedded itself in his shoulder. A shot that close would screw up his hearing temporarily, leaving him disoriented. She shifted into reverse and pressed on the accelerator, causing the two shadowy forms behind her to dive to the side. She then shifted into drive and maneuvered around the sedan in front of her, scratching the front of it and sending sparks flying as she damaged the side of the Monroes' convertible. Sly kept the accelerator floored and didn't look back.

~~*~*~*

Jet sat in his study, a warm glow illuminating the room around him. His elbows rested on the desk and his hands were folded in front of him. He rested his chin on them as he stared at nothing in particular. He was troubled by the news of Roan's return, as was Lilly, and they had spent much of the day trying to figure out how to proceed. He was relieved the feared assassin was finally in custody and the suspected Key had been retrieved, but now they had a completely new set of questions that needed to be answered. Both he and Lilly had met with the Four earlier in the day, shortly after Electra had told them all that had happened. He knew they were going to have to question Roan, a task he wasn't looking forward to.

The soft ringing of the office phone interrupted Jet's musings. He picked it up and put the receiver to his ear.

"Hello?"

"Good, you're there. Jet, I'm afraid I'm going to have to temporarily resign from my informant duties," Sly's calm voice traveled down the line. Jet leaned back in his chair. He could hear a strange clicking on the other end of the line.

"What? Why?" Jet frowned when he heard the sound of a busy street behind her as well as people chattering. "Where are you?"

"I had a bit of a situation on the way to the rebel Lair. Some rather unpleasant men tried to run me off the road," Sly continued. "Now I'm going to have to track them down and kill them. I might even have to torture one or two first just to find out who's behind this whole thing and exactly how they know me, which is going to be *such* a chore. I know how you protectors frown on that kind of thing, so I figured—"

"Wait, whoa. Slow down. Are you all right?" Jet asked, concerned about his former friend. She was a pain in the ass ninety-nine percent of the time, but she was also a damn good informant. Jet couldn't stand the thought of anyone getting hurt because of him, even if it was Sly. He glanced up when Lilly entered the room, shooting him a questioning look. He held up a hand, indicating he would tell her once he was off the phone. Lilly moved to sit in one of the chairs across from the desk.

"Obviously. Jet, do you *really* think you'd be my first call if I weren't?"

"Sly, before you do anything rash," Jet paused, frowning at the strange noises on the other end of the line. "What is that clicking sound?"

"What clicking — oh! This?" The clicking became a little louder. "I'm loading a couple weapons. I'm going to keep your car a little longer. It got a bit banged up in the earlier confrontation."

Jet rubbed his brow, closing his eyes. "You're loading weapons in public?"

"Don't worry. I'm being subtle. I'm not loading a shotgun or anything like that. Haven't gotten any weird looks. The humans are just kind of going about their merry way, not sparing me a second thought."

"Why are you in public?" Jet still couldn't believe she was in a place surrounded by humans. That just wasn't Sly.

"Because where else am I going to find people trying to blend in," Sly answered as if it were the most obvious thing in the world. "Look, Jet, these guys were working for someone and one of them said he had a message for you and Lilly. As if I was your personal secretary. Let me tell you, someone is *definitely* getting punched in the face for that."

"Did he tell you the message?"

Sly paused for a moment. "That's the weird thing. All he said was 'he just wants to say hello.'"

"That's it?"

"Apparently," Sly responded. "I have a couple more guns that I need to load, so I'm going to run. Jet, be careful. These guys . . . they were able to anticipate moves that I hadn't even thought of yet. Also, they didn't have a scent."

"Didn't have a scent? How so?"

"I know it sounds impossible and I can't exactly explain it, but they had literally no scent. No body odor, no cologne, nothing. I've never encountered anything like it before. Maybe this is a new species or a very old one, something along those lines."

"It seems unlikely, but I'll look into it. Thank you for the information, Sly."

"I'll get back in touch once I've resolved this matter. I'll try and save some remains so you can figure out what the hell they are."

"Be careful, Sly," Jet said, knowing he couldn't talk his contact out of doing what she was going to do. He had learned that long ago.

"You too," Sly said before hanging up the phone.

Jet dropped the phone back in its cradle, running his hands over his face. Lilly approached and sat down on the arm of the computer chair, her dark blue eyes holding a look of concern as she waited for him to tell her what had happened.

"Sly is taking a temporary leave so that she can hunt down, torture, and kill some scentless beings," Jet explained, reaching up and intertwining his fingers with Lilly's. "Someone ran her off the road on the way to the rebel Lair. They told her that their employer wanted her to tell us that he says hello."

Lilly leaned down so she could rest her head atop his.

"What are you thinking?" Lilly asked, looking at their intertwined fingers.

"I think someone is trying to get our attention by showing off," he replied. "It feels like a power-play, a way to show us what he or she or they can do. And something tells me Roan might know something about whomever it is. Him popping up with what we thought was the Key and then this attack on Sly? It's a little too convenient."

"We're going to have to pick up where Sly left off," Lilly mentioned. "First, we should meet with Alpha. We might need allies if we're going up against whomever this person is."

Jet glanced up at Lilly. "She won't talk to us, sweetheart. We also have to question Roan and follow up this lead with Cara's mother."

"Then call Alpha and offer to send the Four to negotiate a truce. The rebels and protectors have been at odds for far too long. An alliance with the rebels would be beneficial and Alpha would be a useful ally to have," Lilly replied. Jet smiled at her. His wife was right, as usual. Some things were more important than a feud.

"I'll try," Jet agreed, reaching for the phone. He could only hope the rebel leader would be willing to speak with him. Lilly gave him a supportive smile and moved off to the side, staying nearby to listen to the call.

~~*~*~*

In the lands of Night in the Meadows, two guardians were in the midst of vigorous lovemaking. Illuminated only by the pale light of the moon and the silvery light of millions of stars, their nude interlocked bodies glistened with sweat. The woman straddled her lover, who lay on his back and grasped her hips as he thrust inside her. She had already climaxed twice and as he reached the height of his own pleasure, she did once more.

As Passion rolled off him, Donovan let out a groan of pleasure and chuckled.

"I never need to worry about exercising when you call," he laughed. She grinned as she ran her fingers over his chest and playfully nipped at his ear.

"I'm sure you say that to all the girls," she murmured in her throaty voice. She was breathless, as was he. Their lovemaking always had an intensity that left them both exhausted. They had known each other for years and before her affair with Roan, many had thought she and Donovan would marry. They were a perfect match, even though their personalities were often rather different.

Donovan reached down and trailed his fingers up her thigh, just barely touching her soft flesh. She shivered in pleasure under his gentle touch. She ran her slender fingers through his dark hair as he began to kiss between her long legs. Passion gasped when he found the spot that sent currents of electricity through her body, moaning as pleasure overtook her once more. Donovan had a reputation for being one of the best lovers in the Meadows. He had an almost intuitive understanding of the body and an uncanny talent for being able to find the exact places that unleashed torrents of bliss. His knowledge of sexual pleasure rivaled Passion's own. Passion often wondered if that was why the High Council had paired them, before the whole incident with Roan. Donovan looked up at her once he had finished, running a thumb over his lower lip and smiling at her. The moonlight glistened on the beads of sweat covering his dark skin. Stars shone in his soft brown eyes.

"You are troubled," he observed, resting on his elbow beside her. "I'm guessing it has something to do with why you summoned me out of the blue."

Passion smiled. "Perhaps I just desired an evening of pleasure."

Donovan raised an eyebrow. "If all you desired was sex, you have a number of lovers in your own lands who would be more than happy to oblige."

"Perhaps I desired a male lover tonight," Passion countered, leaning back so she rested on her elbows beside him. "It has been some time since we've seen each other and I have missed you."

Donovan was quiet for a while, studying her. He reached out and gently brushed some strands of hair behind her ear. "If you're worried about Roan's return . . ."

Passion sat up, staring at him with wide eyes. She had not mentioned Roan in her letter to him. Donovan smiled and rolled on his back again, interlacing his fingers behind his head.

"I must admit that I'm a little offended. I have been around for a while, Passion, longer than you. I am a member of the High Council. Give me some credit."

"The guardian men already know," Passion breathed, running a hand over her forehead. "How much else do they know?"

Donovan shrugged. "Just the basics: Roan turned himself in early this morning to the guardian women. He's being held in your dungeons. Worry not. Our secret is still safe."

Passion rolled on her back and ran her hands over her face, letting out a shaky sigh of relief.

"If it somehow comes out," she began.

"It won't."

"But if it does, I'll take the blame. I got us into this mess. The responsibility is mine and mine alone."

Donovan rolled over so that he was facing her. "You'll do no such thing. You did nothing wrong, neither did I. You needed help and I helped you. If the High Council doesn't understand that, then fuck the lot of them."

Passion ran a hand up his face. "You and I both know it's not as simple as that. We could face banishment for our actions. I couldn't ask that of you."

"What kind of man do you take me for, Passion? You don't need to ask. Like I said before, we did nothing wrong. Besides, they're not going to find out," Donovan murmured, turning his face slightly to kiss her palm.

Passion smiled and leaned over to kiss him deeply.

"Have I ever told you how amazing you are?" she whispered.

"I know. I would have made a wonderful husband, but you had to go and get knocked up by a shape shifter," he teased, grinning wickedly. She swatted his shoulder, smiling.

"How are things with your other daughter, by the way?" Donovan asked. "Word is she has a cynicism that could rival mine."

"Isis is doing well from what I hear from the Monroes," Passion replied. "She does have an undeniable cynicism, but could any rival your own?"

Donovan rolled back so he was resting on his elbows. "You sound sad when you speak of her."

Passion shrugged as she sat up. "I'm a stranger to her. I never thought I'd see her again after I gave her up for adoption and now she's living with Jet and Lilly in the mansion. It's a very odd situation and one that's hard to adjust to."

"I see," Donovan said, watching as she stood up and retrieved her dress. She pulled it over her head, tying the sash about her waist.

"Speaking of the mansion, I think I'm going to spend some time there," she mentioned, looking out across the night lands. "I really need to be away from the Meadows, for a little while at least. It may be some time before you hear from me."

"I expected as much. I know of the bond between you and the Monroes. I am glad you have a safe place you can go when you need a break," Donovan said. Passion knelt beside him, trailing her fingers across his chest.

"When I return, we have to catch up," she stated, meeting his eyes again. "I want to hear all about how Lucky became your apprentice."

Donovan snorted. "The High Council has never been fond of me and the dullards have finally figured out the perfect punishment."

"Lucky is a sweetheart and will be a good guardian. Be patient with him," Passion said, half-smiling. She leaned down and kissed him one more time.

"Don't be gone too long," he whispered when she

pulled away. "This place is so boring without you."

Passion smiled and nodded. She stood up and walked off, disappearing in the dark woods.

CHAPTER FIVE

Isis glanced out the window as Jade parked on an empty road. It was so little used there weren't even street lamps or signs. Everything was still and quiet. A goth girl suddenly banged into the passenger window. The girl had metallic purple hair and was covered in what looked like glowstick liquid. She looked like a glowing Pollack painting. She smiled and waved before disappearing into the night.

"Where is this place?" Isis asked, looking over at Jade. Jade merely shook her head as she continued looking out the window. Isis glanced in the back seat where Alex and Shae were sitting. Alex appeared indifferent, whereas Shae resembled a kid in a candy store. She was fidgeting and looking around excitedly with wide bright eyes.

"The club is a little further up the hill, past those trees," Alex answered, gesturing in a vague direction. "The rebels renovated an old hotel into a dance club. They even have a track for drag racing."

"Yeah, yeah, that's very interesting. Can we go already?" Shae asked. Isis stared at her cousin. Shae's enthusiasm left her feeling even more apprehensive about the place and she wanted to know exactly what she was being dragged into.

"What's up with you?" she asked.

"I've been *dying* to see this rebel Lair for ages," Shae answered. She was wearing her best club clothes: tight black pants with a silver belt and a dark purple top with a draping neck.

"For the love of the guardians, why?" Jade asked, mystified. "It's just a club."

"Are you kidding me? The rebels are like the ultimate club goers," Shae replied, adjusting her top a little. "They've practically got a twenty-four hour rave going on most days of the year."

"Sounds like a nightmare," Isis remarked, shuddering at the thought of listening to loud rave music for hours on end. The one she had covered for the local paper when she had been a photojournalist had been enough to sour her on the idea of raves.

"It's not just that, ice queen," Shae stated. "The rebels are all about freedom. Most of them don't even recognize gender norms. Their club has a different room for almost every want or desire. I've heard stories about a glam room, a 30s room, a goth room."

"An S&M room, a jungle room," Jade put in, looking out over the snowy landscape. "They're glorified hedonists, Shae."

"Jade, I'm a protector to the core, but I still think the rebels are interesting and will be extremely valuable allies. We don't need to quarantine ourselves from them," Shae argued. "It wouldn't hurt protectors to take a few pages from the rebel book."

"Uh huh," Jade responded, unconvinced. Isis noticed more shadows moving across the snowy grounds. She hadn't seen anyone come the opposite way, but it was still relatively early in the evening.

"So what are we supposed to do exactly?" Isis asked. Jade had been silent throughout the nearly four hour drive to the club. Jet had also been vague when explaining what he needed them to do. It had been quite clear to Isis that neither Jet nor Jade were fond of the rebels, while Lilly seemed rather optimistic about a potential alliance. Both Remington and Jade had explained the feud between rebels and protectors a while ago, but to Isis, it seemed to be mostly about conflicting philosophies.

"We're here to act as ambassadors on behalf of the protectors," Jade responded. "Our main objective is to negotiate a truce with Alpha. She's the leader."

"In the loosest possible sense of the word," Alex mentioned. "Rebels aren't organized in the same way as protectors or other shape shifter factions."

"Right. Jet doesn't care what we do in there, although I would prefer not to stay overly long," Jade said, twisting in her seat. "Under no circumstances are we to mention Roan's sudden reappearance."

"Don't say anything about the resurrection of the most feared assassin in the world, got it. Can we please go in already?" Shae pleaded as she opened her door and jumped out into the night. Isis grinned and shook her head. Jade sighed and opened her car door. Isis did the same on her side and was practically dragged out of the car by her eager cousin.

"Hey, what the hell," she exclaimed in surprise, nearly slipping in the snow. Shae looped her arm within Isis', slowing her pace a little.

"Can't you just *feel* the energy of the place?" Shae beamed, shivering in excitement. Jade stepped past the two of them, moving up the hill. There was a cluster of trees and a faint light behind them. Their footsteps crunched in the little snow that remained on the ground. Numerous feet had worn the snow so thin that scattered blades of dark grass poked through.

As they made their way in the direction of the Lair, Shae continued to chatter excitedly. She wondered if she should have worn something dressier or more themed. Isis mostly nodded, bewildered, not as familiar with clubbing culture as her cousin. She shivered when an icy wind swept through the grounds. Sharp particles of snow stung her face. Distantly, she could hear the roar of a motorcycle. *Who races in the freaking snow?* Isis wondered, huddling against the cold. She again questioned why Jet and Lilly hadn't sent one of their sons or daughters on this particular errand. According to Jade, they were at the Lair almost every night and were on good terms with the rebels. As they passed through the cluster of trees, Isis heard the sound of retching from somewhere to her right. *Always a good sign,* she thought, massaging her brow as she felt the beginning of a headache.

After another five minutes, an enormous building came into view. Large spotlights illuminated every inch of land up to the clusters of trees. Another gust of wind whipped up a curtain of snow, briefly obscuring the towering hotel from view. It only looked vaguely like a hotel, having undergone extensive renovations. A porch wrapped around the front, illuminated by the warm yellow glow of heated light bulbs. A few shape shifters reclined on the porch, watching the newcomers. Two huge pillars marked the entrance and giant rainbow-colored letters were painted vertically down them, declaring it "The Lair." From where the Four stood, they couldn't see the front door. Isis could barely tell how large the place was. It seemed to stretch as far as the eye could see.

A slender woman in a red hood sat at the base of one pillar with her legs stretched out in front of her. She looked as though she were barely out of adolescence. Isis glanced to the side when a pair of foxes raced across the snow. She could feel Shae almost bouncing next to her. Jade led the way up the steps to the door and to the front entrance where a giant tiger sat.

"Alpha's expecting us," Jade stated, glancing over her shoulder at the strange woman sitting by the pillar. She stood up and made her way around the pillar, trailing her fingers around the smooth surface, her eyes fixing on the

Four. She seemed to study Isis in particular. Isis adjusted her coat, making sure she was hiding as much skin as possible. Her guardian blood caused her skin to glisten faintly in the moonlight. It was so subtle most humans didn't notice it. Shape shifters, however, could easily spot it. When she had first noticed it, the glimmering had fascinated Isis. Now she found it to be more of a nuisance.

Isis turned her attention back to where Jade was talking to the tiger. The large orange tiger approached her, looking her up and down. He then moved over to Alex and repeated the same cursory glance.

"She's expecting us," Jade explained. "Last time I checked, Alpha wasn't fond of waiting."

The tiger looked back at her and snarled, but trotted back to his spot at the door. Jade nodded to the other three and opened the door. The moment the door was open, hard rock music blasted out. Isis cringed at the sudden assault of sound, reluctantly allowing her cousin to pull her inside. They were immediately engulfed in darkness and Isis had to blink a few times before her eyes adjusted to the dim blue lighting. Jade led them over to what used to be a front desk. Two identical women, dressed in red bellhop uniforms, stood behind the desk. The dark blue light made their skin look almost green and their hair was jet black.

"Welcome," said one.

"I'm Morgan," said the other, lifting her right shoulder to better show her glowing nametag, which was pinned just above her breast.

"I'm Tabitha," said the first, mirroring her sister's action.

"May we," began Morgan.

"Take your coats," finished Tabitha, as both women smiled at the Four. Jade dropped her coat on the desk and the other three did the same. The first woman pinned a small slip of paper on each coat, tearing off the bottom of the paper and handing it to the second woman. She in turn handed the strips of paper to the owner of each coat.

"Is it your first time?" began Morgan.

"At The Lair?" finished Tabitha. Isis was beginning to get a little freaked out by the way the twins talked. She and her own sister were identical in appearance, but had never completed each other's sentences. Then again, they had been raised apart for the first twenty-eight years of their lives.

Isis looked around at the darkly lit club. Shape shifters and humans were everywhere. Most locked lips in passionate kisses and many looked incredibly androgynous. Isis could barely see any indications of gender. Everywhere she looked there was brilliantly colored hair, so bright it was almost blinding. The neon shades glowed even in the intense darkness. Splatters of glowing liquid coated the walls like bizarre abstract art. The odd blue lighting seeped into everything: walls and clubbers alike. It softened their features and added to the overall surreal quality of the club. Light beams traveled down the halls, outlining the occasional person who walked past. The rock music continued pounding throughout the hallways.

"She's in her office." Isis could barely hear the twins' voices. She looked back to where Jade was still talking to the two at the front desk.

"Second floor," finished Morgan.

"Feel free to explore," said Tabitha.

"There's something here for everyone," Morgan added with a grin. Jade stepped away from the front desk.

"Enjoy," both twins called after them, waving their fingers in sync.

"I feel like I'm in Dali's imagination," Isis mentioned to Alex as they started for the stairs.

"I'm sure there's a room for that," Alex responded.

They struggled to get through the crowd. A number of neon-haired rebels kept crossing between them, a few pausing to look the four women up and down. Many of them had spiky hair and numerous piercings. They moved and swayed their bodies to the loud rock music. Shae soon mirrored their movement, dancing with a pair of rebels, easily finding the rhythm of the music. Someone smacked Isis' arm and she turned to see Jade motion for her to get Shae. They had business to attend to.

Isis turned and grabbed Shae's arm, tugging her. Shae glanced over at her, annoyed by the interruption. Isis nodded over her shoulder toward where Jade was standing behind her, pointing to her watch. Shae turned back to the pierced dancers and gestured she had to go. One rebel waved and the other blew Shae a kiss before they disappeared back into the crowd of people.

As they made their way to the large staircase, Isis looked into the room next to the stairs. She was surprised to see the floor seemed to be made of glass. It almost looked like the people were dancing on water. Many were dancing so close it was difficult to differentiate one body from another. There was a bar in the back of the large room where two women were doing impressive flair bartending.

There were shape shifters sitting on the steps, some of whom appeared to be under the influence of drugs of one kind or another. Isis couldn't tell whether they were stoned or tripping or both. Some appeared to be in a state of absolute bliss and contentment while others were running their hands over whatever surface was nearest them.

They reached the top of the stairs and found a long hallway with doors lining the walls on both sides. Jade shook her head and went to the left, the other three following close behind. She opened the first door on her right and stepped inside, followed by the other three. When the door shut, the blasting music from the first floor became muffled.

The room they had entered looked like a scene out of a Fitzgerald novel. Shape shifters and humans were wearing twenties fashions, sipping tea and cocktails. Even the furniture looked like it was from that era. In the corner of the room, an old jazz tune played on a phonograph. The walls were a mural of a sunny spring day and the lighting reflected the weather. The people in the room looked up at the four women who entered, staring at their clothes in puzzlement. The room was more like a suite. There was even a second level, where more people dressed in similar fashions stared down at them.

"You've got to be kidding me," Jade mumbled under her breath as she pinched the bridge of her nose.

"Good evening," Shae stepped forward. "We're looking for Alpha's office. Could you point us in the right direction?"

"Very end of the hall, in the Honeymoon Suite," a rotund older man answered in a jovial tone, raising his cocktail to the four women. Isis exchanged a look with Alex, unsure what to think of the Lair.

"Of course it is," Jade said under her breath.

"Thank you," Shae said politely. They left the room, Shae closing the door behind them.

"What is your deal with rebels?" Shae asked Jade.

"Used to come here, years back. I still do visit on occasion. Alpha is Sly's lover and I get along with her well enough. It just frustrates me how rebels don't care about anything other than what's happening in their clubs," Jade replied. "Like I said, they're glorified hedonists."

"And I suppose being lock-step conformists would bring about world peace?" a husky voice asked, surprisingly clear over the throbbing music.

Isis looked behind her to where the voice had come from. A woman leaned against the wall a few feet back. She wore a simple loose-fitting black tank top with a skull and crossbones painted on and tight jeans. There were black fingerless gloves on her hands and thick black cuffs on her wrists. Black studs pierced her ears and one nostril as well. Rings adorned all the toes on her bare feet. Short black cropped hair hung messily on her head, as though she had just rolled out of bed and hadn't bothered to tame it. The woman held herself confidently, her shoulders back and chest up, her spine as straight as a rod. Kohl-lined eyes observed the Four, pausing momentarily on Isis. She arched one dark eyebrow and looked at Jade again.

"I was on stage in the Metal room," the woman explained, moving toward them. "Jade, it has been too long. How are things in your life of servitude?"

"Alpha," Jade responded evenly. Alpha gave a half-smirk and continued down the long hall, motioning for the women to follow. Isis continued to look around, noticing how widely spaced the dark doors were. The rooms had to be huge, most likely suites. She stepped aside when a man dressed in a leather Santa suit hurried past them. Looking to her left, Isis noticed a pair of shape shifter men dressed in vintage military uniforms passionately kissing outside one door. The large gold buttons glinted in the dim light and the tan fabric looked black in the dark. A tall woman with silver blonde hair dressed in an elegant purple and silver gown, passed by the Four, heading in the opposite direction. Isis blinked a few times when she noticed the woman had distinctly pointed ears.

At the end of the hall, there was another dark door, but it was much larger than the others were. Curvy gold vines were painted in the dark wood and the name Alpha had been carved at the top of the door. A track light was pointed at the door, making it stand out in the otherwise dark hall. Alpha removed a key from a chain about her neck, sticking it in the doorknob and unlocking the door. She pushed the door open, stepped inside a large room, and moved aside so the Four could enter.

Isis looked around Alpha's office. There was a large desk in the back. An enormous window overlooking the Lair's grounds dominated one wall. Lights set in the high ceiling and various lamps illuminated the office. Hardwood floors glistened in the warm glow and the entire space smelled faintly of cinnamon and jasmine. Old pictures covered the bright red walls, showing the hotel throughout time. The pictures started in black and white, gradually becoming color in more recent years. Isis noticed women were front and center in every picture. Alpha closed the door behind them and the office was immediately quiet. She moved over to her desk and leaned against it, drumming her fingers on it once.

"Good sound proofing," Shae observed.

Alpha shrugged. "Everyone needs a sanctuary. This office is my sanctuary within a sanctuary."

"I thought this was a club," Isis mentioned. Alpha looked at her for a moment before pushing off the desk and approaching her. Isis watched the woman, a little unnerved by Alpha's attention.

"It's whatever my patrons need it to be. Most of them are outsiders of one kind or another. All races are welcomed at the Lair, supernatural and human, mortal and immortal," Alpha explained, her gaze never wavering from Isis. "The rebels have served as a sanctuary to outcasts for centuries and will continue to do so for many more."

"Supernatural races?" Isis looked over at Jade. Jade continued watching Alpha. She obviously wanted to get down to business.

"Oh my dear, they haven't told you much have they? Yes, there are many supernatural races. Shape shifters, members of the Seelie Court, lycanthropes — we've even had an exile from the Magic Orders," Alpha explained. "But I must admit, we've never had one as interesting as you. Isis, is it?"

"Yeah," Isis said, not enjoying the scrutiny. "But I'm not that interesting."

Alpha let out a short laugh. "You're one of only two known hybrids in existence, the only guardian-shape shifter on Earth, raised by humans, completely unaware of her heritage, and now one of the infamous Four. You have a foot in both worlds. I dare say you underestimate just how interesting you are."

"She's also Gray-A," Shae added. "My cousin is just all

kind of unique."

Isis shot her a withering glare, but Alpha just chuckled. Isis remained quiet, not wanting to get on a potential ally's bad side, which she seemed to have the unfortunate habit of doing.

"How do you know so much about her?" Jade asked the rebel. Alpha looked over at Jade.

"Sly has told me a little, but there isn't a shape shifter alive who doesn't know of the Four. Isis is particularly known among the rebels," Alpha responded, glancing back to Isis. "We've always been fans of your biological mother. She's one of the only guardians who has earned our respect. I do hope to make her acquaintance one day. Seems she'd be the interesting sort to have coffee with."

Alpha sauntered over to a large glass table that was off to the side. Eight large chairs were arranged around the rectangular table. Alpha held out a hand, inviting the Four to have a seat.

"I hope you don't mind a couple of my advisors sitting in," Alpha mentioned as the Four sat down. Isis looked over at the door when it opened and two women stepped inside. One had dark tan skin and blondish brown hair. Her eyes were dark brown in color. She wore a lavender shirt and dark pants. The other woman was tall and black. Her curly brown hair fell to her shoulders and she dressed in neutral shades. Her clothing looked to be leather, but Isis assumed it was made of some other material. Most shape shifters she had met avoided animal hide, which they found to be tasteless. The women sat across from the Four and Alpha sat at the head of the table.

"Ladies, meet Wylie and Amber. They tend bar downstairs and also work as my advisors," Alpha introduced the two rebels. "Amber, Wylie, meet the Four. They're here on behalf of Jet and Lilly, to negotiate a truce between protectors and rebels."

"That's rather historic," the woman in lavender, who had been introduced as Amber, stated.

"It has been many, many years since any protector leaders have wanted to negotiate with the rebels," Alpha agreed, looking back to the Four. "Probably even before my grandmother was the leader of the rebels."

She leaned forward, resting her elbows on the glass, smiling as she looked at Isis. "You see, Isis, rebel leaders have always been women. Women are more suited to rebel against the status quo. We have more to gain and much less to lose. Not so with the other shape shifter groups. They tend to favor patriarchal rigmarole, though I will grant that the protectors at least require spouses to hold equal rank and title. Still cliché if you ask me. Protectors are almost as bad as the guardians with their positively archaic way of life."

"Are we going to talk history or can we start negotiating?" Jade asked. Alpha leaned back in her chair, raising one leg so she could rest her wrist on her knee. A smile played on her lips as she looked at the Four, slowly twisting her chair left and right.

"First, I want to know what brought on this sudden desire for a truce or alliance, whatever Jet and Lilly wish to call it," Alpha began, glancing to her advisors, who also seemed intrigued. "The few times protectors have desired a truce with rebels, whether officially or not, it has meant ill-tidings, mostly wars. Lately, we've been hearing some rather unsettling stories."

"Such as?" Alex asked. Alpha lifted her shoulders.

"Shape shifters have been talking about the sudden increase in disappearing bodies a few months back," Wylie chimed in. "Some say it's still happening."

"Assassins have been acting unusually as well. Ever since the coup and the murder of Adara and Gia," Amber remarked, tapping her fingernails on the glass. "Not many frequent the Lair, but the few that do have all but vanished in the past few weeks."

"Then there's the tales of your own exploits," Alpha continued. "That nasty business with Adara some months back. Word is the protectors were also there, among others. I heard you had an ally with you that night, a strange nameless man."

Isis tried to keep her face expressionless. She wondered whether or not she should ask Alpha about Coop. Perhaps he had been to the Lair. As if reading her thoughts, Alpha briefly glanced over at Isis.

"We've recently located the Key, or what we originally believed to be the Key," Jade stated. "Jet and Lilly aren't oblivious to the unusual incidents that have been happening lately. It's part of the reason why they sent us. An alliance between our groups would be beneficial for both of us. We could combine resources and—"

"You say the Key has been found?" Alpha asked, looking over at Jade. "If that's so, why do Jet and Lilly need or want this truce?"

"Like I said, there is some question about whether or not it is the actual Key. As you mentioned, there are strange things happening," Jade explained.

"If the real Key has not been found, that means there is probably some kind of fight on the horizon. Not many would let that kind of power go unclaimed and it is a fairly recent prophecy. It's going to lure out all kinds of unsavory types," Alpha said. "And Jet and Lilly expect rebels to fight and die for them?"

Isis looked over at Shae. She was no diplomat and had never sat in on negotiations like this, but even she could tell it wasn't going well. Jade calmly folded her hands on the table and looked between Alpha, Wylie, and Amber.

"Let me ask you something. Do you allow separatists in the Lair?"

"You know I would never let that kind of speciest scum in the front door," Alpha responded sharply, as if the very suggestion offended her. From what Isis had learned since finding out about shape shifters, separatists were considered the lowest of the low among most shape shifters. They believed themselves to be the superior species, higher than all others. Separatists felt there would be no peace until humans were wiped out and all the other supernatural species recognized the superiority of shape shifters. The only ones who interacted with them were assassins. As far as Isis could tell, both groups were relatively small. Still, they did manage to cause quite a lot of trouble. She suppressed a shudder. Just the thought of separatists getting their hands on the Key was frightening.

"I thought as much. Separatists have killed many shape shifters in the past, mostly rebels. They hold a particular grudge against them. Why is that?" Jade continued, bringing Isis out of her thoughts. She glanced over at the rebels, trying to glean their response to her teammate's statement.

"Rebels have always had a soft spot for the human race. Easy money," Alpha responded.

"Oh, I think it's more than that. Rebels stand with the underdogs. You said it yourself: this place is a haven for outcasts of all sorts. Most humans have no idea of the other supernatural races, which puts them at quite a disadvantage," Jade continued.

Alpha smiled. "I don't deny my dislike for how humans are seen as a lesser species and frequently used as pawns or worse. But I wouldn't go so far as to say rebels are protective of them. We merely recognize their right to exist."

"Many rebels have fought in wars alongside humans," Alex pointed out. Amber brushed some hair behind her ear and glanced over at Wylie. Isis noticed they seemed amused by the proceedings. She sat back, turning her eyes to the large window. The wind whipped up some snow, rattling it against the panes of glass.

"Of their own volition. No rebel has ever been ordered to go into battle and none ever shall be," Alpha countered. "Do you have a point you'd like to make?"

"We're essentially fighting for the same thing," Jade stated. "Whatever is going on, the separatists have something to do with it."

"Separatists don't have the kind of power required to erase people," Alpha said dismissively. "Even with the assassins, they don't have the numbers or firepower to be a threat to anyone."

"No, they don't," Jade agreed. "I didn't say they were behind it. I said they were *involved* with it. Someone or something does have that kind of power, and chances are they are using the assassins and separatists. It would be beneficial for us to work together in order to get to the bottom of it."

Alpha looked skeptical. She glanced over to Amber and Wylie. Wylie shrugged after a moment and Amber nodded. Alpha turned her attention back to the Four, pursing her lips.

"I'll agree to this truce on a couple of conditions. The first being that Jet and Lilly are not allowed to interfere with rebel life. This truce is between them and me only. I do not lord it over the rebels. I can ask for their aid, but it remains up to them whether or not they give it," Alpha stated.

"They would expect no less. They would only interfere if you asked them to," Jade agreed. "They want this alliance to be a two-way street."

"I'm sure Lilly does. Her husband, on the other hand? Well, I'm not entirely convinced," Alpha said, nodding toward Isis. "I would also like to have a word alone with young Isis."

Isis felt her eyes widen for a moment at the odd request. She turned her attention over to Jade, who looked hesitant.

"Oh relax, Jade. It's just a little chat. I promise to return her to you in one piece," Alpha scoffed. "This truce is off to a magnificent start."

Jade turned her eyes to Isis, questioning. After a moment, Isis nodded once, indicating her acquiescence to the request.

"Fine," Jade agreed, turning her eyes back to the rebel. "Is there anything else you can think of?"

"Not at the moment, but I reserve the right to request anything else I think of later," Alpha answered. "The three of you are welcome to explore the Lair. Wylie and Amber mix a mean drink if you're thirsty. Most of our drinks can be made virgin, if you're abstaining for any reason. There are no maps, but somehow, patrons always find what they're looking for."

Jade removed a small business card from her pocket, pushing it toward Alpha. "Jet and Lilly's personal number, should you need to contact them."

Alpha glanced at it before pushing it off to the side. She motioned to Wylie and Amber.

"Give them whatever they like. It's on me tonight," she instructed. Jade, Shae, and Alex got up and followed Wylie and Amber to the door.

"I'll be at the front desk," Jade told Isis. Isis nodded and watched as her three teammates disappeared behind the large door. The blasting music invaded the room for a moment, then muted once the door closed again. Isis turned her attention back to Alpha, who still looked toward the door.

"Forced into the life of a protector," Alpha snorted. "You have my sympathies."

She got to her feet, calling over her shoulder. "Would you like a drink?"

"No, thank you," Isis replied, watching as the woman walked over to a drinks cabinet. She opened it up, revealing a multitude of liquors and glasses. The sound of ice clinking against glass soon drifted through the office. Isis bit her bottom lip, wondering if she should speak first. The last thing she wanted to do was say the wrong thing and undo all the progress Jade had made. If her past was anything to go by, it was something Isis was more than capable of doing.

"Forgive me for asking, but are you old money too?"

Isis mentioned, looking pointedly at the old pictures on the wall. Alpha glanced over her shoulder, following Isis' gaze to the pictures, and then turned her attention back to the drink she was making.

"Most shape shifters are," Alpha answered with a smile, reaching for a square bottle of expensive scotch. "Our kind seems to have a natural aptitude for finances. Most of the leaders of shape shifter factions come from old money. Jet's lineage has close ties to the guardians, so that helps. Who knows how much money that man has to his name."

Alpha poured her drink, screwing the top back into the bottle. She turned back to Isis, swirling the amber-colored liquid in the stout glass. Approaching the table again, she sat next to Isis in the seat Shae had been in. Sipping the scotch, Alpha studied the younger woman's face.

"Is there anything in particular you wanted to talk to me about?" Isis asked when she realized Alpha wasn't going to speak first. Alpha smiled as she twisted the chair slowly, side to side.

"I got the distinct impression that there was something you wanted to ask me," Alpha answered. "Something you didn't want to ask around your friends."

"I don't—"

Alpha stopped twisting and leaned forward so that they were inches apart. "Isis, I read people for a living, been doing so for longer than you've been alive. You have something you want to ask. Don't insult me by denying it. Out with it."

"I don't know if I should," Isis said, feeling a little uncomfortable. She didn't know how much Jet and Lilly would want her revealing about the mysterious Coop. She hadn't even told the other three what she had found out from Phil.

"Whatever you ask, it stays in this office. You have my word," Alpha reassured her, leaning back in the chair again. Isis swallowed, trying to figure out how much to reveal to the strange woman.

"Have you ever encountered a patron who wore sunglasses inside, even in the dark, and displayed some kind of … superior strength? Even more than was normal for shape shifters?" she finally asked. Alpha stared at her, blinking a few times.

"Come again?"

"I'm looking for someone I met a long while back. He went by the name Coop. He was tall, brown hair, blue eyes, clean-shaven, and he always wore sunglasses. Even when it was dark out. I first met him in a club, which was dark, and he was wearing sunglasses then too," she explained. Judging from the bewildered look Alpha was giving her, Isis could tell she hadn't expected that particular question.

"Was he blind?" Alpha asked, sipping her scotch.

"No," Isis responded, shaking her head. "There was another man similar to him who was also in the club. He went by the name Dane. I was wondering if anyone like them ever came to your club."

Alpha was quiet as she continued studying Isis. She took a long sip of her scotch.

"You're looking for this Coop?" Alpha asked, rattling the ice in her glass.

"You mentioned that we had a mysterious ally at the Obsidian Manor. That was him. He had superior healing capabilities. During the fight, he was shot, in the stomach and shoulder, and grazed as well but he healed almost instantly. My sister told me he was able to punch through guardian glass without breaking his hand," Isis explained, pausing and frowning. "I think something was done to him, something that might be done to other shape shifters. He indicated there were others who needed his help. If that's true, I want to help him."

Alpha sipped her scotch again, a small smile dancing across her lips. "You've just found out about shape shifters and already you want to save them?"

Isis shrugged. "Isn't that what the Four are supposed to

do?"

"Yes, I suppose it is," Alpha said quietly with a soft laugh, looking at her scotch. "I'm afraid I've never met this Coop. However, there were a couple shape shifters who came to the Lair wearing sunglasses who demonstrated some different…traits than is normal for our kind. The rebels called them ghosts because they moved through the world like shades. We never saw where they came from or where they went. They would come sporadically and they were both very aloof. Neither was big on interaction; kind of lone wolves in a way. We never saw them together and they only came periodically, never a set schedule. One started appearing more than twenty years ago, haven't seen him for at least a year. He had a very," Alpha paused, furrowing her brow as she looked into her glass, "interesting ability."

"Which was?"

Alpha looked up at Isis with a half-smile. "He could affect electricity. Sometimes, sparks shot off the top of his head."

Isis looked at her skeptically. Alpha put her glass down on the table and rested her fingertips on the rim, slowly twisting the glass around.

"Wouldn't have believed it if I hadn't seen it with my own eyes. His unique abilities earned him a nickname among the rebels: Shocker. Not sure where he's gone off to. He might turn up again eventually."

"You said there was another one?"

"The other one has only started popping up more recently, within the last five years. We've only seen that one twice. Tall, dark hair, blended in a bit better than Shocker. No special abilities that I noticed, not like Shocker's anyway. The only thing that made him stand out was he moved with an almost boneless grace."

Alpha stood up. "Of course, that's not counting the numerous stories that have passed down among rebels for centuries."

"Stories?" Isis asked, twisting to watch Alpha. She nodded as she went to the window, sipping her scotch.

"There are six recognized shape shifter groups: protectors, rebels, seducers and seductresses, thieves, assassins, and vigilantes. Separatists have never been recognized as a group and were only recently lumped in with assassins," she explained. "The rebels have long told stories of a seventh, known only as the glowing-eyes."

"The glowing-eyes?" Isis asked.

"Named for their eyes, which are said to glow like fire in the night. We don't know much about them, but they are different somehow. Something about the way they move, the way they act. They often turn up around the scenes where shape shifter bodies disappear, usually right before. If the stories are to be believed, they've been doing so since that mystery first popped up."

Alpha walked over to her desk, opening a drawer and pulling out a newspaper. She flipped a few pages in, then folded the paper over, and approached Isis again. She pointed at a black and white picture.

"This is from the opening ceremony of the new bank in town, Grenich," Alpha explained. "Look in the background, in the shade."

Isis did, leaning closer and squinting as she tried to see what Alpha was showing her. She remembered that day. The new bank had gone all out for the big celebration in town and many citizens turned out. It was more like a festival than a bank opening, though the good press was probably priceless for Grenich, which Isis heard was doing excellent business.

"I don't see anything," she said. Alpha pointed at the paper, directing Isis' gaze toward a thick oak tree. It took her a minute to see the strange woman, half-hidden behind the trunk. Her gaze was straight at the camera and even though the resolution was shoddy, there was something about her eyes that stood out.

"Could be an ordinary citizen, but some of the rebels

are claiming she's one of the glowing-eyes," Alpha mused, her own eyes fixed on the picture. "A few rebels were there and claim to have seen her. According to them, she moved with an unnatural ease and no one seemed to notice her. It was as if she were invisible to human eyes. They also told me she had strangely luminous blue eyes, which she kept hidden for the most part. Unfortunately, none of them were able to track her. She was there and then she was gone, as if into thin air. I'd dismiss the story if not for the fact that it matches up with most of the other rebel tales of strange shape shifters."

Alpha looked contemplative as she took a sip of her scotch and moved back to the towering window in her office. "You know how fairytales were like warnings for children?"

"Yeah."

"I think our stories were meant to serve a similar purpose."

Isis frowned. "So what do you think they were meant to warn about?"

Alpha sighed and looked down at her scotch. "About a threat we don't see, one hiding in the shadows, waiting for an opportunity. The one that has been picking off shape shifters and erasing their existence for millennia. The one the Four is supposed to defeat."

Isis swallowed, feeling more nervous than she had in a while. Alpha turned away from the window, approaching the table again. The windowpane rattled when a strong wind hit it, more snow splattering against the clean glass.

"Things are often more connected than we realize, Isis," Alpha stated cryptically. "If you search for this living ghost, I warn you to be wary about what else you might find along the way. Your search will take you to dangerous places and you will be changed. In my experience, shape shifters don't hide without good reason."

"It sounds like you know a whole lot more than you're letting on," Isis observed. Alpha shrugged nonchalantly, sipping more of her scotch.

"I'm good at reading people, but I'm also very good at reading situations," she said. "I can tell you're not one to let questions go unanswered, no matter what the cost. A mystery as old as the vanishing bodies and shape shifters like ghosts … there is something sinister behind it, something ancient. The very worst kind. You probably think you can go at this alone. You can't. Stay close with your team. You will need their help and they, in turn, will need yours."

Isis nodded. "Is that all?"

Alpha looked at her. "Is it?"

"Well, thank you for your help," Isis said, her brow creasing. Alpha grinned and nodded once.

"Do visit again, Isis. You may deny it, but you would make a great rebel," Alpha mentioned. Isis snickered as she got to her feet.

"It was nice meeting you," she said politely. "I'm sure Shae will drag me back in the future."

"There are quieter rooms where you can seek refuge," Alpha reminded her, watching as Isis exited her office and closed the door behind her.

Alpha finished her scotch and went to her desk, dropping down in her chair and putting her feet up on the desk. She opened one of the top drawers, pulling out a small black cell phone. Dialing a number, Alpha pushed off the desk and wheeled over to the large window. As the phone rang, she watched the snowy landscape outside.

"Hello?" the voice of her tenant answered. He sounded tired, as he always did. Alpha watched snowflakes drift around in the dark winter's night. She wondered how much snow would fall.

"The Four were here, negotiating on Jet and Lilly's behalf," Alpha said.

"Odd. I thought they would've sent Sly, given your relationship," the man responded, coughing once. Alpha wondered if he had been sleeping.

"Sly's taking a temporary leave from her informant duties," Alpha said, pausing. "I met Isis. I fear for that one. She is still looking for Coop and she isn't one to give up."

"Didn't you dissuade her?" the man asked.

"Tried to, but like I said: she's not one to give up. Can't tell whether that comes from her mother's side or her father's," Alpha replied with a small smile, twisting her chair side-to-side. It was not in her nature to dissuade people from searching for answers. The man sighed and Alpha could practically hear him rubbing his face in irritation.

"Gotta say, doc, your plan isn't going all that well," she mentioned.

"They've got the fake Key and they've got Isis," the man replied. "We just have to make sure it stays that way."

"If you say so," Alpha humored him, wheeling back to her desk. "I still don't know how you plan to accomplish whatever you're planning without Coop or Roan."

"With some preparation and a little luck," the man responded. "Goodnight, Alpha."

Alpha disconnected the call, holding her phone in both hands and resting it against her chin. She noticed four dark shapes exit the Lair and watched as they disappeared in the cluster of trees. Tilting back in her chair and turning her face to the ceiling, Alpha closed her eyes. The lights flickered once as the wind continued blowing outside.

~~*~*~*

The next night, a red Porsche pulled up the winding secret path leading to the mansion, followed closely by a silver Jaguar. Freshly fallen snow crunched softly under the wheels of the vehicles. The cars stopped at the gate. The window of the Porsche rolled down and a hand pulled open the box before pressing against the handprint scanner. The light traveled down the large hand, beeping as it changed from blue to green, and the gate started to swing open.

The cars eased up the winding driveway, only stopping when they reached the garage door. The passenger side door on the silver Jaguar opened as a shorter man with black hair and an attractive face exited. He hurried over to the door, quietly cursing the frigid winds that swept over the grounds, and searched for the security system box on the side of the door. He quickly found it and entered a code. Inside the garage, a light clicked on as the doors rolled open.

The man bounced from one foot to the other, hands jammed in his pockets as he watched the cars pull into the garage. He followed them in and closed the garage door from the inside. The cars parked side-by-side in two empty spots, the same ones they always parked in on the rare occasions they visited the mansion. Three men got out of the Porsche and the driver exited the Jaguar.

"Ajax, you drive like a geriatric human," the man who had opened the garage door grumbled as he moved to help with the small amount of luggage the group had brought. Ajax glanced over at his younger brother.

"What are you going on about now, Nero?" Ajax asked pleasantly, straightening his coat. He bent over and reached into the small back seat of the Porsche, grabbing one of the bags.

"I'm freezing my fucking balls off in this damn cold and you snail crawl into the garage," Nero groused, rubbing his hands together vigorously and blowing into them.

"You're a shape shifter. Suck it up. Besides, we couldn't very well do ninety into the garage. I doubt Jet and Lilly would be pleased if we smashed into their cars," Nero's other brother, Malone, put in as he tossed Nero a bag.

"It would be funny, though. Seeing Jet's eye start twitching," Devin laughed as he grabbed his bag. Jensen, a friend of the brothers, grabbed his heavy duffle bags from the backseat of the Jaguar and slid one over his right shoulder. He followed them through the garage. He was more dressed up than the others in a dark jacket, dark slacks, and a white shirt. Jensen had been an orphan the Deverells had taken in many years ago. Jet and Lilly had saved both Jensen and his sister — getting them out of a country on the brink of war — and he repaid them with unwavering loyalty. He traveled with the Deverells around the world, acting as Jet and Lilly's global eyes and ears. They reported odd happenings and fought back against any plotting or machinations they came across.

It had been years since the Deverells and Jensen had returned to the mansion. When Lilly called them with news of Roan's return, they knew it was time to come back. Strange things were happening, and Roan's resurrection seemed to herald the start of something big.

"I'm going to find Jet and Lilly and let them know we're here," Ajax said as he opened the door to the mansion.

"I'll go with you," Malone offered.

"I'm going to get settled in. I'll meet up with you later," Jensen mentioned as he made his way toward the main stairway. He had been dealing with an enormous amount of grief for the past few months and there were times he craved solitude. The Deverells found it was best to let him come around on his own.

Jensen jogged up the stairs and made his way toward the room he usually stayed in when he lived at the mansion. Everything was the same in the enormous dwelling, which was both a good and bad thing in Jensen's opinion. He ran a hand through his soft brown hair. His entire body was tense and he was exhausted. He was looking forward to being alone for the night. The past couple months had been particularly hard for Jensen and he wanted to forget them.

He shifted the dark green duffle on his right shoulder. It held weapons, some books, and other odds and ends.

The other matching duffle contained his clothes, all of which were ironed and carefully folded. He was a bit of a neat freak when it came to his belongings.

Jensen turned down the hall that led to his room. He had his own place in town, but he wasn't ready to return there yet. Jensen planned to spend at least a week at the mansion, just to take it easy and put the past year or so behind him.

"You have some goddamn nerve, showing your face here again," an angry feminine voice growled from behind him. Jensen stopped and turned around. He should have known he would never get to his room without being stopped by at least one angry tenant.

A slender woman stood behind him, arms crossed in front of her. Her hair was as dark as Jet's, and she resembled her father, only without the angry eye twitch. She was a little shorter than was typical for shape shifters. She was wearing tight blue jeans, a low cut burgundy top, and pointed tan boots, one of which was tapping the floor. She stood stiffly and he could sense the anger radiating off her.

Jensen squinted, trying to recall her name. He knew *why* she was mad at him, but he couldn't remember for the life of him what her name was.

"Look, Mary …?" Jensen began, throwing out the first name that popped into his mind. He grimaced when she shook her head. *Damn.* "Hillary … Melanie … Tiffany … something with a 'y' right?"

"Hunter," she answered in an exasperated voice.

"Oh wow, I wasn't even *close*," Jensen laughed. Hunter didn't look so amused. It was just his luck the Monroes' youngest daughter would hold a grudge.

"Anyhow, I won your cash fair and square. It is hardly my fault that you weren't as good at poker as you thought," Jensen stated, flashing his trademark charming smile. Normally, it melted people on the spot, but it only seemed to irritate Hunter.

"You also conveniently left out the fact that you were briefly a thief. You tried to pass yourself off as a normal protector," she responded coldly. Jensen shifted the bag on his right shoulder.

"See, that was kind of my bad. I just assumed everyone here knew who I was," he responded with only a hint of sarcasm. "Now, if you'll excuse me, it's been a long few months. I'm very tired, so if you don't mind . . ."

Jensen turned and continued down the hall, not bothering to wait for a response. He wasn't up for a fight. After what felt like an eternity, he finally came to his room. Jensen pushed the door handle down and slipped inside the large room. He dropped his bags on the floor and looked around.

"Dammit, they redecorated," he grumbled. "When did that happen?"

Jensen heard what sounded like splashing water coming from the back of the room. Reaching for his large knife, Jensen stealthily made his way to the bathroom. He knew it was unlikely an assassin or intruder had gotten into the mansion, but he wasn't taking any chances. Jensen had spent most of his years dodging attempts on his life and it had taught him to never let his guard down.

He noticed the bathroom door was opened slightly. A cream-colored glow spilled out in the otherwise darkened room. Faint traces of mist lazily curled out, escaping from the humid washroom. Jensen arched an eyebrow, now intrigued more than anything. He carefully pushed the door open the slightest bit more.

In the bathtub, there was a beautiful woman with short dark brown hair. Jensen noticed a faint glisten to her skin. She was a guardian, but since when did guardians live in the mansion? Most of the woman was hidden by fluffy clouds of sweetly scented bubbles and her eyes were hidden under closed lids. Only her long legs, slender arms, and head were exposed. One of her legs was curved at the knee and her ankle dangled on the edge of the tub. Her arms rested on the sides of the tub and her head leaned back against a rolled up towel.

Hmmm, Jensen thought as he tapped the flat of his knife blade against his lips. He slipped the knife back in its sheath under his arm and moved into the bathroom. Using his natural stealth, Jensen gathered up all the towels and the satin robe on the floor. He moved back out into the main room, dropped them in a pile, and then swaggered back to the washroom. Opening the door all the way, Jensen walked inside and stuck his hands in the pockets of his jacket, leaning his weight against the sink across from the bathtub.

Jensen watched the woman for a moment longer before clearing his throat loudly.

~~*~*~*

Jet and Lilly looked up from the papers they were reviewing when they heard a knock on the study door. The protectors exchanged a look. They weren't expecting any visitors that night. Their daughter, Brindy, reclined on the chaise lounge. She had been engrossed in a book when she heard the knock. She straightened up, looking toward the door.

"Come in," Jet called. The door opened and a man with cropped brown hair and bright green eyes entered. Jet and Lilly smiled, both rising to their feet and walking around the desk.

"Ajax," Jet greeted warmly.

"How are you, my friends?" Ajax replied, embracing Jet. Malone entered shortly after his older brother. He smiled when he saw the protectors, hugging Lilly tightly when she approached him.

"It has been much too long," Lilly said as she stepped forward to embrace Ajax.

"When did you get in?" Jet asked, hugging Malone. It had been years since they had last seen the Deverell brothers in person. They were some of their oldest and most loyal allies and friends.

"Just now," Ajax answered as he embraced Brindy. "Brindy, you're all grown up! I remember when you barely came up to my elbow."

She laughed lightly as she jumped up and embraced Malone. Devin sauntered in behind his brothers, followed closely by Nero.

"Aw, don't tell us we've missed out on the party," Nero said jokingly, laughing when Brindy ran into his arms. "Good to be back in the old mansion."

"Where is Jensen?" Lilly asked, glancing between the brothers. Both she and Jet looked to the open door expectantly.

"He's just gone up to his room. The months have been hard on the poor man. He needs to rest and recharge. Don't worry, he'll make an appearance at breakfast tomorrow," Ajax answered. Jet's smile gradually faded and he exchanged a concerned look with Lilly before turning his attention back to Ajax.

"His room?"

"Yeah, where he usually stays. Why?"

"Isn't that—?" Brindy began.

"Brindy, would you please run upstairs and show Jensen to his new room?" Lilly requested as Jet ran a hand over his face.

Brindy nodded and bolted out of the room, leaving the Deverell brothers looking very confused. Jet looked back to them. They could only hope Brindy reached Jensen before he made it to his old room. *That's a situation that could turn quite ugly,* Jet thought.

"There is much we need to catch up on. Please, have a seat."

~~*~*~*

Isis had been determined to relax. It had been a

stressful few weeks, or months, and her tense muscles were screaming at her. She was worn out from all that had happened. Isis let her mind wander, not thinking about the fact that she owed Steve and his new girlfriend a dinner since she'd had to cancel the last one.

Isis was dozing when she thought she heard her room door opening. She debated for a grand total of five seconds before deciding she was too tired to care. In the back of her mind, Isis was annoyed with herself for forgetting to lock the goddamn door, but she didn't fixate on it. The water was perfect and unless the world was ending, she did not intend to get out of the tub. She jerked awake when she heard someone loudly clear his throat. Her eyes snapped open and she twisted her body to see who it was.

There was a tall, lean man standing by her sink. He looked incredibly debonair, more than any other shape shifter she had met. He wore a nice jacket with a light-colored shirt, dark slacks and matching shoes. The stranger relaxed against the sink — a stance that spoke of confidence. He had brown hair with a slight waviness to it. His sharp blue eyes sparkled with intelligence, a certain amount of mischievousness hidden in their depths. His hands were hidden in the jacket's pockets and a half smile played on his lips.

"Well hello there," he said with a charming smile, his voice deep and smooth with only a hint of a lingering British accent. "Would you mind telling me who you are and why you're bathing in my room? Not that I mind."

Isis shook off the stunned feeling and moved to righteous anger.

"Don't you knock!?" she snapped, sinking a little lower in the tub. "Who the hell are you!?"

The man's smile grew a little, which made Isis see red, and he shifted his weight. He crossed his left leg over his right, his hands still in his pockets.

"My name's Jensen," he said politely, going quiet for a

few moments as he looked at her expectantly. "Okay, this is where you tell me your name. Unless, of course, you want me to call you the mysterious nude woman."

"I'm Isis, now get out!" Isis snapped, her voice bouncing off the immaculate tiles. Jensen smiled even wider, unaffected by her shouting.

"No need to be rude. You're the one who's in *my* room," Jensen replied calmly, sounding bored. Even his words were elegant, indicating he was highly educated. He craned his neck. "There wouldn't happen to be room for two in there by any chance?"

"You are *so* lucky I don't have anything to throw at you," Isis warned, glaring daggers at the man. "And this is my room."

"Your room?" Jensen asked. "Are you new or something?"

"Or something," Isis replied, getting more and more aggravated with each passing moment. She looked around the bathroom, searching for a towel or her robe. "What the hell happened to all the towels? Where's my robe?"

Jensen reached behind him and grabbed a hand towel from rack on the wall to his left. He tossed it to Isis, who easily caught it.

"You're hilarious," she said, her voice dripping with sarcasm.

"And you're using up my hot water, so chop-chop," Jensen replied. She responded by dunking the towel in the tub and hurling it at him. He dodged but she managed to hit his shoulder with the wet projectile.

"Good aim," he complimented as he tossed the sopping towel to the side. He reached up and brushed the stray droplets of water off his jacket, scrunching his nose. Just then, Brindy appeared in the doorway. *So much for privacy,* Isis thought as she tossed her hands up in the air and dropped them back in the tub in complete exasperation, unintentionally splashing herself in the face. She heard Jensen chuckle and wished she had a knife to stab him.

"Oh good. Jensen, I found you," Brindy told him, breathless. "Um, you're going to have to stay in one of the guest rooms."

"Damn. I was looking forward to getting to know Isis," he said with mock disappointment and she scowled.

Brindy glanced over at Isis, confusion clear in her eyes. "Isis, why are the towels out in the main part of your room?"

Jensen chuckled again. "Yes, Isis, what *is* that about?"

Isis glared at him. "You're an ass!"

Brindy looked between the two of them. "Am I missing something?"

Jensen frowned as if in thought. "I don't know. Isis, stand up."

"Everybody get out of my room! Now!" Isis demanded. Jensen smiled as he followed Brindy out of the room. Isis waited until she heard the door close before she got out of the tub. She made her way to the main part of the room, her feet leaving wet footprints the entire way. Stray bubbles clung to her naked skin in random patches and she shivered against the chill in the darkened room.

Isis soon came upon the pile of towels, which was topped off by her robe. She grabbed the robe and wrapped it around herself, jerking the tie angrily until the knot was tight. Crossing the room, Isis locked the door. She held the back of her neck as she rolled it, trying to calm herself down. Jensen was one of the most obnoxious people she had ever met. *Hopefully I won't have to spend any measurable amount of time with him,* she thought.

CHAPTER SIX

"No!"

Shae rolled her eyes as she followed Isis out of her room into the main hall. She had been trying for the better part of an hour to talk her irate cousin into coming to dinner later on. Electra wanted to see her uncles so Jet and Lilly had arranged a small dinner for that night. The hardest part was convincing Isis to attend, especially after the previous night's incident with Jensen. The halls were mostly quiet. The entire mansion had been buzzing with rumor and speculation since Roan's return.

"Come on, ice queen. You *have* to meet your uncles," Shae protested, attempting to use the old nickname to persuade her cousin. It failed miserably.

"If he's going to be there, I won't be," Isis said stubbornly. Shae ran a hand through her hair. She had to find some way to convince Isis to come to dinner. The Deverells were important allies and would probably be working closely with the Four.

"Just do what you always do during holidays. Ignore him," she suggested. "Come on, Isis, please. Passion and Electra are going to be there. He's not going to act like an ass around them."

Isis spun on her heel. "Have you *met* him?"

Shae shrugged in response. "Briefly. We passed each other in the hall when I was coming down to talk to you. He seemed very polite, not to mention sexy."

"He's a jerk!"

"Isis, you can't skip this. Steve's going to be there. You promised him that you would meet Tracy. Come on." Shae quickened her pace and moved in front of her cousin, blocking her escape and ignoring the irritated glare Isis gave her. "I promise you, Jensen will be on his best behavior. Even if he's not, who cares? Are you going to let some random man rule your life?"

It was a low blow, but Shae was desperate. Isis dropped her shoulders and looked over at her cousin.

"One dinner and I don't have to see him again?" she asked tiredly.

Shae put her hand up. "I give you my word: one dinner, that's it."

"Fine," Isis grumbled as she stepped around Shae and continued on her way. Shae smiled, pleased with herself. The hard part of her night was over.

Meanwhile, downstairs in the kitchen, Jet watched as Passion went through a cabinet, shuffling things around until she found what she was looking for: a bottle of red wine. Around them, the kitchen was alive with activity. A few different cooks were putting together the dinner that would be served later that night. The brightly lit kitchen smelled of a variety of different foods.

Passion put the bottle of wine on the counter and began going through the drawers. She had opted to wear a red sweater and black dress pants for the dinner. She refused to wear a dress when she wasn't in the Meadows. Jet sat on a stool, elbows resting on the counter top. Passion nearly bumped into one of the chefs as she searched for whatever she was looking for. The chef easily sidestepped her, throwing a look in Jet's direction. The sound of sizzling food filled the air and the warmth from the stoves kept out the winter chill.

"Passion, maybe if you told me —" Jet began as he watched Passion continue searching through the drawers.

"Where is your damn —?" Passion snapped her fingers a few times as she tried to think of the word. "Cork-popper?"

"The cork*screw* is in the top left drawer behind you," Jet replied. "Do you want to talk about his return?"

"No, I most certainly do not," Passion said testily as she retrieved the corkscrew. She turned back to the wine and stabbed the sharp tip into the cork. Jet watched as she easily pulled out the cork with a loud pop and then tossed the corkscrew back into the drawer. She grabbed the wine bottle and poured herself a full glass.

"You know the problem with the Meadows?" Passion asked, pointing the bottle's neck at Jet. He smiled and shook his head. Though it certainly wasn't under the best circumstances, he was happy to have Passion around again. It felt like old times, before he had told her daughters about their heritage. Since then, there had been a certain amount of tension between them. It wasn't obvious, but Jet could feel it. His betraying her trust had left an indelible mark on their friendship.

"No, Passion. Tell me what the problem is."

She waved the bottle around slightly. "Nowhere *near* enough alcohol."

"No, but the guardians do have vastly superior wines." Jet watched as she took a long swallow of wine.

"But you can't get drunk on them," Passion countered in a singsong voice. "Earth is infinitely better at creating substances to numb the body and mind for short spans of time."

Jet watched helplessly as she strode from the kitchen, wine bottle and glass in hand. He looked back to the bustling kitchen, unsure of what to do for his friend.

~~*~*~*

Isis couldn't believe someone had the gall to seat her across from Jensen. She had a sneaking suspicion Jensen would've found some way to sit across from her anyway. She sat in between Shae and Electra, trying her best not to look across the table at Jensen. The meal was passing with little incident. Electra was talking amicably and animatedly with her uncles, Jet and Lilly occasionally chiming in. Passion sat toward the head of the table, a bottle of red wine and a glass in front of her. She had already finished one bottle and Isis found herself wondering what a guardian's alcohol tolerance was.

Lilly was at the other end of the table, looking radiant as ever in a pine green dress with silver trim. Steve sat toward the end of the table with his girlfriend, Tracy, sitting next to him. She had been overly friendly when she first met Isis, which Isis ignored. Tracy was a small petite woman with dishwater blonde hair and intense dark eyes. She was wearing a dressy pink top and gray skirt. She glanced over at Isis and smiled. *At least she didn't wave,* Isis thought as she smiled politely back. She was surprised Tracy had been invited, especially since Roan was likely to pop up in conversation. Shape shifters didn't seem to use the classified label as freely as humans did. Then again, he was in the Meadows and his return was likely to be known soon enough.

Isis picked up her glass of water, listening to Electra laughingly tell a story from her youth. The sudden feeling of a shoe brushing against her shin caused Isis to gasp loudly and go completely rigid, dropping her glass of water all over the table. All eyes turned to her and she felt herself flush bright red as she picked up the overturned glass, mopping at the water with her cloth napkin.

"I'm sorry," Isis muttered, attempting to kick Jensen under the table. He easily dodged the kick, giving her an innocent look that only added to her anger.

"Passion, have any guardians spoken with Roan yet?"

Ajax asked, thankfully taking the attention off Isis. Passion laughed humorlessly and took another long swig of wine from her glass.

"Nobody's spoken with your brother yet, aside from Adonia. We're still waiting on approval from the High Council," Jet answered. Ajax nodded and turned back to his food.

"Are you five going to stay for a while?" Lilly asked from the other end of the table. Isis bit the inside of her cheek when she felt the same foot begin brushing against her other shin. She refused to embarrass herself again.

"As long as you need us to," the man who had been introduced to Isis as Malone replied. He and Devin seemed to be the quietest of the brothers. Malone struck her as the more intense of the two.

"Wish I would've slept with you. Doubt you would've tossed a man off a roof," Passion mumbled into her wine glass, causing everyone to turn and stare at her. Nero, the youngest Deverell, began laughing. Passion tilted her head back and finished off the glass.

Jet grabbed the nearly empty bottle from in front of her. "Passion, please eat something."

Passion grumbled something under her breath and used her fork to move the untouched food around on her plate. Electra had her hands over her face.

"Isis, how are things among the humans?" Nero asked. When Isis had first been introduced to him, she couldn't help but stare in shock. He appeared to be only a few years older than she was, and yet she knew he was more than half a century older. Isis was still getting used to the concept of immortality being a real thing.

"I still can't get over the idea of being raised by humans and having no idea what a shape shifter was," Tracy chimed in, smiling when she glanced at Steve.

Isis was still in the process of dabbing up the spilled water. She shrugged in response, subtly palming something off the table.

"Not really that weird. Both species occupy the same space," Isis replied, placing the object she had grabbed under one of her slender legs. "You both inhabit the same planet, after all. You do pretty much the same exact things. You're a lot more similar than you realize."

"You were some kind of photographer, right?" Jensen asked, raising an eyebrow. Isis glanced across the table at him, surprised. He swirled the dark red wine in his glass.

"Uh, yeah. I worked for the local paper in town," she replied. "How'd you know?"

He smiled as he sipped wine from his glass. "Lucky guess."

"Actually, we have spoken with Steve on an occasion or two," Devin said, glancing down at Steve with a friendly grin. He cleared his throat and glanced over at Isis, trying to gauge how angry she would be at the revelation. Isis could feel Jensen's foot prodding her knee again, but she ignored it.

"Well there's a thought that's going to keep me up for a year or two," Isis replied a bit tensely. She didn't like the idea that strangers had taken such an interest in her life. The thought of being spied on was still creepy.

"They just wanted to make sure you were safe," Steve explained. "Lilly and Jet said it was all right to speak with them."

"He's right, Isis," Jet added and Lilly nodded in agreement.

Isis glanced at Steve and then back to her uncles before looking down at her food again.

"Bloody hell!" Jensen suddenly shouted in surprise, jerking backwards. He reached down and rubbed his leg. He glared at Isis, his sky blue eyes narrowing in accusation. She smiled pleasantly back at him as she took a sip of water from her newly filled glass, her eyes daring him to say something.

"Jensen, what's wrong?" Jet asked, confused by the strange outburst. Lilly also watched him with concern.

Jensen straightened his jacket and ran a hand over his hair.

"Nothing. Just a leg cramp," Jensen replied as he composed himself, smoothing the front of his nice shirt and adjusting his jacket.

"Must've been quite painful to make you squeal like that," Isis commented, innocently. Jensen's only response was another cold glare and she merely smirked in response. Isis jumped a little when she felt Shae pinch her arm. She almost knocked into Electra, who stared at her sister's odd behavior.

"Behave," her cousin warned under her breath. Isis rolled her eyes, but turned back to her dinner. She put the fork she had hidden under the table back in its original place.

"So, will the lovely Sly be around later?" Nero asked.

"I doubt it. She has taken a temporary leave," Jet responded. "I'm not sure when she'll be in contact again."

"No!" Nero dropped his fork and looked between Jet and Lilly. "What happened?"

"Nothing," Jet answered. "I will tell you later, if you wish."

"But Jade and her make such a great couple," Nero continued, grousing. Isis looked down the table to her teammate. Jade grinned behind her glass of wine, taking a small sip.

"We're still together, Nero. You're only interested because you want a three-way," she teased. Nero looked at her and grinned mischievously.

"Jade, your cynicism *wounds* me," he replied, clutching his chest for dramatic effect.

Both Malone and Devin chuckled at the repartee between the two. Most of the people at the table seemed amused by the conversation. Isis heard a soft buzzing toward the end of the table and glanced over to where Steve and Tracy were. Tracy reached for her purse and pulled out a small phone, frowning as she looked at the screen. She typed something and then put the phone back in her purse.

"I'm sorry. I have to leave," she said, standing up. "My friend in the hospital needs me to bring something to her."

"Oh that's too bad," Jet said as she and Steve stood up. "It was nice meeting you, Tracy."

"Likewise," Tracy said. "I had a lovely time. Isis, we should definitely find some time to get together again."

Isis stared at her, not sure how to respond. Tracy seemed relatively normal, but Isis wasn't one for hanging out with strangers. Shae was better at socialization. She also knew Tracy wanted to make a good impression on Steve and Isis didn't particularly enjoy being used. Still, she felt she owed it to Steve to at least make an effort.

"Okay," she replied. She figured it would be easy enough to get out of should she change her mind. Sipping her cold water again, Isis ignored Jensen smirking at her.

"Great," Tracy beamed, flashing her perfect pearly whites. "Bye, everybody."

"I'll walk you out," Steve offered. They left the dining room.

"Seems like a pleasant girl," Ajax mentioned when they left. "I haven't seen any of the Monroe children around tonight."

"They're at the Lair," Jet said, sipping his wine.

Ajax's eyebrows rose slightly. "The rebel club? Alpha doesn't mind?"

"We've negotiated an alliance with the rebels," Lilly stated. "The Four were able to do so a couple nights ago."

"Alpha took quite an interest in Isis actually," Jade mentioned.

"Really? Thinking of going rebel, Isis?" Jensen asked.

"Didn't come up," she responded evenly.

Jensen leaned forward. "So then what was Alpha so interested in?"

Isis shrugged, feigning indifference. "I don't know. Maybe it was just my winning personality."

"What did she want, Isis?" Jet asked.

"Just wanted to talk to the new girl," she lied. Jet raised an eyebrow, obviously skeptical. Isis looked back down at her plate, remembering Alpha's warning to keep her team in the loop. Steve came back into the room, taking his seat again. Isis tilted her head, noticing faint rings under his eyes for the first time. He noticed her looking at him and smiled in a way that was meant to be reassuring, but only made him look more worn out.

"Steve, you've been sleeping on the job," Jensen teased. "The rebels have corrupted young Isis here."

"What?" Steve asked, frowning in confusion.

"How is the search for Coop going?" Ajax asked, changing the topic.

Jet shook his head. "No trace. The man has disappeared."

"Perhaps Roan would know something," Malone suggested. Jet nodded, twisting a fork in his hand.

"I'll ask when Lilly and I are granted permission to question him, though I doubt he'll be forthcoming if he does know something," he said. Isis looked back at her plate, wondering if they would ever find out anything about Coop. The man had disappeared without a trace, into thin air. *The rebels called them ghosts because they moved through the world like shades,* Alpha had told her. Isis barely heard the rest of the dinner conversation. She was lost in her own thoughts.

~~*~*~*

"What is that guy's problem?"

Jade looked up from the strawberry cheesecake Shae, Alex, and she were picking at. Isis sat on the opposite counter, head resting against the cabinet behind her. Behind them, the quiet sounds of dishes being washed was beginning to peter out.

"Who? Nero? He's an unapologetic flirt and can't stop

thinking about sex for more than two minutes. I daresay he meets the diagnostic criteria for nymphomania," Jade responded before eating a small bite of the rich cake from her fork. The dinner had been over for a few hours. Electra had finally been able to convince her mother to return to the Meadows. Jet and Lilly were meeting with the Deverells and the Four had retired to the kitchen to pick at what would have been dessert. The Deverells had passed on dessert, much more interested in discussing the eventual questioning.

"No. Jensen," Isis grumbled. "The guy is a pretentious ass. It's like he thinks he's a gift to the world or something."

"Ah come on, Isis. He's all right," Alex responded.

"He didn't molest you with his foot for most of the evening," Isis argued. Alex paused for a moment.

"Well, you got me there," Alex chuckled as she stabbed her fork into her designated slice of cheesecake. "He used to live here, didn't he, Jade?"

Jade nodded. "A long, long time ago. He came with Nat after their parents were murdered. Shortly before the Second World War, the Aldridge line was completely wiped out. They had always been the Monroes' main allies in Europe. They went back quite some time, back before the Tudors come to think of it. Unfortunately, someone decided the line had gone on long enough. Someone had begun picking off the family and then one night, there was a brutal attack. The remaining Aldridges were slaughtered around the world in one of the most devastating coordinated attacks protectors have ever experienced. We're still trying to figure out exactly who was behind the strike. Only Jensen and Nat managed to escape the bloodbath. Jet and Lilly had to pull *a lot* of strings and call in all their debts, but in the end, they were able to smuggle them over. Jensen and Nat actually arrived the night Cassidy and Hunter were born."

Jade paused, pushing a bit of cheesecake around with

her fork, thinking. "The protectors were all stunned. The Aldridge line was ancient, going back to the first protectors. They had survived numerous coups, battles, and other dangerous times. To have practically an entire line wiped out in a few short years — it was unthinkable. No one ever expected such a thing to happen. Protectors all over the world mourned the death of the Aldridge family, as did the guardians. Jensen and Nat lived at the mansion for a while, mostly for their own safety. Jensen was always restless, but Lilly convinced him to spend a few years at the mansion, where he was protected by guardian magic. The Monroes became like a second family to Jensen and Nat. Eventually, Jensen decided to go with Orion and the Deverell brothers to hunt down the people responsible for the death of his family. Nat chose to stay here."

Jade rubbed the bridge of her nose with the back of her hand, closing her eyes briefly. Isis glanced over at Jade, knowing the story of the original women thought to be the Four and how it was a sensitive topic for Jade. She had photographed the gruesome murder scene of one of the women, just before the body vanished.

"You all right, Jade?" Shae asked, concerned.

Jade nodded. "I'm fine. Right, Jensen. I'm not sure if he ever found all those responsible, but he decided to continue travelling with the Deverells, even after Orion's death. They occasionally stopped by the mansion, but their visits became less and less frequent. I introduced him to his lover, Bryn, during one of their short visits. I haven't seen him in ages and only spoke to him briefly to tell him what had happened to Nat and Bryn. He was never thrilled with his sister being part of the Four, but I think he was just concerned for her safety. I know Nat always worried about him, even though they spoke almost daily. Truthfully, I wasn't sure if he'd ever set foot in the mansion again. He loves the Monroes, but the loss of his sister was devastating."

Things went quiet in the kitchen. Isis shifted her weight

and thought back to their time in the Lair.

"I asked Alpha about Coop," she blurted out. All three women stopped eating and looked over at her.

"You what?" Jade asked, putting her fork down.

"I thought it might be worth asking," Isis explained. "Alpha had already figured out that I wanted to ask her something. I couldn't think of anything else to ask."

Jade leaned back, checking the kitchen for any lingering staff, then looked over at Alex, nodding toward the open kitchen door. Alex walked over and kicked the doorstop out from under the propped open door. As the door quietly swung shut, she rejoined the other three at the counter.

"How badly did I screw up this time?" Isis asked, dreading the response.

"What did Alpha say?" Jade asked, sounding more intrigued than pissed off. Isis took it as a good sign. She hopped off the counter, leaning against it.

"She said she hadn't seen Coop, but two men with similar habits had been to the Lair before," Isis began. "They wore sunglasses in the dark club, moved with an unnatural grace, but neither were regulars. She said one was able to affect electricity. The rebels called him Shocker because sparks sometimes shot off the top of his head."

Isis hated telling them that part. Judging from the looks they gave her, they found it just as ridiculous as she did. The scents of the meal lingered in the kitchen. The night was quiet and still outside.

"She mentioned that the rebels called these men ghosts or glowing-eyes. They have been telling stories about similar shape shifters for centuries. They think they're another group of shape shifters, one that isn't recognized," Isis continued. Shae moved around the counter and stood next to her cousin, resting her hip against the smooth surface.

"Alpha warned me not to look for Coop on my own," Isis finished with a shrug. "I figured I should bring up what she said."

"Did she tell you if the rebels know anything else about the glowing-eyes?" Alex asked, obviously interested in the story.

"She mentioned that they tend to show up right before a body vanishes into thin air. Apparently a couple rebels thought they saw one at the celebration when the Grenich bank opened," Isis answered, looking back at Jade. "Alpha also mentioned how searching for answers would lead me to encountering darkness unlike anything we've encountered so far."

Alex looked over at Jade. "Think she's trying to rattle us?"

Jade slowly shook her head. "No, I don't so. I've heard rebel stories about strange shape shifters before. Not the ones relating to the missing bodies, but it's not a huge leap to connect the two."

"So what do we do?" Shae asked.

"Firstly, none of us are going to investigate anything on our own. No matter how small a lead, we investigate it together," Jade began, pointing at Isis. "I mean it, Isis."

Isis raised her hands. "All right. You have my word: no investigating solo."

"Next, we should keep information about Coop as quiet as possible. Any information we find out we keep between the Monroes and us. If we're looking for him, chances are we're not the only ones. I don't want anyone finding out about us before we find out about them."

"Sounds reasonable," Shae said. Alex and Isis nodded in agreement.

"I also want to find out more about these rebel stories if we can," Jade mentioned. "Hunter or Cassidy will probably be able to help us with that. Let's just hope the rebels wrote some of them down."

"If they did, I'd be happy to look them over," Alex said. "And on that note, I think I'm going to call it a night."

"Me too," Jade said. "You two have a good rest of the evening. I'll talk to Hunter in the morning."

Isis and Shae watched as they left. Once they were gone, Shae turned back to Isis. The kitchen was dark around them and the only light came from a single fixture above the counter.

"So, what did you think of Tracy?" Shae asked. Isis could tell from her tone that she had been waiting to ask her that all evening.

"Did Steve look tired to you?" Isis asked, looking over at her cousin.

"He's a detective. He's been working weird hours."

Isis shook her head, not satisfied with Shae's response.

"It's more than that. He has worked weird hours before," Isis pointed out. "He looked completely worn out. I've never seen rings under his eyes before."

Shae paused. "You know, now that you mention it, he did look a bit under the weather. You should call him later."

"I will," Isis said, pausing when she noticed her cousin was still looking at her. "What?"

"His girlfriend, what did you think?" Shae repeated and Isis shrugged. She hated it when people asked her opinion on others. She never knew how she was supposed to respond and it always seemed like no matter what she said, it was wrong.

"She seems nice enough," Isis answered, moving for the doorway. Shae followed her.

"Wow, you actually liked someone. That's a change," she joked. Isis gave her an annoyed look as they made their way to the main staircase. She barely heard the numerous questions about her uncles as they walked in the direction of her room, lost in her own thoughts again. Once they reached her room, they said their goodnights and Isis stepped inside. She closed the door, locked it, and went across the room to the large window. Isis looked up at the moon. Some dark clouds hung in the sky, obscuring the many stars.

She closed the curtains, blocking out the light from the snow, and moved back across the room to her nightstand, pulling open the drawer and retrieving a thin spiral. Isis pulled up the right sleeve of her dark sweater exposing her bare arm, where she had swiftly jotted down the number of Halley Waterson, Cara's mother, the only lead they currently had on Coop. She wrote down the phone number in the corner of a page. Jet had briefed them on the search earlier that morning, mentioning the possible lead. He was planning to make contact later in the week and might need the Four to do a follow-up. Of course, Lilly and he would probably have their hands full with Roan and the task would likely be assigned to the Four.

Once she put the spiral back, Isis held the pen for a minute. She tapped it against the palm of her other hand, debating what to do with the information. She had promised Jade she wouldn't investigate on her own, and Isis fully intended to keep her word. However, she questioned the wisdom in having four people question one source. From what Jet had said, it sounded as though Halley could be jittery. Alpha also told her shape shifters didn't usually hide unless they had no choice, meaning Coop had probably gone underground for a reason. He implied there were people after not only him, but Isis as well. Surely a small investigation with fewer people should be considered. After all, the fewer people who knew about a person in hiding, the less likely said person could be found. That was the whole philosophy behind witness protection.

Isis kicked off her shoes and folded her legs under her, leaning against the headboard of her bed. Her mind was racing as she tried to sort out the wisest course of action. After a moment, Isis got off the bed. She wasn't going to figure out the answer in an evening. The best course of action at present was taking a hot shower and turning in for the night. She could think about it more in the morning.

~~*~*~*

Early the next morning, Roan sat at the desk in his cell. His bright green eyes were glued to the book lying on the desk and he slowly twirled a pencil around his fingers. He was waiting for one of two people and knew it would be some time before either of them made an appearance. So he remained focused on his book. It was an account of the War of the Meadows as told by one of Jet's ancestors.

> *In the beginning, there were two guardians charged with watching over death: Death, for natural death, and Chaos, for violent causes. Chaos became corrupted by the power he had over life and death. He began to play very dangerous games with life and death, bringing back those who had already died and then concealing his actions by killing them again. The ones he brought back were completely under his control, lacking any form of free will. They became mindless servants of the one who brought them back. When Death discovered the actions of Chaos, he confronted him. Chaos deceived him and promised to stop. But he did not. When Death witnessed his brother resurrect a young child, he went to the High Council to inform them of the grievous actions of his brother. It was done with a heavy heart, but Death knew Chaos could not be allowed to continue violating the laws of nature.*
>
> *Chaos was called before the High Council to plead his case. He argued it was the right of guardians to interfere with Earth matters to figure out the processes of life. He believed it his duty to figure out how death worked and why. Chaos viewed the Earth as belonging to the guardians and the guardians alone. Despite the High Council's best attempts, Chaos steadfastly refused to cease his experimentations. The High Council, realizing he was*

afflicted with a dangerous madness, stripped him of his title and banished him from the Meadows.

Chaos sulked in the shadows for decades, studying the dark art of necromancy, and eventually amassed an army of resurrected servants. When he had gathered thousands, he opened a portal between worlds, and went to war against the Meadows.

In the first wave, the guardians suffered heavy losses. Though they had the advantage of intimate knowledge of the lands, the army of Chaos had the advantage of not feeling any pain. For years, the battle raged and finally the guardians called upon their shape shifter allies to aid them in the war.

Roan flipped the thin pages rapidly, skipping to the end. Scratching his brow, his eyes scanned to the bottom of the page and the very last line. He circled a word in the last sentence and scratched a brief note on the edge of the page, then dog-eared the page.

The sound of footsteps in the hall reached his ears and Roan closed the book, getting to his feet. Adonia stepped in front of the glass. She was wearing a soft orchid dress that seemed to enhance the guardian shimmer in her skin. Her wise dark green eyes looked at him expectantly. Roan bowed his head as a sign of respect.

"You've requested to see the Monroes again. Why?" Adonia asked.

"To warn them about something," Roan replied, his eyes never moving from hers. She studied him, clearly suspicious.

"About what?"

Roan studied her, tapping his book lightly with his fingers. "Why haven't they been to question me yet? I know Jet dislikes me, but surely he's not so petty that he would just ignore what information I might have. And I know Lilly certainly wouldn't let petty grievances prevent them from questioning a valuable source."

"You know it's much more complicated than that. The High Council is still considering their request to see you. That takes time."

Roan laughed in frustration and walked toward the back of his cell, shaking his head. "Unbelievable. Unbe-*fucking*-lievable."

"You haven't answered my question: What do you need to warn the Monroes about?"

"Look, as much as I respect your ancient laws and traditions," Roan began, "the information I have is urgent and potentially time-sensitive. I have to speak with them."

"And I told you: I cannot just go over the High Council without good reason," Adonia responded.

"Adonia, listen to me. The Monroes need to know about the Key. From what I hear, the protectors are more focused on finding some random shape shifter. If they keep poking around without knowing what they're getting into . . ." Roan paused and shook his head. "The protectors are valuable to the guardians. How many can your people afford to lose?"

Adonia crossed her arms over her chest. "Is that a threat, Roan?"

"Merely a warning from years of experience," Roan replied. "If the members of the High Council continue dragging their feet, the Monroes will run into a fight completely blind. Believe me when I say, no good will come of that."

"If you have a message for Jet and Lilly, I will gladly pass it along to them," Adonia offered, brushing some hair over her shoulder. Roan licked his lips, shaking his head as he looked to the side.

"The information I have may cause some guardians to act … unwisely. However, if you could give them something for me, I would be much obliged."

"What do you wish to pass along to them?"

Roan moved to the slot that was normally used to pass meals through and put the book in it. "Give them this."

Adonia took the book from him and flipped through it. "I'm certain they already have this in their library."

"Adonia, please, just give them that book."

She glanced at him and nodded before turning to leave. Once she was out of his sight, Roan turned back to his cell. He bit his lower lip to prevent himself from screaming in frustration. *Damn guardians and their damn traditions! They're a bureaucratic nightmare,* he thought angrily. That book was a last resort and he wasn't sure the Monroes would even understand the message he sent. Roan paced around his cell like a caged animal, running a hand through his hair. He could already tell things were going to get complicated. And complications never yielded anything positive.

~~*~*~*

Jensen wandered around the mansion early the next night, dressed in his usual nice clothing. The sound of his shoes clicking on the tile was one of the few sounds in the halls. The shape shifters who lived in the mansion were going about their own business. Jet and Lilly were meeting with the Deverell brothers about Roan. Jensen had been invited to sit in but declined. It was just a regular meeting and he found those to be incredibly dull. He had considered joining the protector leaders' children at the rebel Lair, but decided not to at the last minute. Absurdly loud house music would not be enjoyable. He hadn't seen the Four around. He reached the door that led down to the training room and heard the faint sound of someone working out. Jensen raised his eyebrows, glanced around the hallway, and then started to descend the stairs to investigate the noise.

He reached the bottom of the steps and looked at the sight before him. Isis was working out, punching and kicking one of the punching bags that were suspended by solid chain links. The bag rattled violently with the intensity of the strikes. She was wearing dark workout clothes that gave her skin an almost luminous quality, but the lights in the room were too bright to highlight her faint guardian glisten. The harsh lights glinted off the small droplets of sweat that had begun to bead on her skin. Jensen swallowed as he shifted his weight, struggling to maintain his indifferent demeanor.

Isis stopped striking the bag and took a step back. "Can't say that I'm surprised you're a voyeur as well."

Jensen grinned. "It was my shoes on the steps, right?"

She twisted around, looking at him with those bright green eyes of hers.

"What can I do for you, Jensen?" she asked as she unwrapped the tape from her knuckles. Jensen leaned against the wall.

"I can think of *all* kinds of answers to that question," he stated. She rolled her eyes as she reached for her water bottle.

"Oooh, you've gone and made me weak in the knees," she responded in a snarky tone before taking a long drink from the blue bottle. "I bet all the girls fall for that line."

"You'd be surprised," Jensen said, approaching her.

"Doubt it," she scoffed as she moved to leave the room, meeting him halfway across.

"Do you enjoy solitude or something?" he inquired. Isis paused, leaning back to look him up and down. He stood a couple inches taller than Isis, but she wasn't the sort to let a person's height intimidate her.

"Do you?" she asked.

He raised an eyebrow. "I asked first."

"Just a natural loner, I guess," she replied. "I enjoy having time to myself."

"Hm, interesting," Jensen mused as he began to circle her, clasping his hands behind him. She turned with him, keeping him in her sight. He stopped and she did as well. Jade had mentioned earlier that Isis was a skilled fighter and Jensen was curious to see how accurate the statement was.

"I answered your question. What's your excuse?" Isis asked, holding his gaze. A mischievous smile crept onto his face.

"I was raised by humans and they ingrained a lone wolf mentality in me," he replied, imitating her voice. Isis scowled and stepped around him, muttering something under her breath.

"What was that?" Jensen asked, turning to watch her leave. She stopped and spun on her heel so she faced him again.

"I said that it is completely impossible to be civil to you!" she snapped and he stared at her. It didn't take much to aggravate her. Then again, he was sure the past few months had been incredibly stressful.

"Sorry, I don't recall asking you to be," Jensen responded, a little annoyed. He hated it when people used civility to develop a martyr complex.

"No, you wouldn't," Isis shot back.

Jensen shook his head. "I don't even know what that means."

"It means you are without a doubt the most arrogant person I have ever met! And believe me when I say, *that* is an impressive accomplishment."

"You certainly have me figured out," Jensen responded sardonically. "If I'm arrogant, you're judgmental and narrow-minded."

Isis blinked. "Excuse me?"

"You figured me out after knowing me a grand total of what? A few days? You're practically the definition of judgmental," Jensen answered harshly.

Isis shook her head and turned to leave. "You don't know a damn thing about me, Jensen. And you have no idea what or how I think."

Jensen scowled as he watched her storm up the stairs. He hated people who thought they were always right. Nero came down the stairs a few moments later, frowning and glancing behind him.

"Wow, my niece looked furious. You two get in a tussle or something?" he asked, gesturing behind him.

"She started it," Jensen half-lied. Truthfully, he didn't remember who started the argument. Nero sighed and hooked his thumbs in the pockets of his faded jeans. He was wearing a plain white shirt, the top buttons undone. Nero rarely dressed any way other than casual.

"She's my niece and you're my friend. Can't the two of you just get along, or at least act civil toward one another?" he asked.

"I will if she will," Jensen responded, trying not to sound childish and failing miserably.

"You're much older than she is, man," Nero reminded him. Jensen shook his head and turned his attention to the punching bags on the far wall.

"Ajax wants you to keep an eye on her," Nero began. Jensen spun around, narrowing his eyes at his good friend. Nero just shrugged.

"No," Jensen said.

"Something is up. Whatever it is, Isis might be in the middle of it. This Coop approached her, not any of the others. She might be important. We're going to be busy helping the Monroes and Isis has been known to sneak out. Last time, she wound up in the middle of a full-blown assassin coup. She got lucky once and who knows if that luck will hold out. Please, Jensen," Nero pleaded. Jensen rolled his neck, hoping to relieve some of the tension.

"I'll think about it. But I think she is more than capable of taking care of herself."

"Fine. Thank you." Nero went quiet for a few moments. "So that's my older brother's daughter."

"She definitely takes after her mother more."

Nero chuckled and nodded in agreement. Jensen moved over to the boxing ring and leaned against it.

"It's creepy though, isn't it?" Nero continued as he moved over to lean against the ring next to Jensen.

Jensen frowned as he looked at Nero. "What is?"

"How much they look like Selene," Nero responded. "I thought Lilly was exaggerating, but looking at them, you can see the resemblance."

Jensen gave him a very skeptical look. Selene, one of the earliest night guardians, was said to be the most beautiful and bravest woman among humans, supernatural races, and guardians. She was also an important legend to both the shape shifters and the guardians. She had fallen during the War of the Meadows, but had been allowed to return to life. Selene had vanished shortly after, never to be seen or heard from again.

"I don't see it," Jensen said, shaking his head. "Their hair is much lighter and you've mentioned that their eyes do that weird thing where they change colors. They definitely look more like Passion."

"You are such a nitpicker," Nero laughed. Jensen shrugged and smiled. Upstairs the faint sound of footsteps signaled the mansion dwellers were going about their nightly routines.

~~*~*~*

Jet was on the phone when the messenger Appeared in his office. Lilly stood from the chair she had been sitting in and approached the messenger, who handed her the book she held. The messenger disappeared in a bright flash of silver light. Lilly approached Jet, studying the cover of the book and held it out for him to see.

"That sounds good. I'll check in next week," Jet said to the person he was talking to before hanging up. Lilly opened the cover and a slip of paper fell out into her hand.

"Apparently, Roan requested that Adonia give this to us," she said after reading the note.

"Why? We have this book in the mansion library," Jet mentioned, his brow creasing as he opened up the cover and began paging through the book. It was a full account of the War of the Meadows, told by one of his ancestors.

"Jet, a page is dog-eared, over here in the middle," Lilly pointed out, opening the book to the folded page. They both read the small print of the page, which told of the end of the War, just before the reconstruction and rebuilding of the Meadows.

Finally, Chaos was vanquished and the guardians and their allies emerged victorious.

The word "vanquished" had been circled and there was a penciled note in the margin in Roan's handwriting.

Learn from the past, Monroes. Sometimes we miss small things that are actually quite important.

CHAPTER SEVEN

"Ladies."

Isis bit the inside of her cheek as Jensen's voice reached her ears. She and Alex had been practicing sparring when Jensen had wandered into the workout room. Alex went to the edge of the boxing ring and Isis twisted to look over at him. Wearing his usual cocky smirk and dressed to the nines, as always, Isis doubted the man had any normal casual clothing. His nice shoes barely made a sound on the mats as he crossed the room and stopped at the boxing ring. Jensen rested his hands at the edge of the ring, looking up at Isis and smiling.

"What's up, Aldridge?" Jade asked as she approached from the opposite direction. She was sweating from the intense kickboxing she had been practicing. Her dark workout clothing was practically soaked through.

"Where's the fourth?" Jensen asked, turning his gaze to Jade.

"Back here."

Isis looked over to where Shae had been doing pull-ups. She let go of the bar and dropped to the floor in a crouching position. She straightened up and jogged over to the other four shape shifters.

"Jet and Lilly want a word right away," Jensen's eyes wandered back over to Isis. "Looks like the four of you, the Deverell brothers, and I are going to have a bit of fun tonight."

"Meaning?" Jade asked.

"Alpha called. Seems some rather unusual men have wandered into the Lair. She thinks it might be worthwhile to have the Four investigate," Jensen explained.

"We're all going on a mission together?" Isis asked.

"The Deverells and I will be there just in case things get hairy. Never know when you're going to need backup," Jensen replied, tilting his head. "Don't look so down, Isis. I'm sure Alpha's looking forward to seeing *you* again."

With that, he put his hands in his pockets and sauntered away, whistling an upbeat tune. Isis looked up to the ceiling and shook her head.

"I hate him," she stated. "So much."

~~*~*

Isis put her earpiece in, pressing the on button. She grimaced at the burst of static that drilled through her head. She sat in a sedan with the other three. The Deverells and Jensen were in a van behind them, equipped with a computer that downloaded the input from their listening devices. Alpha had also allowed them to hook into her security system so Ajax could receive video feed as well. The group parked on the road outside the club. Isis glanced out the back window and noticed four large wolves leap out of the van and lope off into the trees surrounding the Lair.

"Check, can you hear me?" Ajax's voice filtered through the earpiece. Jade looked at the other three, checking to make sure everyone's listening device was working. They all nodded, indicating they heard him.

"We've got you loud and clear, Ajax," Jade responded.

"Malone, Devin, Nero, and Jensen are going around

back. They'll meet you inside," Ajax reminded them. *Goody,* Isis thought. She had asked Jet earlier why Steve couldn't come with them. She would have preferred having someone she already knew watching their backs, but unfortunately, Steve was on shift.

"Right, we'll head in now," Jade's reply brought Isis out of her thoughts. Isis played with the charm at her throat, glancing out at the snowy landscape again.

Jade opened her door and stepped out of the car, followed by the other three. As usual, Shae was the most dressed up in black slacks and a cranberry-colored V-neck top. Jade wore cargo pants and a green camouflage tank top. Alex wore glistening jeans and a plain gray top. Isis had chosen to dress in a similar way, but she wore a black sleeveless top.

Alpha had forbidden them from bringing firearms or any kind of bladed weapons in her club. It seemed to irk Jade, but made perfect sense to Isis. Hotel or not, if there was a panic, it would be a disaster. Isis listened as Jade went over the Monroes' instructions. They were only to use force if the strange men started anything. Alpha didn't want a rumble breaking out in the Lair. If there was trouble, they were to rely on hand-to-hand fighting and only use their batons as a last resort. As they emerged from the trees into the spotlights, Jade turned around.

"According to Alpha, there are six men and they're pretty unremarkable except for a couple things: they don't have any kind of scent and they seem to be able to move faster than is natural," Jade explained.

"Isn't that how Sly described the men who attacked her?" Alex asked, her eyebrows rising. Isis glanced to the side when she heard rustling. Two redheaded women chased each other out in the snow, giggling, and shifted into a pair of raccoons. They disappeared in the trees.

"Okay, how is it possible to not have a scent?" Shae's question brought Isis' attention back to her teammates.

"Not everything produces an odor, but this is really

unusual," Jade answered. "According to Alpha, they've kind of spread out around the club and just seem to be watching everything. She has requested we be discreet and not draw attention to ourselves."

"Question," Isis spoke up. "I'm still not clear on the whole 'not having a scent' thing. I don't smell people. I don't think my sense of smell is that heightened."

"It's probably a lot more heightened than you realize, but you don't notice it. Trust me, if you encounter something scentless, you'll probably know," Jade explained.

"Unless her senses are muddled from all that time she spent among humans."

Isis clenched her jaw when Jensen's voice filtered through their earpieces. She cleared her throat and ignored him. Shae and Alex snickered but Jade remained serious.

"We've got five floors to cover, so we're going to spread out," Jade explained. "We'll be switching up throughout the time we're here. Sometimes we'll be alone, sometimes with one of the Deverells, et cetera."

"What about Jensen?" Alex asked.

"I'll just wander around with the rest of you," Jensen's voice came through the earpieces again. Isis could hear the throbbing music in the background. She had a feeling his "wandering" would be on her heels, annoying the living hell out of her. Isis listened as Jade went on about staying in communication and in sight of at least one other person. Jade finally finished and nodded over her shoulder, indicating they should go inside.

They went up through the pillars. Isis noticed the same young woman from the first time the Four had ventured to the Lair. Instead of a red hood, she wore a dark purple one. Her crystalline blue eyes followed them and her short wavy hair peeked out from the hood. Isis kept pace with the other three as they hurried to the front door. The same large tiger sat there, but this time, he didn't hassle Jade. She pushed open the door, waving the other three in.

They were immediately engulfed in dark blue lighting. People danced everywhere with glowing bracelets and necklaces, some holding glowsticks. Neon hair blazed in the darkness, glowing under the blacklights. It was much more crowded than the last time the Four had been there. The warmth inside was in stark contrast to the frigid cold outside.

Jade swiftly gestured directions: she and Alex would start upstairs, Shae should go to the bar area, and Isis should go out to the main dance area. Isis nodded her understanding and started making her way through the crowd of people toward the main dance floor. She noticed a hallway that ran along the dance floor and slowly made her way around it. Some couples sat at tables and some at booths, sipping various drinks. Isis paused halfway through and moved to the railing, standing at it for a moment. She watched the people on the floor, moving and swaying to the music. Her eyes wandered up to the second floor where there was a similar open hall looking down on the dance floor. She noticed Alpha standing off to the side, watching the goings on below. She had a beer bottle in one hand and leaned on the railing. She noticed Isis and raised her bottle slightly. Isis tilted her head in acknowledgment and Alpha sipped her drink.

Out of the corner of her eye, Isis noticed a shadow. She turned her attention to the side, leaning back. In the corner of the hall stood a man in a light gray business suit. He was the most non-descript person Isis had ever seen. The strange man was pale with sandy-colored hair, brushed forward. His expression was mostly flat, showing little emotion, but from the angle she was at, it looked like he was sneering. Isis glanced across the floor in the opposite direction and noticed a similar-looking man standing on the other side. Her eyes wandered back to the first man when the strobe lights started. Isis just caught a glimpse of movement in the flashing lights. She tensed up and reached for her baton when the strobe lights stopped.

The place where the man had been standing was empty. Isis looked all around, her gaze wandering across the wide floor. She stared when she saw the first man standing beside the second all the way across the hall. No one moved that quickly, it was impossible. Even if he had taken a shortcut across the floor, he still only should have made it halfway through the crowd in the time the strobe lights were going.

"What's got your interest?"

Isis grabbed Jensen's jacket and dragged him over to the steps that led to the dance floor, ignoring his questions. She pulled him onto the dance floor, looking at the other dancers, and then yanked him against her. Isis started to move her body in a similar slinky motion, running her hand up into his soft dark hair. She turned around to face him, noticing the expensive-looking vest and light shirt he had worn. He looked nothing short of bewildered. She put her face next to his, nuzzling his neck and smiling as she ran her fingers over his chest. She turned him a little so that she could watch the two strange men in her peripheral vision. One was looking out over the floor. The other seemed to notice Jensen, but was doing his best not to show it.

"Have you completely—?" Jensen began.

"I'll explain in a minute. Now would you please shut the hell up and try to blend in?" she hissed behind her smile and then turned so her back was against him again. Jensen pressed himself against her and began kissing her neck. He ran his hands down her hips.

"Watch those hands," she warned sharply.

"Look around, darling. Modesty isn't exactly on display here," Jensen murmured, kissing her neck. She could practically feel him smirking. Isis grabbed his hands and placed them on her hips, squeezing the small bones in his fingers as an added warning. They continued moving and swaying to the music. Isis swallowed, trying to ignore the heat. Her temperature seemed to rise. Jensen's subtle aftershave wasn't helping matters. She didn't think a person could smell that nice.

"You mind telling me why we're grinding to awful dubstep music or is this your way of coming out as a rebel?" Jensen whispered in her ear. Isis turned her face toward him, resting it against his chin and smiling as if he had just said something sexy.

"You see the two guys in suits standing in the hall to my right?"

Jensen turned his head so he could look where she indicated. She nipped at his ear, pleased when he stiffened again. It was quite fun having the upper hand on him.

"The plain guys who look like they work for an insurance company?"

"That's them," Isis whispered. "One of them somehow made it all the way across the floor in the space of maybe a minute."

"Impossible."

Isis glimpsed another man out of the corner of her eye on her right. She grabbed the front of Jensen's shirt, pulled him closer, and kissed him passionately. She could feel him go completely rigid as if he wasn't sure whether or not he should pull away. After a moment's hesitation, he opened his mouth and met her tongue with his. She opened her eyes, looking in the direction of the man. He was sitting on a bench that ran adjacent to the dance floor, isolated from the few other people. He had darker hair than the first man she had seen, but was equally nondescript. His eyes wandered over the dancers. Before he looked in her direction, Isis closed her eyes and turned her attention back to the kiss. She still gripped Jensen's shirt in one fist with her other hand on the back of his neck. Her body started to tingle as if electricity were racing through her. Jensen also seemed to be getting a little excited.

Isis pulled out of the kiss and glanced over to where she had spotted the third man. The space was empty. She looked over to the hall where the first two men were still standing. She let go of Jensen's shirt and straightened up. Jensen cleared his throat and smoothed his shirt, tugging on his vest, as he tried to regain his composure.

"One just disappeared," Isis said, looking around. "These guys move fast."

Jensen followed her gaze around the dance floor, trying to find whomever she was looking for. There were a bunch of neon-haired rebels, other shape shifters, and a few other supernatural species. The music continued throbbing above them.

"I'm going to have a look on the second floor," Isis stated, nodding at his crotch. "Might want to sit down for a minute there, Jensen."

She smiled and waved her fingers as she walked backwards toward the steps. She jogged up them and disappeared around a curve in the hall. Jensen whistled once and ran a hand through his hair again. He looked back toward the two men she had pointed out earlier.

One was gone.

~~*~*~*

Malone and Devin stood on the second floor, watching the action below. Alpha had passed by earlier, heading for her office. She barely even acknowledged them. The music continued throbbing. They watched their youngest brother grind with a couple rebels.

"He's in his element," Devin mentioned. Malone smiled and nodded toward two other figures on the floor.

"So is Isis apparently," he stated. They laughed when their niece pulled Jensen into a passionate kiss, obviously flustering him. Malone squinted and leaned down.

"She's looking at something," he observed.

"Have you two seen anything suspicious?" Jade's voice barely filtered through the music.

"No, but it looks like Isis might have," Devin called back, watching as Isis left Jensen on the dance floor.

Jensen took a moment to straighten his clothing and glance around the dance floor. A few rebels danced about him, but he waved them off.

"I've seen all six, but they move fast and they don't stay in one place for long," Ajax's puzzled voice was a little clearer. "Who the hell are these guys?"

"Or what?"

Devin looked over his shoulder when his brother straightened up. He followed his gaze down the hall to where a strange stone-faced man in a dark gray suit stood. A small smirk began to cross his lips. The lights started changing: red to yellow to green to blue back to red, bathing the dance floor in different vibrant colors. The man suddenly disappeared in a blur. Malone and Devin looked around, trying to locate him again.

"Do you see him?" Devin asked as he turned around once.

"Where did he—? There," Malone stated pointing over Devin's shoulder. Devin turned and spotted the gray suit immediately. He stood near some rebels on the other side of the hall. He wove around them and disappeared down one of the dark halls. Malone and Devin hurried after him. They moved around the patrons in the crowded hallway, ignoring the complaints as they climbed over a few. They rounded the bend and spotted the man standing in a packed elevator as the doors closed. He smiled and shook his head once.

"No way that's a shape shifter," Devin said. Malone shook his head, looking behind him.

~~*~*~*

Alex walked down the second floor steps, moving to the first floor. She jumped back when she felt a hand slide up her leg. A white-haired woman grinned foolishly, obviously under the influence of something. Alex stepped away from her, turning her attention back to the stairs. She didn't understand the appeal of narcotics at all.

"Alex, did you see anything on the second floor?" Jade's voice was barely audible over all the other noise.

"Negative," Alex responded as she reached the bottom of the stairs. "Where are you?"

"Third floor," Jade answered. "Malone and Devin are going to head up to the fourth. Shae's going to join me in a — Hey! Back off!"

"Are you all right?"

"I'd be better if we were not here," Jade grumbled. "Can you meet up with Isis while I sweep the third again with Shae?"

"That's what I was planning." Alex paused when she entered the glass-floored bar. In one corner, she spotted the outline of a tall man. The light flashed yellow, revealing a man in a suit. He appeared to be looking at nothing in particular. Alex made her way over to the bar, keeping the man in her peripheral vision.

"Guardians I wish I had a gun!" Jade's irritated voice came over the com. Alex reached the bar and caught Wylie's attention. She moved over to the protector, still drying the glass mug she held.

"It's about time you showed up," she shouted over the music.

"Is that one of them?" Alex asked, nodding over her shoulder. Wylie glanced in the direction she indicated. She put the mug back under the bar and leaned forward, resting her hands on the bar.

"They came in shortly after sunset," she explained. "Been wandering around ever since."

"Are they armed?"

Wylie shrugged. "Don't know."

Alex glanced over at the man again. "Jade, I've got one in … wait. Where did he go?"

Both Wylie and Alex straightened up, noticing the empty space where the suited man had stood. Alex moved around the people in the bar area until she reached the spot where the man had been standing. She looked out the open doorway toward the dance floor. She didn't see the man anywhere. Alex moved out to the dance floor, glancing up at the open floors above. A small movement on the fifth floor got her attention. She gritted her teeth and swore as she began running down the hall.

"Jade, you need to get to the fifth floor now!" Alex yelled as she tried to push her way through the crowd.

"What? Why?"

"I just saw Onyx!"

~~*~*~*

Jensen cautiously made his way down a dark hallway on the first floor. The few dim lights blinked from bright red to yellow to blue to green in the same repeating pattern. Jensen felt naked without a gun or blade on him. He kept glancing over his shoulder, unable to shake the feeling of being followed. He stepped around a pair of women dressed in matching white nurse costumes. *Men who don't have scents. That's not going to be a pain in the ass at all,* Jensen thought dryly as he continued down the endless hall. The rebels just had to set up base in a hotel.

He ducked around a vine that was hanging from the ceiling, apparently entering the jungle section of the hotel, which was unexpectedly quiet. *Odd, I wonder why the crowd hasn't filtered in here,* Jensen thought as he glanced around, keeping his guard up. He had just finished his thought when a solidly built man in a gray suit tackled him. The man slammed him into the wall and then threw him to the floor. Jensen felt all the air rush out of his body and stars burst in his vision when his head contacted with the floor. He forced himself to regain his bearings and kicked out at the man, hitting his knee. The man smiled and kicked him in the side. Jensen let out a gasp as pain ignited in his ribs. *He should have gone down. Nobody could withstand a kick like that*, he thought distantly as he tried to pull himself up, using the wall. The man smirked as he reached down and grabbed hold of Jensen's throat, squeezing tightly as he slammed his head back to the floor.

"Aldridge," the man growled, squeezing even tighter. Jensen fought to break the grip, clawing at the man's arm and kicking at whatever body part was reachable. It was as if the man were made of stone. He was completely unaffected by Jensen's strikes. In desperation, Jensen attempted to gouge his eyes.

"Hey!"

The man looked up and was instantly struck in the face with a baton. The grip immediately vanished from Jensen's throat and he greedily sucked in oxygen, coughing harshly as he rolled to the side. Jensen turned his head and watched as Isis landed an impressive amount of strikes and kicks on her suited opponent. She managed to evade and deflect most of his strikes. A cross punch went past her face and she brought her baton down on the elbow. He let out an angry growl and tried to backhand her, which she easily ducked under. She pushed off the wall and used the momentum to strike him hard in the face again. Isis brought her baton down on his knees and cracked him hard in the back of his head. He jumped to the side and suddenly, in a blur, was gone. Isis turned around a couple times, alert and ready.

"Where did he go? Did you see where he went?" she asked, not looking at Jensen. He coughed in response and gestured vaguely in the opposite direction. Isis quickly went a short way down the hall, looking for the man.

"He's gone," she said as she returned to Jensen's side.

"You don't say," he gasped out around a cough. Isis gave him a dry look and pressed the button on her earpiece.

"Jensen got his ass kicked by one of the suited men," Isis reported, as she looked him over for visible injuries.

"Did not," he managed to protest before coughing again. "Had him right where I wanted him."

"Strangling you to death on the floor?"

"*You* lost him," Jensen pointed out. Isis pressed down hard on his sore ribs and he let out a cry, curling in on himself.

"That seems like it's probably broken," she observed. He narrowed his eyes at her.

"What the hell were you doing?"

Isis helped Jensen to his feet, allowing him to lean on her for support. "I noticed one of those guys watching you. I knew you'd follow me, so I managed to lose you and then followed you. I figured your secret admirer might tail you, so I just watched and waited."

Jensen stared at her. "You used me as bait?"

"I was right here. You were never in any danger of serious, lasting harm. Well, unless he somehow managed to sneak in a gun or knife or something," Isis responded as she helped him around a large crowd of people dressed in leather. Jensen tilted his head. It had been a decent plan, but he couldn't help being a little offended at being used.

They gradually emerged in the main dance area when a shot rang out over the loud music. Isis shoved Jensen to the floor when another shot rang out. Jensen grunted in pain when he hit the floor and he wondered if the night would ever end.

"What the hell is going on in there?" Ajax's worried voice came over the coms. "Was that a gunshot?"

People screamed and started running in a panic. Jensen opened his eyes and pushed himself up to his knees, glancing over in Isis' direction. She was pressed against the wall, clutching her upper arm. Blood was leaking out from between her fingers.

"Stay down! Get behind that wall," she shouted over to him. He pressed himself against the opposite wall, peering out at the dance floor. Jensen closed his eyes and turned away from the corner when another bullet slammed into the wall.

"Jade, she's up on the fifth floor," Isis reported.

"I know. Shae and Alex are meeting me up there. Devin and Malone are coming down to you. Are you okay?"

"I'm fine. Go get her," Isis yelled. Jensen went further down the hall into the darkness, crossing over to the side where Isis was. He approached her and tugged at her shirt. She glanced at him and he nodded over his shoulder, gesturing for her to come back into the shadows. Isis cautiously backed up into the safety of the dark, her eyes glued to the open halls above them.

"Malone and Devin are going to try and reach us," she mentioned, distracted. The bright overhead lights came on in the club and the music cut out abruptly.

"Are you okay?" Jensen asked, attempting to see her arm. She looked over at him with a skeptical expression. She turned her attention back to the bright open floor, which was practically deserted.

"Where's the back exit?" Isis asked. "I need to get out there."

"Across the hall," Jensen answered. "Would you please let me see your arm?"

"I'm fine, Jensen. Would you please stop hover — OW! What the hell is wrong with you!?"

She punched his arm when he pressed just above the wound. He grimaced in pain and glared at her.

"If you just let me see your arm, I wouldn't have to do that now would I?"

Isis glared at him, but took her hand away from her arm. He hissed in sympathy as he looked at the bleeding wound.

"It's a graze. The guardian healers will be able to repair it in five minutes," she said, watching down the hall. Jensen stared at her.

"You do realize that you are susceptible to blood loss, right? Guardians can heal many wounds, but you have to be alive in order for them to do so," he said. "This needs to be wrapped."

"We lost her," Alex's voice came over their earpieces. "She must have gone out a window and blended into the crowd. Was anyone hit?"

Isis ran her good hand over her face, wondering if protectors were capable of catching assassins. She looked over at Jensen, who was still examining her wounded arm. *I just saved him twice. Guardians, I must be losing my damn mind,* she thought.

"Isis was grazed," Jensen responded, glancing up when Malone and Devin appeared in the entrance of the hall.

"Well, the men in suits seemed to have vanished as well," Ajax's voice came over the communications link. "I can't find any trace of them on the security feeds, which cover a disturbing amount of the club by the way."

~~*~*~*

Onyx was annoyed as hell. She separated from the rush of fleeing patrons, heading off toward where she had parked her car. Tucking the bag with the sniper rifle under one arm, she listened to her footsteps crunching in the snow.

A sudden pinch in her back was followed by an impossibly strong current of electricity. Onyx let out a cry as she fell to the ground, paralyzed. Her entire body shook uncontrollably in the cold wet snow. She gasped as she tried to get her breathing under control.

"Had a friend of mine toy with a regular Taser gun," a nonchalant voice spoke from somewhere over her. A dark-haired woman emerged in her field of vision. She held the bulky Taser in her left hand, examining it.

"My friend has a thing for electricity — just *loves* juicing things up. Did you know it's not necessarily the volts that are dangerous? Amps, now that's what you've got to watch out for," Sly continued as she examined her gun. "Two amps can kill a human. I'm not sure how many can kill a shape shifter, but I just hit you with two and a half."

She looked at Onyx with disinterest. "You seem to be alive, so it obviously didn't kill you. Lucky me."

Onyx attempted to say something, but found herself unable to form words. She couldn't move her limbs and her body still trembled. Sly dropped a coil of rope from her shoulder and kicked Onyx onto her stomach.

"I knew you wouldn't be able to resist taking a shot at the last Aldridge," Sly continued as she began to hogtie Onyx. "What's the price on that man's head? Gotta be more than five million by now, right? Your leaders are such big spenders to the point of ridiculousness. I've always wondered though — who put the bounty on the Aldridges in the first place? I imagine that information is a little above your pay grade."

"What … want?" Onyx managed to sputter. Sly finished tying a knot, jerking it extra hard for good measure. *Knew that stint as a dominatrix would come in handy one day,* she thought as she crouched down by Onyx's head, resting her wrist on her knee. Her lips began to curl up in a smile.

"That's a *very* good question, Onyx, one I'm glad you asked. You see, I was nearly run off the road by a group of men in suits. Scentless nondescript men in suits. In fact, I think they were here tonight. At first, I was planning to kill them, maybe torture a couple to send a message. However, this struck me as a little rash. After all, whoever sent them would probably just send more. So then I thought, 'who's usually behind the really fucked up shit that happens in this town?' Which led me to *you*," Sly explained, pressing her index finger in the back of Onyx's head and shoving it down. She looked out across the field, watching as the last patrons vanished into the trees. "You have always been embarrassingly predictable and therefore easy to track. Now, I doubt you know as much as you think you do, but I have a feeling you at least know the name of the puppet-master. And that's exactly what you're going to tell me."

Onyx glared at her, her lips set in a thin straight line, and Sly smiled as she stood up again, holding a length of rope in one hand. She started forward, dragging her captive behind her.

"Fine. We'll do it the hard way."

~~*~*~*

Blackjack sat in the Obsidian manor, lounging on Adara's old seat when he heard the sharp click of heels on the stone floor. He glanced up at the petite figure that made her way down the long entrance hall. She looked professional in her long gray skirt and light pink top. Her short blonde hair was brushed to the side and her dark, intense eyes didn't waver from him. The shoulder holsters were the only thing that looked out of place on her slender frame. A few feet behind her, two men in gray suits followed in lock step. She raised a hand and they stopped instantly, standing at attention.

"We have a problem," the woman stated as she stopped in front of his chair. Blackjack swung his leg down from where it rested on the chair's arm.

"Which would be?"

"You gave my boss your assurance that you and your … associates could conduct yourself professionally if the price was right," she responded, stepping up to the chair and running her fingers over the cold arm of it. "He has been more than generous in his payment."

"And I have kept my word. Onyx and I have stayed out of the way—"

Her cell phone rang shrilly and she held up a finger, silencing him. A pleasant smile crept across her ageless face as she answered the small gray phone.

"Hi, Steve. What's up?" she said affectionately, her tone changing. The seriousness was gone and her voice raised a couple octaves. Gone was the subtle hint of an ancient accent and in its place was American vernacular.

"I'm just at the office. Looks like I'll be working a double again. Sorry, babe. I'll see you tomorrow though, right? Okay. All right. You too. Yeah. Bye."

Tracy hung up and tucked the phone in her pocket again, turning her narrowed eyes back to Blackjack. He shifted uncomfortably under her scrutiny.

"Mr. Blackjack, you have certainly not kept your word. We had set up a demonstration at the rebel Lair, a demonstration your female associate ruined by opening fire in a crowded club."

Blackjack's jaw clenched. He had warned Onyx to stay out of it, but apparently the bounty on the last Aldridge was too tempting to resist. *She has absolutely no self-control. If they don't kill her, I'll do it myself,* Blackjack thought as he cracked his neck.

"I apologize, Tracy. You have my word that—"

"Don't waste your breath," Tracy cut him off, glancing around. "Where is she? I would like to have a word with her myself."

"I haven't seen her since she left earlier today."

"Imbecile," Tracy growled, twisting her body to look back at the men in suits. "Find the other assassin, bring her back here."

The men were gone in a blur and Blackjack tried to swallow the nervousness in his throat. Tracy smiled as she turned her attention back to him.

"Do you like them? They do this thing called blinking. It's a skill that allows them to move at speeds unmatched by man, animal, or machine. The Corporation used to use them to gather . . . wayward sheep, in a manner of speaking. Their eyes have some limited hypnotic ability, enough to freeze a living creature in their tracks. Once they do that, they simply pick them up and carry them wherever we desire. Of course, the quarry experiences some mild side effects. Disorientation, dizziness, mild nausea, memory loss. Your kind even experiences spans of missing time, anywhere from minutes to an entire day."

She leaned down over the chair, gripping the armrests. Her face was inches from his and he shrank back.

"Those two? Mere reconnaissance. They don't bite, don't even carry weapons. Domesticated cats are more dangerous. They die after one use. That speed is very taxing on the system, so we only have a limited number of them left. However, most of our stock is a bit more … aggressive, shall we say. They are also much hardier. This territory remains yours because my master allows it. Make no mistake, you throw a wrench in our plans again, there will be consequences."

She straightened up again, smoothing her blouse. "I have other matters that require my attention. Clean up your mess."

Tracy strode down the steps and made her way back down the hall. Blackjack swallowed again and let out the breath he hadn't realized he was holding.

~~*~*~*

"I believe I specified *discretion*. Instead what I get is a group of protectors stomping in here like a herd of goddamn elephants!"

Isis watched Alpha storm around her bar, pouring herself a shot of whiskey. Jade, Shae, and Alex sat on nearby bar stools. Alex was flipping through the pages of a book Alpha had lent her — a collection of rebel legends. Malone and Devin were sitting on a vintage lounge off to the side. Jensen was standing near the bar, behind Isis. He had finished wrapping her arm earlier. She had lost track of Nero, but she assumed he had found some room in the hotel to his liking.

"Well, you tell your leaders that they are going to reimburse me for all the business I lost tonight. And they are paying to fix my goddamn wall!"

Alpha tilted her head back, drained the whiskey, and slammed the shot glass back on the bar. Wylie and Amber stood behind the bar as well, off to the side.

"Alpha, Jet and Lilly couldn't have known Onyx would show up," Jade began calmly. Alpha let out a bark of laughter and gestured over at Jensen.

"You bring that one along and you think an assassin isn't going to show up? With the bounty on his head offered by the assassin leaders? Fuck, *I* was tempted to take a shot at him!"

"I feel I should be offended by that," Jensen mentioned, leaning against the bar. Isis turned her head.

"How much is the bounty on you anyway?"

"None of your business," Jensen answered, sounding mildly indignant. Isis arched an eyebrow, grinning.

"That much, huh?"

"You never saw these men before?" Alex asked suddenly, not looking up from the book.

"If scentless men that move faster than fucking Superman were regulars, I think I would have noticed," Alpha responded.

"These guys just show up out of nowhere and then do nothing? If they can move that fast, they could have easily taken us out. So why didn't they?" Alex mused out loud, rubbing her forehead and looking over at the other three.

"Didn't they tell Sly that someone wanted to say hello to Jet and Lilly?" Shae observed. "Maybe someone's trying to show us what they can do."

"There's a frightening thought," Malone said.

"Has the High Council granted Jet and Lilly's request yet?" Alpha asked irately. "Since you can't seem to find Blackjack or Onyx, the assassin you do have in custody might be able to shed some light on all these weird events. Roan did have a lot of power within this territory at one time and returning from the dead is pretty goddamn weird."

Isis felt her eyebrows raise a little, surprised at how much Alpha knew. Although she supposed it made sense that the Monroes would share important information with her, since she was an ally now.

"Not yet," Jade answered.

"For fuck's sake!" Alpha threw her hands up in air. "Since you're all quite useless and the Lair is closed for the night, could you kindly get the fuck out? I've got to clean up. Unless of course you want to trash anything else?"

"Can I borrow this for a while?" Alex asked, holding up the book. Alpha waved her off.

"Isis and I need to go to the Meadows to get patched up," Jensen mentioned. "We'll meet you lot back at the mansion."

Wonderful, I get to spend even more time with him, Isis thought irritably. *First I save him, then I get shot, and now he's going to follow me to the Meadows. Could my night possibly get any worse?*

~~*~*~*

Onyx sputtered and coughed when a bucket of ice water was tossed in her face. She was bound tightly and hanging upside down from a heavy metal hook, but felt more in control of her body than she had earlier. She looked around. Everything was shadowy and Onyx wondered whether or not it was still night. The only light was the extremely bright floodlight pointed directly at her face.

"It's an abandoned slaughterhouse, been empty for decades." Sly's voice came from somewhere in front of her. The sound of a chair being dragged across the old floor echoed throughout the empty space. Sly soon appeared, swinging the chair around so it was in front of her. She straddled it backwards, sitting down in front of the assassin.

"It's perfect for when you need to hang someone upside down and beat them like a piñata," she mentioned, grinning as her eyes wandered up and then back down.

"Did you know that high amps of electricity screws with our ability to shape shift? Yeah, you're not going to be able to change form for at least a week. So I don't have to worry about you scampering away before I get a chance to ask you my questions."

"Fuck you, Sly!"

Sly clicked her tongue and shook her head. "That's not very nice, Onyx. I've been very polite, all things considered. The least you could do is answer a few simple questions."

"I won't tell you shit."

Sly chuckled, brushing her long fingers through her hair. "Then I'm going to have to start cutting things off. Or I might gouge out your eyes to start. I'm in the mood for a little violence tonight."

Onyx glared at her. "Then I'll just bleed out and you'll have nothing."

"I could start by skinning you," Sly continued on, standing up and walking around Onyx. "Or perhaps I'll just spend some time beating you with a baseball bat. I did always enjoy the classics. Who are you working for, Onyx?"

Sly blinked, and suddenly, she was in the middle of her forest. She spun around once, startled and disoriented. The fresh cold air filled her lungs and the call of birds sounded distantly. She looked down at her watch and stared at the time, not believing her eyes.

It was the afternoon.

"What. The. Hell?" Sly said softly, looking up again. Her eyes fell on a strange gray lump a few feet away. She moved closer, caution coloring every step. Sly was stunned to discover it was a body — one of the scentless men. She carefully crouched down and felt for a pulse. There was none. She pulled her hand back, rubbing her suddenly cold fingers together. After a minute, a small smile began to curl her lips. *Missing time, a change in scenery, and a mysterious dead body. Interesting. Very interesting,* she thought.

CHAPTER EIGHT

In the early hours of the morning, the sun rose a brilliant shade of red and the frost glistened in the light. Isis was in her room, shuffling through her nightstand drawer. She took out the spiral with all her information and notes on Coop and shoved it into her messenger bag along with her baton before tossing the bag onto the bed. She walked over to the wardrobe, pulled out her coat and threw it on, buttoning it up. She moved back to the bed and grabbed the bag, throwing the strap diagonally over her shoulder. Pulling out a set of keys, Isis opened the door to her room, looking up and down the hall. It was still early in the morning, so most shape shifters were still asleep. She knew her three teammates would be. Jet and Lilly were always swamped with one thing or another. They had yet to meet with Roan. Isis could tell Jet was beginning to get frustrated with the High Council and she imagined Lilly was as well. The protectors had also been unable to get in touch with Halley. Isis had a feeling the daughter would have warned her mother about the Monroes. However, Halley's daughter wouldn't know about Isis.

She closed the room door behind her and hurried

down the hall to the main staircase. Isis was going to walk into town and have a cup of coffee at the local diner. She had called the Halley — the wife of the man who looked like Coop — the day after the encounter with the men at the Lair. After a lot of cajoling, Isis had finally convinced the nervous woman to meet her in town for coffee. The woman was harmless enough from what Isis could tell. She sounded as though she was scared of her own shadow. To be on the safe side, Isis had made sure the place they were meeting was as public as possible. She hated going back on her word to Jade, but something about this mystery was tugging at her. She was connected to it somehow and she wanted to know how. She wanted to get answers about Coop, preferably sooner rather than later.

Isis made it downstairs and jogged to the front door, glancing once more over her shoulder to make sure she hadn't been seen. Around her, the mansion was silent. She unlocked the large front door, opened it as quietly as possible, and slipped out.

~~*~*~*

Isis sat in the diner, working on her second cup of coffee. She hadn't been sleeping a lot lately and she was certain the only reason she was still on her feet was the sheer amount of caffeine she consumed. The diner was mostly empty; still too early in the morning for most people. There were a few older men sitting at the counter, working on large breakfasts. An older grandmotherly woman sat in the next booth over with a younger woman sitting opposite her. Some college students sat in another booth behind them. The waitress seemed to know them and often stopped at the booth to talk with them. Isis could hear the sounds from the kitchen as a cook went about preparing food. There was a scent of eggs, different grilled meats, and fresh baked goods hanging in the air.

The windows were clean, as was the black and white checkered floor. For the most part, the diner was pleasant except for a woman who was trying to keep her unruly toddler under control on the opposite end of the diner. The kid kept screeching "Donut!" and Isis found herself wishing his mother would just give in to his demand.

She glanced out the window, squinting against the brightness of the sun-kissed snow and checked her watch again. Halley was almost ten minutes late. *Shape shifters don't hide without good reason*, Alpha had told her. Halley was very scared of something. Isis sighed, deciding to give the woman ten more minutes. She wasn't in a hurry and appreciated the change of scenery.

Isis' eyes fell on a maroon sedan parked in the small lot. She had glimpsed it once or twice since entering the diner and hadn't paid it any heed. Now that she was looking closer, the windows were unusually tinted. Isis squinted as she looked at the car. It was almost as if the windows were completely blacked out. As she continued to stare, Isis could almost make out a pair of binoculars. Was someone watching her …?

"Well, fancy meeting you here."

The sudden loud greeting caused Isis to jump about a foot in the air. She almost knocked over her coffee as she looked up at Jensen, who was standing over the table, grinning. He was wearing his usual nice clothes: pants, vest, light shirt, jacket, and nice shoes. Isis wondered if he ever wore anything other than tailored clothes. He looked like he was heading to some high society function and it made him stick out like a sore thumb in their plain surroundings. Everyone in the diner had turned at Jensen's loud voice and they were now staring at the two of them. The students started snickering. For the second time since meeting Jensen, Isis felt her face get hot as she flushed in embarrassment. She covered her face with her hands, mentally saying every swear word she knew. Jensen obviously couldn't care less about the attention he was attracting. He clicked his tongue as he sank down in the empty seat opposite Isis.

"Oh darling, you are so *busted*," he continued loudly. He didn't even attempt to keep the amusement out of his voice. Isis once again kicked herself for saving his life.

"I'm not a prisoner and last time I checked, I don't have a curfew," she grumbled under her breath from behind her hands.

"No, you don't. So why on Earth did you sneak out of the mansion without telling anyone?" Jensen asked pointedly. "You're supposed to let at least one person know where you're going. That's just common sense with all the weird things going on, especially for a member of the Four."

Isis dragged her hands down her face, shaking her head. Jensen looked over at the college students sitting nearby. The women had definitely taken notice of him, as had one of the men.

"She's a *very* bad girl. Might have to spank her later," Jensen mentioned, nodding over his shoulder at Isis, winking at them. He turned his sky blue gaze back to Isis, smiling in a way that made her want to slap him.

"What the hell is wrong with you?" Isis hissed.

"Is the coffee any good in this place? I assume you've come here often enough to know," Jensen replied in a conversational tone, as he reached over and lifted up one of the thin laminated menus. He made a face of disgust and grabbed a napkin from the dispenser, brushing a sticky substance off his fingers.

Isis squinted at him. "What are you talking about? I've never been here before."

"No?" Jensen folded his hands. "So you just kind of sneak all over?"

He smiled charmingly at the waitress when she came over. "Just a coffee for now, thanks."

He looked back at Isis. "I assume you realize you have a tail."

Jensen tilted his head toward the window. Isis scratched the back of her neck, subtly glancing over her shoulder.

"The maroon sedan out there. Been following you since you reached town," Jensen continued. "Not bothering to hide, which is a bit troubling, if you ask me."

"I didn't," Isis mumbled, turning her attention back to him. The waitress stopped by the table, filling up Jensen's coffee mug. He grinned and winked at her, picking up the steaming mug and sipping, his eyebrow raising in surprise.

"That's not half-bad. Though I still prefer imported roasts, fresh-pressed," he mentioned, turning his attention back to Isis. Isis stood and tossed some bills on the table before heading for the exit, pulling on her coat as she made her way to the door. She heard Jensen follow close behind.

"Where do you think you're going?" he asked. She opened the door, letting a blast of cold air into the warm diner. Once she was outside, Isis pulled out her baton and flicked it down, expanding it to its full length.

"I'm not big on being followed," she growled. "You may have heard that I had a bad experience."

"I see. So your solution is to smash the hell out of a car in front of numerous eyewitnesses?" Jensen laughed. "Quite the cool-headed strategist you are."

"You got a better plan?"

The sound of screeching tires brought their attention to the parking lot just in time to see the maroon car speed away and disappear around a corner. Isis pressed her baton on the ground, collapsing it again. She looked over at Jensen, who was watching the direction the car had sped off in. It was the first time she had seen him expressionless. The confidence was gone and his eyes narrowed. Isis shook her head and changed her direction, walking the opposite way. After a moment, she heard Jensen jog after her.

"Okay, I think we may have gotten off to a bad start,"

he said as he caught up to her, shoving his hands in his pockets. The cold winter air nipped at their faces.

Isis laughed, glancing around to make sure no one else was following her. "You don't say."

"Hey, I'm not entirely to blame here. If you weren't so quick to jump to conclusions . . ." Jensen trailed off, letting the sentence hang in the air.

"I really have nothing more to say to you," Isis replied as she carefully stepped around a patch of ice.

"You walked here, right?"

Isis glanced at him, confused. "Yes, I walked. Why?"

"Because I drove, and it's rather chilly out. Think of it as an olive branch."

Isis looked down at the dirty snow as they crossed the street, doing her best to ignore Jensen. Once they had crossed, Jensen moved so he stood in front of her. Isis glared at him, getting increasingly aggravated.

"What do you want, Jensen?"

"I would just like to give you a ride to the mansion. In a nice heated car," Jensen offered, sincerely. "Come on. You don't want me to follow you in the car, do you?"

Isis glanced off to the side. She didn't like cold weather – never had – and a nice warm car sounded inviting. She also knew Jensen would find some way to embarrass her if she didn't take him up on his offer.

"Fine," she agreed. "But I don't want to hear you the entire way back. One word, just one, and I will get out of the car. Even if it's still moving."

Jensen grinned and nodded, moving out of her way so they could continue walking side-by-side. Isis followed him to a parking lot behind a shop across the street, making a mental note to call Halley. She worried someone might have gotten to the skittish woman first. She should probably let the Monroes know as well. *Jet is going to be pissed at me,* Isis thought.

Jensen made his way over to a silver Jaguar. He pressed a button on the car keys and the car chirped twice. Isis moved to the passenger side of the car. Jensen slid into the driver's seat, a self-satisfied smile playing on his lips. As soon as Isis buckled her seatbelt, he locked the doors.

"So, are you going tell me why you snuck out today?" he asked, grinning. "You didn't think we'd just sit in stony silence the whole way back to the mansion, did you?"

Isis glared at him. "Are you going to tell me why you got weird when that car drove away?"

Jensen laughed. "Weird, there's something I've not been called before."

"I'm tired, it was the best I could come up with," Isis muttered in response, closing her eyes as she put her head against the window. Jensen smoothly pulled out of the parking lot, moving onto the deserted street. He stopped at the crosswalk to allow some pedestrians to move to the other side of the street.

"Don't think you're going to get out of this by pretending to be asleep," he said as he glanced over at his passenger. "I've lived much too long to fall for *that*."

"How old are you anyway?" Isis asked without opening her eyes.

Jensen shrugged as he inched the car forward again, making sure no more people were crossing. "No idea. I stopped counting years ago. Time doesn't concern me."

"The usual response of immortals," Isis said as she opened her eyes partway, noticing Jensen's overly cautious driving. *Great, he's dragging this out for as long as he can. That's just wonderful,* she thought irritably.

"Not necessarily, I just don't care all that much," Jensen replied as he stopped at a red light. "Anyone ever told you how human you sound?"

"I was raised by them, sue me," Isis shot back, looking up at the red light in an attempt to turn it green through sheer will power. It didn't work.

"What were you doing out?" Jensen asked again.

"Why is it any of your damn business?"

"Okay, then I'll just start guessing. Were you doing

some amateur sleuth work?" Jensen began, lightly pressing on the accelerator when the light turned green. "Why would one of the Four go out on her own? Hmm, lovers' tiff perhaps?"

Isis snorted and shook her head, hating the world for a moment. Only in her life would the seeming resurrection of her assassin biological father mean she would be saddled with a shape shifter as obnoxious as Jensen. The car ride back would only be roughly fifteen minutes, but it couldn't end soon enough in Isis' opinion.

"But if that's not it, what else could it be?" Jensen continued, gasping suddenly. "Is it possible that you're trying to catch my eye? Are you manipulating me into following you? While I'm flattered, I'm afraid it would be rather awkward, what with my being so close to your uncles. And of course there's the fact that you're considered a guardian."

"I'm crushed. Really, utterly devastated," Isis answered in a flat voice.

"No, no, I think I'm onto something. It's all starting to make sense now: taking a bath in my room, the little lover's nip under the table, taking a bullet for me. You're a kinky little thing, aren't you?"

"Your ego is unbelievable," Isis scoffed with a shake of her head. "I was taking a bath in *my* room. I *stabbed* you with a fork because I wasn't in the mood for a game of footsie. If that's your idea of a lover's nip, then someone's been mistreating you, sweetie. I was *grazed* by a bullet, saving your sorry ass after you got beat down by a guy who looked like an insurance collector. And sorry to break it to you, Jensen, but you are not my type."

Jensen chuckled. "*You* have a type? One that doesn't run on batteries?"

Isis scowled. "You're an asshole, you realize that right?"

"From what I've heard you're a hardcore cynic bordering on being misanthropic," Jensen continued.

"You don't play well with others, hence my insinuation."

"Oh right, I forgot. You and my uncles have been stalking me since I was born," Isis said.

"You do love to exaggerate, don't you? Believe it or not, the world doesn't revolve around you. Ajax checked in with Steve every now and again. He wanted to make sure the poor man didn't have a nervous breakdown."

Isis shot a cold glare in Jensen's direction. "Since you know my story, I'm curious about what yours is."

"I'm a man of mystery, no story, no past," Jensen replied, some amusement fading from his voice. Isis shook her head and looked back out the window.

"The last Aldridge? Oh no, there is definitely a story there," she responded. Jensen glanced at her before turning his bright blue eyes back to the road. The traffic had picked up.

"So you talked to Jade?" he asked, attempting to sound nonchalant.

"There's quite a section on your family in the library at the mansion. Tell me, how did you survive that massacre? Did you just annoy the assassins to death?"

Jensen turned to glare at her, his jaw clenching. Isis turned her eyes from the window, waiting for whatever snarky remark or insinuation Jensen would throw at her in response. Instead, he just looked back out the windshield, his expression becoming disturbingly blank. *Shit, I might have crossed a line,* Isis realized, feeling a faint hint of guilt. Turning her eyes back to the windshield, she noticed they were approaching an ugly little green Volkswagen. Isis frowned when she noticed the car wasn't slowing down and glanced over to Jensen, noticing that he still seemed to be lost in thought.

"Jensen? Jensen! Fuck!"

Jensen blinked, shook his head, and swore loudly as he slammed on the brakes, narrowly avoiding a rear-end collision.

Isis had pressed herself against her seat, bracing her

body for the impact. She clutched the door handle and the seat, her wide green eyes turned to Jensen. She immediately regretted bringing up his past. It had been a low blow, even for her. His face was still blank, free of any readable emotions as he kept his eyes straight ahead. She swallowed and attempted to relax her stature. A few minutes passed in complete silence.

"I'm sorry," Isis apologized. Jensen made a noncommittal noise in response. Isis ran a hand over her face, wishing she had just ignored him.

"Goddamn weather," Jensen grumbled. Isis grinned a little at the memory of saying those exact same words to Steve whenever winter rolled around.

"Not a fan of snow?" she asked.

"No," Jensen answered shortly. "And the cheesy decorations don't help matters either. Damn humans and their damn holidays."

Isis couldn't help but laugh at his bitterness. It was funny, and a bit refreshing, to hear those words come out of someone else's mouth. Jensen glanced over at her, frowning.

"What's so amusing?"

Isis waved him off. "I've said something along those lines to Shae and Steve every single winter since I can remember. I hate the holidays almost as much as I hate the cold."

"Ah, must be a trait you inherited from your mother," Jensen seemed to think aloud. "You know passion, heat?"

"Yeah, I got it," Isis said, still smiling.

"I cannot believe you walked in this."

Isis shrugged. "I've walked longer."

"In the cold?"

"Yes," Isis replied with a grin.

Jensen smiled and shook his head, pausing at a stop sign. "Do you realize how much trouble you're going to be in when the Monroes find out you went out wandering without telling anyone?"

Isis returned her gaze to the snow outside. She knew she had to tell Jet and Lilly what had happened, but she was dreading it.

Jensen glanced over at her, surprised by her silence. "I know it's horribly cliché, but it is for your own good. Plus, I owe the Monroes a lot. My life, actually."

Isis watched the landscape as they got closer to the mansion. She wondered if Jet would make her wear an ankle monitor from now on.

Jensen was quiet for a while, glancing at his passenger. "Tell you what, you swear that you won't sneak out again and this trip can be our little secret."

Isis turned to look at Jensen. "You'd do that for me?"

He smiled, keeping his eyes on the road as he turned onto the secret path that led up to the mansion's gate. "Sure, why not?"

"I don't get it," Isis said. "What do you want?"

"Ajax wants me to keep an eye on you. I want to get some sleep. I do owe you a favor for helping me in the Lair, so if you promise me you won't go sneaking out again, then we'll be even," Jensen replied. Isis arched an eyebrow. Jensen's deal was too simple.

"Fine, I promise not to go sneaking out again," she said as honestly as she could manage.

"Good," Jensen replied as he pulled up to the mansion's gate. He placed his hand on the scanner and drove down the winding driveway once the large gate swung open.

~~*~*~*

In her small townhouse, Halley Waterson sat rigidly at her kitchen table, a small mug of coffee clutched tightly in her bony hands. The morning light illuminated her small home, harshly brightening the natural colors of the walls and floor. Halley was in a simple pastel rose-colored bathrobe with matching slippers. Her soft brown hair was tied up in a lose bun; strands fell out and framed her face. Some gray streaks peppered her otherwise light brown hair, an odd occurrence for a shape shifter.

At the other side of the small table, a petite woman sat. She looked young, especially compared to Halley, but she was ancient. A sharp smile was plastered on her lips as she watched the woman across from her. Behind her, Halley could hear the tall man the woman came with moving about in the room behind them. He had a handsome face, chiseled features, and dark eyes. He wore a designer brown suit, one that probably cost more than Halley's entire modest wardrobe. His short brown hair was curly and well managed. He was imposing; an aura of hidden power seemed to radiate from him. But he wasn't the one who scared Halley.

The woman he came with looked like an ordinary young woman. Youthful and slender, her short blonde hair barely touched the nape of her neck. The front of her hair swept to the right. Her manicured nails were a pearly rose color and she drummed them on the table every now and again. She wore tight, dark blue jeans and a simple light pink blouse. A wicked-looking handgun, complete with silencer, sat on the table in front of her, probably a gift from her masters. This woman existed for one purpose and one purpose only: to protect the Corporation, no matter what the cost.

Halley almost dropped her mug when the phone rang suddenly. The beautiful blonde woman in front of her only smiled wider as she got up and moved to the message machine that rested on the kitchen counter. *Please don't call me,* Halley begged whatever guardian might have been listening. The woman effortlessly hopped up on the counter, sitting beside the small machine with the bright red light. Halley's daughter often made fun of her for being the only person left with an actual answering machine. The thought of her daughter made Halley even more afraid, knowing these people wouldn't hesitate to use her to get what they wanted. The Corporation was ruthless when they wanted something.

"Halley, this is Isis. You didn't show up, which has me a little worried. Please call me on my cell when you get a chance."

Halley closed her eyes when the phone beeped as Isis hung up. The blonde woman put a finger to her lips as she turned back to Halley, a thoughtful look on her face. She was toying with her prey; a cat with a helpless mouse.

"Hmm," she began as she approached Halley, her designer shoes clicking sharply on the tile. "Who was that, love?"

Halley glared up at the woman defiantly. "Goddamn you, Tracy."

"Sounded a lot like the guardian hybrid. I met her once, you know. Intrepid little thing, a bit cold, but can't hold that against her."

Tracy put a hand on the woman's chair, resting her other one on the table as her dark eyes bore into the woman's frightened blue eyes. "I know you weren't planning on speaking to her about your late husband's former employers. Especially after how generous they were to you, not to mention Cara. She recently had a child, didn't she?"

Tracy straightened up again and moved over to one of the windows, leaning her weight against it. Halley kept her eyes forward, unwilling to show them how scared she was.

"Mr. Carding is very concerned that you might be tempted to tell the protectors what you know," Tracy continued on. "I'm here to make sure that doesn't happen. Mr. Brown, if you would be so kind."

Before she could react, Halley felt Mr. Brown grab her arms with one of his strong hands and force her head back with his other arm.

"Tracy, please, I won't tell her anything. Why would I?" Halley pleaded with the blonde woman. Tracy pulled out a medium sized switchblade. She had the blade out with one deft flick of her wrist, examining it for a moment. She turned her eyes back to Halley.

"Oh, I wish I could believe you, love. I really do. Your family has been so good to the Corporation. But this little slip has to be punished," Tracy cooed as she straddled Halley, twirling the knife in her dexterous fingers. "We're not cruel. We simply wish to make this world — our world, a better place. To show his thanks for your loyalty to Grenich, I have been authorized to give you a choice. I can take either your tongue or Cara's. This hurts us much more than it will you, but unfortunately, it is unavoidable. Know that I take no pleasure in executing this punishment. You would be wise to keep this in mind: the next time something like this happens, the Corporation will not be so generous."

~~*~*~*

Half an hour later, Caleb Brown sat in his dark blue sports car, waiting for Tracy to finish up with Ms. Waterson. The blonde soon strode out of the house and across the small porch. She jogged down the stairs, her clothing completely clean. Caleb had been alive for centuries, but Tracy's effortless skill never ceased to amaze him. She was a marvel and it was no wonder she was so high up in the ranks. She was ancient, older than most of the guardians, and yet her existence was not known to the shape shifters or guardians. The only ones who knew of her, other than the higher ups, were deep in the Corporation — usually the ones who didn't have much longer to live. She was the Corporation's angel of death, as lovely as she was deadly.

Tracy opened the passenger door and slid her petite body in. She smiled at Caleb as she closed the door and buckled her seatbelt. Producing a balled up white handkerchief from an inner pocket, Tracy laid it on the dashboard.

"Bleeding's stopped," she said as she crossed her ankles in front of her, ever the modest lady when in the presence of an employee. "She'll be fine, but she won't be speaking to anyone for a *long* while. I doubt she'll speak to anyone ever again."

"You sure about that?"

"No, not entirely, but Halley's predictable. She'll kill herself before she endangers her daughter. She knows I'm a woman of my word."

"Have we located the escaped experiment yet?" Caleb asked. "The L-series who has been such a nuisance lately?"

"He's not our concern. I'll take care of him if he tries to interfere, which I very much doubt he will. Our products are many things, but they are definitely not stupid," Tracy responded casually, glancing behind her. "Can we hurry, please? I've got a date tonight and I can still smell some faint traces of blood on me. Better safe than sorry."

"Ah yes, Steve," Caleb said with an amused chuckle as he started the car. "How is that little love affair going?"

"He's a valuable asset. I can get to her through him, I just haven't figured out how I'm going to do that yet. Her aloofness is proving to be a challenge," Tracy responded as she ran a hand through her short blonde hair. She didn't feel sentimentality. She used it against the people she hunted. It was a powerful motivator.

"Onyx and Blackjack are getting restless. Wouldn't want a repeat of the incident at the Lair," Caleb commented. Tracy grimaced in disgust and Caleb snickered. He knew how much she disliked the two assassins who "owned" the territory.

"Please don't remind me of those damn fools. I don't understand why he insists on using assassins as city guides. They just get in the way and wind up making a huge mess, which I inevitably have to clean up," Tracy grumbled.

"I thought you didn't question the higher ups."

"I don't. I want to finish this job so we can win the war and He can reclaim what's His. The last thing we need are more loose ends," Tracy replied.

"The protectors bought right into the red herring," Caleb said as he pulled onto the street. "It was almost too easy."

"Yes, almost," Tracy murmured. "Let's make sure they stay in the dark on this one, all right?"

"I'll alert the others," Caleb replied as he made a right turn. He knew how displeased his bosses would be if someone were to throw a wrench into their carefully laid plans.

"I'll get in touch with the assassins, see when they want to take care of her. I should contact you soon, so be ready to move fast," Tracy said as she stretched her arms above her head. Caleb couldn't help but sneak a peek at her toned body.

"Just this last one and we'll have all the possible Keys," he mentioned. "Think this hunt is over?"

Tracy smiled. "Almost."

~~*~*~*

Roan sat in his cell, quiet as always. The lights rarely dimmed except at night, which was proving to be an annoyance. His eyes were glued on the wall outside his cell, but his gaze was distant. He was in a trance, searching for something not in his cell. After being immersed in the world of assassins for so long, Roan had an almost uncanny ability to see into the hidden corners of the world. It was a skill he honed while recovering from his wounds after his fight with Draco, when he had disappeared and was thought dead. He knew he would need this skill if he were to be any use to his rescuer … or to Passion. *And our daughters,* he thought. Roan had never thought he would be a parent. Children never really appealed to him. Then he had met Passion and suddenly, the thought of settling down wasn't such a horrible idea.

He had rescued Isis a few times in the past months and had been amazed at her tenacity. She had so much potential, so much strength. She was probably going to be an incredible protector, one who would go down in history. *If the Corporation doesn't get her,* he thought darkly. Roan was beginning to lose his patience waiting for the High Council to grant Jet and Lilly permission to see him. The bureaucracy in the Meadows was downright infuriating. They didn't have time for this rigmarole. Their enemy was gathering more power, amassing more weapons, and extending his reach every single day. They were wasting time they didn't have.

Roan came out of his trance and got to his feet, pacing around the cell for a few moments. He ran his long hands over his face, wishing he had some mundane task to occupy him. *Or a cigarette*, he thought wistfully. Quitting cold turkey hadn't been horrible, Roan had done it before, but there were times he missed it. His well-honed ability wasn't helping him now and it was frustrating. The protectors were up against something they had never faced before and the High Council was still taking forever to get anything done. And he was trapped in a cell, unable to do anything other than watch and wait to see what would happen.

CHAPTER NINE

"You're leaving your middle open again."

Isis glanced over to where Jensen sat on a folding chair near where she was practicing on a punching bag. He was eating a Gala apple — which she was sure was another one of his tactics to get under her skin — and grinning at her between bites. A few weeks had passed since the two had met. Jensen followed Isis almost everywhere, staying true to his word that he would keep her from sneaking off. Isis seemed to finally understand his sense of humor and didn't complain about him as much anymore. If anything, she actually teased him back.

"Don't look at my middle," she said. Jensen let out a long-suffering sigh and tossed the apple core into a nearby plastic garbage container. He was dressed in his usual nice clothing, looking ever the dapper gentleman. Jensen grabbed the towel he had brought down with him and scrubbed what little stickiness remained on his fingers.

"Shae, will you please watch your cousin so you can tell her she's leaving her midsection open?" Jensen called over to where Shae was sparring with Alex.

"Isis, listen to Jensen," Shae called back, smiling. She lunged to the side when Alex aimed a roundhouse kick at her stomach.

"Too slow," Shae taunted. Alex smirked before dropping into a perfect spin kick, successfully knocking Shae off balance.

Isis gritted her teeth when Jensen sighed loudly again. Critiquing her techniques was his new favorite pastime. *Even though I saved his sorry ass, he still thinks he's a more capable fighter,* Isis thought, shaking a damp strand of hair out of her eyes. She often practiced sparring with him and found him to be a skilled partner. It irked her to no end how he seemed to be perfect at everything. *Everyone in my life is a freaking know-it-all,* she thought as she turned toward Jensen.

"What now?" Isis snapped at him. Jensen smiled, getting up and taking off his jacket. He carefully laid it over the back of the chair.

"I just want to ensure you don't get hurt out there. It's a dangerous world," he said as he approached her. "En garde, Isis."

Before Isis had a chance to respond, Jensen lunged at her. She stepped to the side, narrowly avoiding getting tackled. He went into a perfect diving roll and then back kicked, knocking her to her knees. Isis turned her neck slightly and kicked out, aiming for his groin but only succeeded in striking his upper thigh. It was enough to knock him back a couple steps, allowing her time to get to her feet and prepare for his next attack. Jensen circled her and she mirrored his movements. He nodded, impressed by her quick reaction time.

Jensen lashed out with a powerful punch, which she deflected easily. Isis did a high side kick, aiming for his gut. She followed through with a sweeping kick that knocked him off his feet. Isis stood up, ready to gloat, but he suddenly struck out with his feet, catching her square in the stomach and knocking her on her back. Jensen crawled over to her and pinned her wrists to the mat, grinning in that cocky way of his.

"See," he panted. "Leaving your middle open."

"Are you pleased with yourself now?" she asked, smiling.

"Yes, very," he responded.

"Ahem." A voice came from behind Isis' head. She closed her eyes, already knowing who it was. Isis tilted her head back so she could see behind her.

Electra stood there, arms crossed over her chest, an amused expression on her face.

"Am I interrupting something?" she asked, raising one eyebrow.

"Nah, just getting your sister on her back, which isn't too difficult a feat," Jensen replied. Isis raised her knee, hitting him in the groin. Jensen let out a grunt as he fell to the side.

"Electra, what's up?" Isis asked as she got to her feet and brushed herself off.

"Nothing, just thought I'd come down here and visit with my favorite sister," Electra replied, still smiling. Isis gave her a look that said, *Come on.*

"I'm your *only* sister," Isis pointed out, looking to the side when Shae hopped out of the boxing ring. Alex was leaning against one of the corners, taking a long swig from her water bottle.

"You and Jensen seem to be close," Electra observed, looking to the side where Jensen was just finding his feet again.

"Him?" Isis asked, laughing. "Maybe in his dreams."

"Uh huh," Electra replied. "Do you know if Jet and Lilly have received any new information on Coop?"

Isis shrugged. "Not that I know of."

Just then, Jade jogged down the stairs. "The Monroes called a meeting in five minutes, mandatory."

For the first time, Isis was glad for a mandatory meeting. The last thing she wanted to discuss was Jensen or Coop, which seemed to be two of Electra's favorite topics.

"Oh well, I've got to run," Isis said, stepping around her twin.

"Sure you don't need a cold shower first?" Electra asked in a playful tone.

"Good one," Isis called back. Electra chuckled and glanced over her shoulder, watching Isis disappear up the stairs. Jensen bowed his head in respect as he passed by.

"Your secret's safe with me," Electra teased. Jensen frowned and twisted back.

"Don't know what you're talking about," he said.

"Sure you don't," Electra replied, glancing toward the back of the room. "You forgot your jacket."

"Ah. Thanks," Jensen said as he jogged back to retrieve the jacket. He tossed it over his shoulders and buttoned the two bottom buttons. He started for the stairs again, smiling politely at Electra as he passed her by.

~~*~*~*

In the meeting room, Jet was sitting with Lilly at the large table. He was tapping the Key against the table, producing a soft rapping noise. Lilly was shuffling through a few papers, her brow creasing as she paused at one particular paper.

Jet glanced over at her and then lifted the flashdrive, examining it. It had been too easy to retrieve, and it worked just a little too perfectly. Jet was certain it wasn't the actual Key and Lilly agreed with him, though she felt the flashdrive had some importance. He was almost positive not even Roan knew where, or even what, the actual Key was. *We would know for sure if the damn High Council would get its act together,* he thought irritably.

Jet put the flashdrive on the table as he got up, glancing over at Lilly when she looked up from her papers, offering him a gentle smile. Jet knew she was as frustrated as he was, but she was better at acting diplomatically. He wrapped his hands behind his head. Adonia had told them Roan needed to speak with them and kept requesting to do so. The assassin undoubtedly had important information, but he refused to speak to the guardians, which might be why the Council was taking so long to grant Jet and Lilly permission to question him. It didn't surprise Jet that he was being so cagey. Roan had never been an open book, even before he became an assassin. Jet was just thankful the man was in a cell where he belonged. Roan knew something, and it was their responsibility to find out exactly what it was. They had to know what they were up against. Running into a fight blind was not only stupid, it was suicidal. He wished the guardians would let them do their jobs. *The guardian men anyway,* he thought. There was no doubt in his mind it was the older guardian men on the High Council holding up the decision.

"Worry not, my darling," Lilly's calm melodic voice drifted to his ears. "The Council can be maddeningly slow, but they shall grant our request. We will be speaking with Roan soon enough."

Jet dropped his arms to his sides and turned to his wife, smiling. "I know, my dearest Lilly. I just feel as though time is of the essence. Delay could very well cause us more problems."

Lilly nodded in understanding, turning when at the sound of the door handle's click as someone entered the room. Ajax stepped inside, nodding to his friends in greeting. He moved over to the table, his eyebrows knitting together when he saw the small flashdrive in front of Jet's empty seat. He picked it up and looked at it, his eyebrows rising in surprise as he gently bounced the small object in his palm.

"Rather cold, isn't it?" he observed, his eyes turning back to Lilly and Jet.

"We noticed the same thing," Lilly replied with a nod. "We're not sure of the cause."

Ajax shrugged as he put it back on the long table. He

was dressed in a suit as if he were headed to the office or some kind of important meeting. Ajax always dressed professionally for meetings. He was a lot like his late brother, Orion, in that way.

"The Key?" he asked, nodding to the flashdrive. Jet exchanged a look with Lilly before turning his eyes back to Ajax.

"We don't think so, not anymore. The more I think about it, the less convinced I am."

Ajax frowned. "What do you mean?"

"It was too easy to retrieve and Roan told Adonia that the real Key is a living being. That's just something to throw us off track," Jet responded as he sat down next to Lilly again, interlacing his fingers with hers. "What he didn't say was who made it or why, and I'm not sure he knows for certain."

"You believe him?" Ajax asked, glancing at the Monroes. Jet nodded, resting his head between the thumb and index finger of his right hand. Lilly also nodded once.

"May I ask why?"

"We got a call yesterday from a contact who works in the local hospital. A shape shifter came in the previous night. Her tongue had been cleanly sliced out. You want to guess who that shape shifter was?"

Ajax's eyes widened. "The woman whose husband vanished? The one you think may have familial ties to Coop?"

Jet nodded again.

"We're sending the Four out tonight to check on Cara," Lilly explained. "We believe someone is covering up their tracks. Our contact said that the woman had already been cared for, sewn up, as if the removal of her tongue was just a warning."

"Hell of a warning," Ajax commented. "Any theories about who might be behind it?"

Jet shook his head. "That's what we're trying to figure out. It would help if the guardians would just let us talk to your brother. Lilly and I are beginning think everything that has happened is connected somehow, from the Key to Roan's return, maybe even Isis meeting Coop."

"You think Roan would know who's behind everything?" Ajax asked as he leaned back. "If someone's really manipulating everything like you suspect, that individual would have an enormous amount of power and sway. If Roan were connected to someone like that, he might have just been the cleaner."

"I know, but right now, it's all we have. Roan wouldn't turn himself in for nothing. According to Adonia, he has something he needs to tell us," Jet agreed.

"He sent us that cryptic note in the book we showed you, but we're not sure what it meant," Lilly put in, clasping her hands in front of her.

"Obviously, we'll take his words with a grain of salt, but we'd be fools to not hear him out," Jet finished. He sat back as the rest of the Deverells entered along with Jensen. Shae, Alex, Jade, and Isis followed shortly after.

"Jet, can we speed this along? Jensen and I have dates tonight," Nero griped. Jet shot him a look as the younger protector took his seat. Isis glanced over at Jensen, smirking. He kept his eyes on Jet and Lilly.

"It shouldn't take more than a few minutes and then you can all leave to do whatever you want," Jet said, adding, "except for those of you who are going to have jobs tonight."

Lilly slid a small sheet of paper to Jade. "You four are going to this address and checking on the occupant. Don't disturb her, just drive past and make sure everything is fine. Only go up to the door if you absolutely have to. She's trying to lead a normal life and we have to respect that."

"A human wannabe?" Nero asked, shaking his head. "Can't say I understand that. Seems downright unhealthy."

"Honestly, the amount of disdain shape shifters seem to have for humans," Isis muttered as she looked at the paper.

"Said the cynical misanthrope," Jensen pointed out and Isis laughed sarcastically.

"We're still waiting for permission to question Roan," Jet mentioned. "Ajax, would you want to sit in when it's finally granted?"

Ajax shook his head. "Not unless you deem it necessary. Roan and I had no special rapport."

"Roan was always the loner of the family," Malone added. Isis looked over at Nero, the youngest of the brothers. He was leaning back in his chair and twisting it from side to side.

"Do you have any opinion on him?" Isis asked curiously. Nero looked surprised at the question and shook his head.

"Nah, Roan and Orion were both off doing their own thing by the time I was old enough to have any opinion on either one of them," he answered.

"Nero's always been the baby of the family," Devin explained, winking at his niece. "We protected him from all the skeletons in the Deverell family closet."

"This is at least a two-hour drive," Jade mentioned, her shoulders slumping a little.

"We know it's a bit inconvenient, but we would feel better if we knew she was all right," Lilly explained. Jade rubbed her forehead.

"Then could we go now?" Jade asked. "I'd prefer to beat as much traffic as possible."

Jet nodded and Jade stood, nodding for the other three to follow.

~~*~*~*

Isis entered her room, moving for the nightstand where she kept her smaller throwing weapons. She knew Jade would likely bring a gun. Though she'd had shooting practice, Isis still wasn't entirely comfortable with firearms.

She was a decent shot, but she wasn't a great one. Isis glanced over her shoulder when she heard her door open. Jensen was standing in the doorway. He sauntered over to the bed and hopped up on it, resting on his elbow.

"Shouldn't you be getting ready for your date?" she asked, putting her baton in her messenger bag.

"Nah, I prefer to watch you," he answered as he looked up at the ceiling, bored. "Shouldn't you bring a gun? Doesn't everyone in this country carry one?"

"Just out of curiosity, who is the lucky lady?" she asked, ignoring his question. Jensen looked over at her, grinning.

"Why? Are you jealous?"

Isis scoffed. "You wish."

Jensen sobered. "I really wish Jet and Lilly were sending the Deverells on this errand instead of the four of you."

"Why is that?" Isis asked, snapping the bag shut.

"Something isn't right," he said, looking down as he tapped his thumbs together. "This woman's mother had her tongue cut out. Ordinary shape shifters aren't randomly tortured like that."

Isis stared at him, unable to conceal her shock. *Halley had her tongue cut out? Oh god, I hope it's not because of me,* she thought, swallowing the sick feeling that rose in her throat. Jensen frowned as he studied her face. His eyes widened when it dawned on him.

"Guardians, *that's* who you were going to meet at the diner," he observed as he sat up. Isis went quiet for a moment.

"Yes it was. She was late. Dammit, I should have realized something was up when she didn't show," Isis said, picking up her messenger bag. She scrubbed her hand down her face, holding it over her mouth for a minute.

"What did she get herself into?" Isis asked herself as she shook her head and turned to leave.

"Hey, wait a minute," Jensen got off the bed and

reached out, grabbing a hold of her wrist. Isis spun around and found herself standing uncomfortably close to Jensen. She stared at him and they locked eyes for a moment. Jensen cleared his throat and looked down at his hand on her wrist.

"This is … a little awkward," he mentioned.

"Uh, yeah," Isis replied, waiting for him to step back and release her wrist. He seemed stuck in the spot.

"I should probably let go."

"Probably."

"Right," he said, hesitantly releasing her wrist. She took a step back, wracking her mind for something to say. The silence felt uncomfortable. Jensen didn't seem to know what to say and she didn't either.

"I've got to go," Isis finally said, turning to leave and nearly walking into the door. She gritted her teeth in embarrassment and gripped the edge of the door, pulling it open wider.

"Have fun on your date," she called over her shoulder as she left. As she hurried down the hall, Isis let out a breath. The air suddenly seemed warm.

~~*~*~*

Shae glanced over at her cousin, who was drumming her fingers on the handle of the car door in a near neurotic manner. The sun was setting fast and it was already quite dark out. The night was as bitterly cold as the day. The temperature rarely rose past the teens in the winter.

"Guardians have mercy, Isis," Alex finally said as she turned around in her seat. "What is *with* you tonight?"

"Huh, what?" Isis said, finally coming out of her trance.

"You've been drumming your fingers on the damn door ever since you got in the car," Jade answered, glancing at Isis in the rearview mirror.

"Oh, sorry," Isis muttered, taking her hand away from

the door and resting her elbow on it. She rested her head on her hand and started drumming her fingers on her leg.

"You were rather flushed when you came downstairs," Shae suddenly mentioned with a grin. Isis furrowed her brow and looked at her cousin.

"Come again?"

"Just noticed that you looked rather warm when you came downstairs. As if you were feverish, which of course is impossible for shape shifters and guardians," Shae replied, her eyes wandering over to Jade and Alex. "Jensen also looked rather warm, even from a distance."

Isis snorted. "If you're suggesting that Jensen and I—"

"I'm not suggesting anything, merely an observation," Shae replied in a tone that was much too innocent. Isis shook her head, laughing softly.

"Sorry to burst your bubble, Shae, but Jensen and I are friends, nothing more. We just had a bit of an … odd moment," she explained.

"Sexy odd?"

"Awkward odd."

Shae looked a little disappointed. "Shame."

Isis made a non-committal noise in response, her attention focused on the landscape. Jade finally pulled up the small driveway in front of a dark house. She frowned as she double-checked the address.

"We're here," she said, puzzled.

"Are you sure?" Alex asked as she looked at the dark home. There were no signs of life inside the house from what they could see. None of the lights were on and the windows were bare. Isis looked at the house out of the corner of her eye and suppressed a shiver that crept up her spine. She glanced toward the basement windows and noticed dead plants poking out of the ground around the house.

Jade shrugged. "Jet and Lilly asked us to check it out, so we better get to it."

She opened the car door and stepped out, as did the

other three.

"Shae and I will knock on the door," Jade said. "Alex, you and Isis check around back and be subtle. Try not to look like you're casing the joint."

Isis followed Alex around back. The shadows swiftly swallowed them up. Jade turned to Shae and nodded her head in the direction of the house.

~~*~*~*

Things were peaceful in the Meadows. Most of the guardians were focused entirely on their endless jobs, as was their way. In the Pearl Castle, messengers rushed around the beautiful space, delivering messages and running errands.

Electra sat on her mother's bed, relaxing on the red satin sheets. She was watching Passion, who sat off to the left in front of a vanity mirror. Passion was running a soft brush through her perfect honey-colored hair, which was over her left shoulder.

"You're going to see him, aren't you?" Electra asked as she leaned down so that she was resting on one elbow. Passion flipped her hair over her right shoulder, running the brush through it, glancing at her daughter in the mirror.

"Jet and Lilly need answers. I can get them before the High Council gets around to granting their request, which will be more than a decade at the rate they're moving. I am more experienced at handling Roan than anyone. I know many of his tells," Passion said, pausing. "And I have to confront him face-to-face. If I don't, I doubt I'll ever have any kind of closure."

"Have you told Grandmother and great-Grandmother?"

Passion smiled. "Of course. I wouldn't just waltz into the dungeon. There are some rules even *I* won't break."

"Not many," Electra muttered. Passion gave her a dry

look in the mirror as she stood up and turned off the lights around the mirror.

"I will be back soon," she said as she walked over to the bed and kissed Electra's forehead affectionately. "Don't follow me."

Passion hurried down the stairs to the main hall of the Pearl Castle. She passed by a number of messengers as she made her way to the stairs that led down to the dungeon. Once she reached the bottom level of the castle, Passion strode through the dungeons and down the hall leading up to Roan's cell. She was trying to keep her face clear of emotion and could only hope she was successful. Passion tried to find the inner stoicism possessed by her mother, grandmother, and even her daughters. She paused for a brief moment, took a deep breath, and then continued on without stopping.

He was sitting with his back to her when she reached the cell. His reddish blond hair shone under the light. His jacket lay across the bed on which he rested his feet. Passion swallowed, finding her voice.

"Roan," Passion said firmly. He twisted partway to look over his shoulder, green eyes widening a little. After a moment's hesitation, Roan stood up and turned around fully so that he faced her. He approached the glass slowly, his expressive green eyes never leaving hers. Passion needed to tilt her head up in order to meet his gaze due to those long legs of his, which made up most of his height. He was as thin as ever; "lanky" came to mind. He still had a pale complexion, as though he hadn't ventured out into the sunlight often enough. Passion glared at him. Though she thought she had prepared herself to speak with him again, she could feel her anger bubbling to the surface.

"You're still angry at me. You have every right to be," he began in his smoky voice.

"You don't have the right to tell me how I feel," she snapped, unable to feel anything other than fury.

He cringed. "Okay, you're a lot angrier than I

remember."

"Where have you been hiding?" Passion demanded, crossing her arms over her chest.

He looked down at his feet briefly, lifting his shoulders in a small shrug. "I've been everywhere, sticking to the shadows for the most part."

"Again with the vague answers, Roan? That's not going to cut it," she said, narrowing her eyes at him. The very sight of him made her angrier than she ever thought possible. "At least tell me this: how do I know you're not an imposter? Last time I saw you, you were sans a pulse."

He smiled a brief sad smile, which he quickly wiped from his features when he saw Passion was not amused. "That's not entirely true. After you left I still had a faint heartbeat, but it was so faint no one would have been able to detect it. Someone came to my aid. They cared for me until I had recovered."

"That's rather convenient. Does this mystery person have a name?" Passion asked, not buying his story for a second.

"I'm sorry, Passion. I can't tell you that," Roan apologized. His tone was always sincere when he spoke with her, which was starting to grate on her nerves.

"Why not?" Passion demanded.

"For their protection," Roan answered, albeit hurriedly. "Passion, please, you have to convince the High Council to let Jet and Lilly see me."

"Yeah, because they seek my counsel all the time for decisions," Passion scoffed derisively. "You have two daughters, did you know that?"

Roan flinched as if she had struck him. He looked at her with an apologetic expression, but she continued to glare at him. Her eyes held anger and scorn for the shape shifter in front of her, fury making her see red. Passion was sure her eyes had changed color and were probably redder than blood.

"Well?" she demanded when he didn't respond. Roan

swallowed and nodded, taking a deep breath.

"Passion, I meant everything I said when you tried to help me," he said softly. "You have no idea how sorry I am for everything that happened. I would give anything to take back my past actions. I turned myself in with the hopes of doing some good, hopefully atoning for some of my crimes—"

"Don't! Don't you dare!" Passion snapped, forgetting her composure again. She put her hands on her hips, dropping her gaze for a moment, gathering herself. Passion looked up at him again, her composure regained. Around them, the dungeon remained calm and peaceful.

"You can't go back and undo all the damage you did," she started carefully. "But if you are telling the truth and looking to atone for your past, you can start by helping Jet and Lilly. Tell me what you need to tell them. No more of these cryptic answers or riddles or vague roundabout responses."

"Passion, I can't do that. I have to speak with the Monroes directly."

"Fine," Passion said, pausing and searching his face. "Why did you come back now, of all times? Why not all those years when the protectors were still looking for you?"

"Isis was in danger. I had to protect her."

Passion shook her head, dropping her eyes again. She couldn't believe him. Roan was an assassin, the worst that had ever roamed the world. He had murdered his own brother in cold blood, killed a man in front of her, and now he claimed he had wanted to protect their daughter. Roan wasn't capable of compassion. No, he was playing some kind of game.

"My rescuer … Passion, something very bad is coming. That flashdrive, what you think is the Key — it's not. It's a decoy meant to throw the Monroes off track, which I'm sure they've already figured out. I told Adonia before: the actual Key is a living, breathing being and if he or she falls into the wrong hands … it means the end of everything. The Key will be capable of great destruction and their wielder will have unlimited power to the point of being invincible," Roan stated, his green eyes as intense as Passion had ever seen them.

"How do you know?"

Roan glanced to the side, stepping closer to the glass and lowering his voice. "There are things in this world that not even the guardians know about. These things pose the greatest threat to the survival of both supernatural and mortal species. Look, I can't tell you what they are, Passion. But I've seen what they do in this hunt of theirs. I've seen things that are so appalling they've been right out of some horrific nightmare. Only they were real — too real."

Roan dropped his eyes to his feet, shaking his head as if to rid it of some horrible image. Passion stared at him, wondering how much of his words were the truth. She tried to meet his eyes again.

"Roan, if what you're saying is true, the only way you can help is by telling me exactly what it is you know so I can tell Jet and Lilly."

Roan leaned forward resting his hands against the glass, his eyes remaining on the floor. He shook his head, swallowing.

"I can't tell you anything specific."

"Why not?"

Roan looked back up at her with a rueful smile. "Because I know you. You act on emotion. When your loved ones are threatened, you go off half-cocked. You'd get into this fight in whatever way you could. Passion, if anything ever happened to you, I could never forgive myself."

Passion narrowed her eyes at him, her nostrils flaring.

"Know this, Roan. If these indirect answers result in the death of another innocent, that's more blood on your hands," Passion stated.

She turned and stormed out of the dungeons, aggravated she hadn't been able to get the answers Jet and Lilly needed. Passion could feel Roan watching her as she left and thought she heard a quiet apology just before she reached the door, but disregarded it.

CHAPTER TEN

Jade and Shae stood in the front room of the empty house. There was a layer of dust on everything, as if no one had lived there in years. They exchanged a look before Shae moved into the kitchen, her shoes clicking on the hardwood floor. All the appliances were in place, covered in dust and cobwebs, just like everything else in the small home. The floors were bare, no sign of furniture. The windows that weren't covered were obscured by grime and dirt. Shae frowned as she crouched down and ran her index finger across the hardwood floor. She held it up to her face and rubbed her thumb against the soft gray dust that stuck to it.

"I got nothing," Jade said as she moved into the doorway. "The place is completely abandoned."

"Jet and Sly were here a couple weeks ago?" Shae asked.

"Yeah," Jade answered, scratching the back of her neck. "It looks like no one has lived here in at least ten years though."

Shae stood up again, wincing when her knees cracked.

"Nothing around back," a voice came from the door leading to the yard. Jade and Shae looked over to where

Alex and Isis were standing.

"Everything is dead back there," Isis added. "And yes, I know it's winter. But there are some coniferous bushes out there or whatever those year round plants are called. They're all brown and … dead."

Alex moved inside the house, followed by Isis who closed the door behind them.

"Am I the only one who finds this entire scene to be *very* weird?" Isis asked no one in particular. The other three shook their heads.

"Do we know of any other instances like this?" Alex asked.

"What? Like disappearances?" Jade replied. Alex shrugged.

"Like that, or," she paused, running a thumb over her lower lip as she dropped her eyes for a moment. "When I was growing up, I remember Remington telling me a story about things so evil that wherever they walked, death followed close behind."

Jade stared at her. "There's a nice little bedtime story."

"I liked myths of shape shifters. That particular story was from the War of the Meadows, I think," Alex replied.

"Remington's kid likes mythology, who woulda thought?" Shae put in.

"Weren't the plants in my old apartment dead?" Isis asked, looking over at Jade. "That day we went back to get my stuff with Electra, when I came to live at the mansion?"

"You know, I think they were," Jade said, looking around at the empty house and shivering. The house was very cold, but there was also a strange heaviness to the air.

"Let's get out of here," Jade suggested. "Nothing more we can do. Whoever lived here is long gone."

"Great," Isis said, hurrying toward the front door, eager to leave the creepy house. Shae went next, then Alex, with Jade bringing up the rear. Jade glanced around the house one last time and then closed the door behind her.

They never noticed the pair of eyes watching them from the upper level of the home. Tracy absentmindedly ran her fingers over the pommel of her sword as she watched the Four leave. She smiled a little, relieved. For a moment, she had been afraid things were going to get a little bloody. It would have been most unpleasant. Tracy raised her arm and glanced at the small watch on her delicate wrist. Ten o'clock, she had places to go. She strode from the house and melted back into the night.

~~*~*~*

Ajax knocked on the door of the home of a Ms. Halley Waterson. Malone stood nearby, leaning against the railing of her small porch with his arms crossed over his chest, his coat rustling softly in the wind. He glanced at the modest watch on his right wrist.

"It's been about five minutes, man. I don't think she's home," he mentioned as Ajax knocked again.

"I doubt she'd venture out any time soon," Ajax replied, glancing over at his brother before turning his eyes back to the door. "After getting one's tongue cut out, grocery shopping is probably not high on the list of priorities. Just a hunch."

Malone spread his hands and shrugged, but remained quiet. Ajax, on a whim, tried the doorknob. It was unlocked. He glanced back at his brother, his brow furrowing.

"If you had recently been tortured, would you leave the door open?" Ajax whispered.

Malone straightened up, concern creasing his features. His hand drifted to the sheath he kept hidden on his waist. The Deverell brothers didn't carried firearms when out on simple missions, but they always kept at least one blade on hand. There were plenty of separatists and assassins who would enjoy putting them down.

"Ms. Waterson?" Ajax called out, taking a cautious step into the house. Nothing but silence greeted him, which unnerved him more than he cared to admit. The house was dark and most of the curtains had been drawn. Malone stayed right on his brother's heels, his hand resting just above a carefully concealed knife. He tapped Ajax's left shoulder, pointing to his nose when his older brother turned to look at him. He was picking up a faint scent, so faint that even with his sensitive nose he was unable to identify it. Ajax nodded, indicating he had also noticed the odor. He pointed, signaling it was coming from somewhere in front of them. They paused at a corner and Ajax peered around the bend.

There was a short empty hall. Ajax cautiously crept out from behind the bend, noticing a flight of stairs leading to the second floor. He carefully made his way up the stairs, his ears and eyes alert for even the smallest movement. Reaching the top of the stairs, Ajax noticed three doors. One was open a crack, light spilling out. Ajax had a feeling of dread as he made his way to the door. He pushed the tall door open and sighed at the scene before him.

There were a few open empty pill bottles on the floor. As Ajax took a step inside the bathroom, he could see the tub was filled with dark red water. The protector could see Halley's body at the bottom of the tub, her glassy blue eyes staring at nothing.

"Is she …?" Malone asked, entering the bathroom behind his brother. Ajax nodded, taking out his gloves from his pocket and pulling them on. He crouched down and picked up one of the bottles, twisting it in his hand so he could read the label. Putting it back in its original spot, Ajax picked up another one.

"Powerful stuff, recent prescription. Judging from these meds, she probably died a couple hours ago," Ajax murmured, putting the bottle back on the floor. "No signs of struggle, so this was probably self-inflicted."

"Guardians have mercy," Malone said, scrubbing a

hand over his mouth as he studied the dead woman. She had been a beautiful shape shifter. Even in the bloody water, he could see her hair was chestnut-colored. Malone craned his neck and he squinted as something caught his attention.

"Ajax? Are those gray streaks in her hair?"

Ajax looked over his shoulder, standing again. "It looks like it. She must have been under a severe amount of stress for quite some time."

"It had to have been a while, right? I can't remember the last time I saw a shape shifter with graying hair. I mean, we're constantly hunted and getting in less than pleasant situations and none of us have any gray hair."

"It's unusual, but not unheard of. Come on, let's get out of here. I'll have the Monroes send their contact in the police department to take care of her."

Malone followed his older brother back out into the hall and out of the small house. Death was not a natural occurrence for shape shifters, but that didn't mean it was uncommon. Both Ajax and Malone had seen their fair share of death — more than they would like. The Deverell family had experienced plenty of tragedies over the years and there were few of them left. Unfortunately, in their lives, death was unavoidable.

~~*~*~*

Jade pulled up the driveway to the mansion. The winter nights lacked the heavy darkness of warmer months, due mostly to the glistening snow that still coated everything. A kind of serenity had fallen over the mansion, as it usually did in the colder months. Most of the shape shifters who resided in the mansion had gone south for the winter, preferring the warmth of the sun to the chill of the snow.

"Well I'll be damned," Jade said as she stopped the car in front of the garage. "Hey Isis, the object of your indifference seems to be back from his date."

Isis glanced out through the windshield. Sure enough, Jensen was in the driveway near the garage, leaning against his sleek silver Jaguar. He had his long coat on, the collar up so it shielded the back of his neck. His back was to them, but they knew he heard the purr of the car Jade was driving. He turned his head a little at their approach, but gave no other indication he heard them. His hands were hidden in the pockets of the jacket.

"Isis," Shae suddenly said as Jade pulled into the garage and parked the car. "If you're not going to take him, can I have him?"

Isis laughed as she got out of the car. She moved toward the open garage door, which spilled bright yellow light across the freshly shoveled driveway. Isis stopped on the other side of the car.

"You're back awfully early," she observed. Jensen turned around and leaned his hip against the side of the car, a small grin crossing his face.

"Are you complaining?" he asked.

"Yes, actually," Isis responded with a half-smile. "Thought I'd have a night of peace for once."

Jensen chuckled. "Nero doesn't have a type, but I'm afraid I can be a bit pickier. They were nice enough, but her interests were vastly different from mine. It made for very poor conversation, I'm afraid."

"Uh huh," Isis said, arching an eyebrow. "I would have taken you for a player."

Jensen squinted at her, still smiling. "Are you suggesting I'm easy?"

Isis leaned down, holding his gaze. "I'm sure you've been called worse."

Jensen laughed again and looked back up. Isis followed his gaze into the clear night sky, which was like purple velvet decorated with millions of tiny diamonds. The two stood together for a moment, enjoying the peace and quiet. The moment was interrupted by the screech of tires.

They both turned to where the noise originated, further down the drive.

In the distance, they could just make out a red Porsche squealing to a stop at the gates, pausing only for them to swing open before tearing up the driveway. It drove inside the garage and screeched to a halt.

"That was the Deverells' car," Jensen said, moving to stand next to Isis. She glanced at him, noting the look of concern on his face, and then looked back toward the garage. A flustered-looking Malone and Ajax exited the Porsche and hurried into the mansion.

"That can't be good," Jensen said as he made his way toward the open doors, followed closely by Isis.

~~*~*~*

Alpha ran a hand through her short black hair as she made her way down a secret corridor. The hall was hidden in the back of the club, accessible only through a locked door in her office. Cobwebs decorated every corner and clutter lined the walls, remnants from old rooms that were no longer in use.

Alpha continued down the hall until she reached the end where two ordinary doors sat across from each other. She took out a set of keys that were attached to her belt and unlocked one door, stepping into the single windowless room. The occupant glanced up at her. The glow from his laptop illuminated his weary face.

"Alpha, what is it?" he asked, tiredly.

"Halley's dead, Cara's missing," Alpha stated, never one to pussyfoot. The man sat back, running his hands over his unkempt face. His five-o'clock shadow rasped against his rough palms.

"I know," he replied.

"What do you mean, you know?" Alpha hissed as she slammed the door shut behind her. "Have you called Coop?"

"My contact with access to the Corporation told me the Watersons would be targeted. If I know, I assume Coop does too. He knows my contacts," the man replied, still unbothered. Alpha stood, gaping, for a moment, not believing her ears.

"That was his *family*! How much higher does the body count have to get before you actually *do* something?"

The man leaned forward, his eyes blazing. "Alpha, stay out of it. You don't know what this place is capable of, what the head will do to ensure his success. I'm doing everything I can to make sure that doesn't happen, but I can only do so much. Yes, there are going to be casualties, probably a lot, but it's unavoidable in war."

Alpha shook her head, leaning against a nearby chair. "I heard Roan's in the Meadows."

"He is, doing his part," the man answered in a gruff tone. "Now if you don't mind . . ."

He gestured toward the door. Alpha glanced at the door and then back to the man. She remembered a time long ago when he had been a doctor, the most well-mannered and compassionate protector she had ever known. Sure, he was part of the establishment, but he still treated everyone with respect, even rebels. That Corporation had changed him, tainted him like it did all shape shifters who got in too deep. The man hunched over the desk again, his eyes fixed on the laptop screen once more.

"When was the last time you went out?" Alpha asked softly. The man rubbed his eyes and groaned.

"I don't have time and I can't risk being seen," he replied, trying to ignore her. She approached the desk, standing above him.

"You're wound tighter than a spring. You need to take a break," she pointed out.

"I eat and drink when I need to," he said with a dismissive wave of his hand.

"You need fresh air, the touch of another living being,"

she replied, walking around the desk. She slowly pulled herself up on the desk near him. "There are a number of rebels that would gladly relieve some of your stress."

The man squinted up at her, puzzled. "Are you offering to sleep with me?"

"You aren't my type, but I would happily arrange companionship for you with another rebel who would be more amenable," Alpha said, leaning closer to him. "You will be no good to anyone if you have a nervous breakdown, which is exactly where you're heading."

The man rubbed his aching eyes again. "Thank you, Alpha. I will think about it."

Alpha shook her head as she stood again, knowing he would never take her up on the offer. As she was moving to the door, Alpha noticed a basket full of dirty clothes. Papers and books covered every surface in the small room, and maps adorned the walls. There were pictures and pages of strange symbols pinned up in different spots. If she didn't know him, Alpha would have thought she was standing in the living space of a madman.

"Has he ever taken rebels?" she asked off-handedly, glancing back to where he hunched over the laptop. He was illuminated only by the screen and a pitifully small lamp.

"He doesn't view shape shifters according to factions," he answered without looking up, not bothering to sugarcoat his response. "As far as anyone can tell, he just grabs whatever shape shifter he wants. To him, we're a bunch of mindless guinea pigs."

"Do you really think you can stop him?"

The man paused for a moment, looking up at her again. "Do you want the truth?"

Alpha nodded once, crossing her arms over her chest.

"I don't know," the man answered. Alpha moved to the door, pausing to look at one of the maps. It was covered in colorful pins, a few strands of yarn connecting assorted pins. She looked back at the man one last time and then left the small room, closing the door behind her.

~~*~*~*

Isis paced around her bedroom the next night, troubled. Jet and Lilly had told the Four of what Ajax and Malone had found when they visited Ms. Waterson's home. It had taken every ounce of strength in Isis' body to conceal just how disturbed she was by the news. She was worried she had gotten Halley killed and the guilt was weighing heavily on her.

Isis went to the doors to the balcony, throwing them open and letting the frigid winter air flood her room. She stepped out onto the frosty ground and into the night. Standing at the balcony railing for a minute, Isis looked out over the mansion lands. The cold air stung her face and body, knifing through her clothes. She shivered in the cold, but kept looking out at the night. If she had gotten Halley killed, even unintentionally, what did that make her? Could she have put Coop in even more danger? Isis should have heeded Alpha's words and kept the other three in the loop at the very least. She closed her eyes, a million thoughts warring for control in her mind.

Another freezing wind swept over her and Isis went back into her dark room. She closed and locked the balcony doors, striding to the nightstand where her messenger bag was. Isis grabbed it and switched off the lamp. She needed to go for a walk, just around the mansion grounds, to clear her head.

Isis left her room, closing the door behind her, and hurried down the hall. She jogged down the steps and moved through the main hall. She ignored the few shape shifters she passed. At the moment, she wanted to be alone. She suddenly found herself at the garage door. Looking over her shoulder, Isis opened the door and slipped into the garage. Once inside, she pressed the button that would open the large door at the opposite end.

She jogged down the three short steps and made her way toward the ascending door.

"Didn't we already have the 'no sneaking out' talk?" a familiar voice asked from her left. "I really thought we had come to an agreement on that topic."

Isis twisted in the direction of the voice. Jensen was standing near his Jaguar, studying her with that arrogant smirk of his. It faded when he saw the look on her face.

"I'm not sneaking out. I-I just need some fresh air. I won't leave the property, I promise," Isis replied softly, looking off to the side. Jensen shifted his weight and glanced out toward the night, running a hand through his hair.

"Listen, you want to take a short trip?" he asked. She felt her mouth drop open and he snickered at her expression.

"You've got a caged bird look about you," he observed. "It's rather unsettling."

"I-I . . ." Isis couldn't think of anything to say. She hadn't expected him to be that perceptive. She wanted to get the hell out of the mansion, if only for an evening. Isis didn't necessarily care where either.

Jensen moved around the car and opened the passenger side door, nodding toward the empty seat. "Come on, I have a place in town. I was heading there anyway. Been away too long, the landlord's going to start getting suspicious."

Isis paused before blurting out, "I'm not going to sleep with you!"

Jensen couldn't help but laugh at the random declaration, which was made even more amusing by the blush that rose to her cheeks. She covered her eyes and muttered obscenities under her breath. She couldn't believe she had just said that. *Of all the idiotic things I could've said, that had to be the worst,* Isis thought in embarrassment.

"Well now that we've gotten that out of the way, hop in," Jensen said, still laughing.

Isis moved over to the car, sinking into the smooth seat. The car was just as nice on the inside as it was on the outside. The interior was warm and inviting, comfortable. Jensen shut the door and moved around to the driver's side.

"Thank you."

"Don't mention it," Jensen replied as he closed the driver's side door. He started the engine and pulled out of the garage. The two made their escape out into the cold winter's night.

~~*~*~*

Jensen unlocked the door to the large, sparsely decorated apartment, holding a bulky handful of mail. The apartment was bare for the most part. Sheets had been thrown over the few pieces of furniture he owned. His lover, Bryn, had been fond of the place, seeing it as her home away from home. Jensen swallowed the lump that came unbidden to his throat as he stepped in and opened the door wider, allowing Isis to enter. He closed the door and locked it. She looked around the open space.

"It's nice," she complimented. "How long has it been since you've last been here?"

"Years. Kept up on the rent, in case I came back," Jensen responded as he began sorting through the pile of mail. "There's no food, but you can order out if you're hungry."

"Not really hungry," Isis said, running her hand over the smooth sheet that covered the table. "You didn't think you were coming back?"

Jensen shrugged. "I always expect that. Hope for the best, prepare for the worst. Plenty of nasty individuals out there who wouldn't mind wiping out the last of the Aldridge line."

He pushed the mail aside, which was mostly junk as he

had expected, and tossed his keys on the counter before hopping up on one of the bar stools, watching Isis. She glanced over at him and when their eyes met, the electronics in the apartment came to life, startling the two protectors.

"Damn," Jensen grumbled as he made his way over to the TV set and turned it off. "Must be an electrical surge or something."

"Jensen?"

"Hm?" Jensen said, not taking his attention from the stereo that he turned off. He moved next to the lights, turning them down a little so the light wasn't so harsh.

"Why aren't guardians and shape shifters allowed to have relationships?" Isis asked as she sat down on one of the two stiff chairs at the small table. Jensen shrugged as he moved over to the table, taking off his jacket and draping it over the opposite chair before leaning over it.

"You've heard the legend of Selene, right?" he asked, loosely clasping his hands in front of him.

"Bits and pieces," Isis replied, leaning back in her chair. "I know that she was one of the earliest guardians to fall in love with a shape shifter, and it didn't end so well."

Jensen smiled, wondering why she hadn't been told more. It was one of the most important legends among both guardians and shape shifters.

"You could say that. There are many different versions of the story of Selene. In one, Selene and her lover both died in the War of the Meadows, which I'm sure you heard of. Chaos tried to conquer the land of the guardians after his exile. Many great shape shifters fought alongside the guardians, my ancestors included. In fact, Selene's lover was a distant relative of the Aldridges. After the fall of Selene, the grief of the guardians was so profound and intense it began to affect the Earth. They wept for days on end and their tears flooded the water realm. Darkness fell over the Meadows and Earth experienced nothing but starless nights. The High Council met and it was decided that the guardian who watched over death would allow Selene to return to life. However, when she was restored, she could find no peace in the Meadows and eventually vanished, never to be seen or heard from again. This was way, *way* back when. We're talking the Dark Ages. After Selene disappeared, the High Council decided there would never again be romantic liaisons between shape shifters and guardians."

Isis snickered at Jensen's words, ever the refined gentleman. He wasn't such bad company … on the rare occasions he wasn't completely full of himself. He smiled when she laughed. It felt as if they had known each other for years rather than just a few weeks.

"Bed or couch, which would you like?" Jensen asked as he straightened up, undoing the buttons on his sleeves. Isis stood up, studying him for a moment.

"Do you agree with the sacred rule, law, whatever it is?" she asked him as if she hadn't heard his question. Jensen looked at her, taken off guard by the question.

"Not for me to decide," he replied with a shrug. "I'm a mere protector, a humble servant to the guardians and loyal to the Monroes."

"Ah," Isis nodded, smiling in amusement. Jensen stepped forward, intending to step around her. He paused, so close to her he could feel her breath through his shirt. She looked up at him, her green eyes alight with invitation. The silence between them seemed to stretch on for an eternity, until neither of them could take it any longer.

Isis stood on her toes and captured Jensen's lips with her own. She wrapped her arms around his neck, clasping her wrists so one hand was free to massage the back of his head. They started backing up toward his bedroom, locked in hungry passionate kisses. They collided with the walls, using the small pauses to fumble out of clothing.

Jensen stopped first, whispering, "Wait, wait."

Isis' eyes connected with his again. "What's wrong?"

"We can't do this, Isis. Do you have any idea what the

consequences would be if the guardians were to find out?" Jensen said in a mournful tone, his lips inches from hers. She tilted her head as she looked at him.

"Are you *that* afraid of the guardians?" she inquired. The almost instinctive fear of shape shifters toward guardians was beginning to get on her nerves. The darkness of the hall enveloped them as they stood, locked in an embrace.

"Them, your uncles, Jet, Lilly," Jensen replied with a quiet laugh. "Isis, they're our leaders. I know it's different with humans, but—"

"That doesn't give them the right to tell us how to live. Not if we're not hurting anyone," she replied, running her fingers through his soft hair with a mischievous smile. "Please don't tell me you're a traditionalist. Because that would be a turn-off."

Jensen chuckled as he looked at her. He smiled as he leaned down and kissed her again. They continued their trek toward Jensen's room, their hands exploring every inch of the other's body.

Isis ran her hands over Jensen's abdominal muscles as he pulled off his shirt. His chest was smooth and yet still masculine. His entire body was warm, like a heavy comforter on a frigid winter night. They finally reached the darkened bedroom, and Isis suddenly felt Jensen's powerful arms wrap around her slender frame and she wrapped her long legs around his waist. Then she was falling backwards, onto a soft bed with cool smooth covers, the mattress firm beneath her.

High above them, outside the apartment, the moon was the only witness to a sacred law being shattered.

CHAPTER ELEVEN

Enormous clocks that didn't tell time surrounded her on all sides, caging her in. A black cat burst through the face of a clock, wearing an hourglass on its collar. Suddenly she was trapped inside a gigantic hourglass, the dark red sand rising above her throat to her chin. The sand was running out, but it would still bury her.

Isis' eyes snapped open and her breath caught in her throat. She glanced to her left when Jensen mumbled something in his sleep and turned over, taking a good portion of the covers with him. Isis swallowed and looked back to the window on her right. She thought about the nightmare she had just woken from and curled up under the remaining blanket, putting the images out of her mind. Isis glanced over at Jensen's back. He hadn't been her first lover, but he had definitely been one of the best, though she had no intention of telling him that. *The man doesn't need any more ego,* she thought with a grin.

Isis glanced to the side when she heard a strange rattling on the floor. Something was vibrating in the pocket of her jeans, which lay haphazardly on the ground. She groaned, a feeling of dread overtaking her. Isis had a feeling who was calling and why.

She got out of the bed, taking the top cover with her to act as a makeshift robe. The sun was so bright on the snow it hurt her eyes and Isis shivered in the chilly air. She didn't remember the apartment being so cold the previous night. Then again, she had been otherwise occupied. She knelt down and retrieved the phone from her discarded pants.

"Hello?" Isis answered.

"You are in *so* much trouble," Shae stated, though Isis could hear the laughter in her voice. "Get your ass back here."

"On my way," Isis said.

"And I want every last detail," Shae demanded. Isis could hear her grinning. She glanced over her shoulder to where Jensen still slept. *Definitely going to be doing that again,* she thought.

Isis smiled and hung up, gathering her clothes as fast as she could. She bit her lip when she remembered Jensen had brought her to the apartment. Isis looked back at him, reluctant to wake him up. She smirked, an evil little smirk that frequently crossed her features when she knew she was about to do something that would get her in trouble.

Isis swiftly pulled on her clothes and hurried out to the main area of the apartment. Sure enough, the keys to the Jaguar were on the counter, right where Jensen had left them the previous night. Isis snatched them and grabbed her shoes, slipping them on. She sorted through the junk mail, grabbing a good-sized envelope and a nearby pen. Scribbling a quick note, Isis put it where she knew Jensen would see it on the counter. She moved to the apartment door and undid the locks, opening the door. Nero stood on the other side of the door, his hand raised as if he had been about to knock. He tilted his head as he studied her. Isis smiled at him and jostled the car keys in her hand.

"Hey Nero," she greeted as she ran out the door, passing the youngest Deverell. "I left Jensen a note on the counter, but in case he doesn't see it, let him know that I borrowed his car."

Nero stood there, a little taken off guard by his niece's hurried words. He nodded and watched Isis disappear around a corner, still in a state of puzzlement. Shrugging, Nero stepped into Jensen's apartment and closed the door behind him. He moved to the bedroom door and saw his good friend sprawled out on the bed. Nero moved back down the short hall to the small closet that contained most of his friend's shoes and coats, as well as a broom, mop, and bucket. Nero grabbed the dull green plastic bucket and made his way to the bathroom. He put the bucket under the tap and turned on the water, wincing at the loud sound of rushing water. Luck was on his side — Jensen remained asleep. *He's always been a heavy sleeper,* Nero thought.

Once the bucket was half-full of cold water, Nero turned off the tap and moved to the bedside. Jensen remained in blissful oblivion.

"Rise and shine!" Nero shouted as he dumped the water on him. Jensen let out a yell of surprise as he jumped out of bed, concealing himself with one of the bed sheets. He was dripping wet and looked nothing short of infuriated.

"What the hell is wrong with you!?" Jensen snapped. He kept a tight grip on the sheet that was wrapped around his waist.

"You slept with my niece!? My innocent niece! Be thankful I'm not challenging you to a duel," Nero stated with feigned indignation, putting the bucket down.

"You're mental!" Jensen yelled, groaning when he heard pounding on his door, which could only mean one thing. *For fuck's sake*, he silently cursed. Jensen tossed the sheet to the side, moving toward the bedroom door and retrieving his dark blue robe. He wrapped it about himself, tightening the sash as he made his way to the front of the apartment.

Jensen opened his door to reveal one of the nosier neighbors and he struggled not to roll his eyes. She was anything but happy. The vein in her head throbbed and her pale face was turning an interesting shade of scarlet.

"Yes, Mary?" Jensen asked, scrubbing a hand down his wet face.

"You seem to think this is your own personal home. There are other tenants who live here and you're disturbing them," Mary fumed.

"What are you on about? It's," Jensen paused to glance over at the clock. "Ten in the morning, everybody is up and about by now."

"You miss the point. I was watering my plants and the next thing I know, you start shouting at the top of your lungs. Now there's water all over my kitchen," Mary continued on.

"I fail to see how that's my fault."

"I don't know what kinds of shenanigans you people take part in, but that's your business. The whole world doesn't need to know about it."

Jensen leaned against the doorframe, crossing his arms over his chest, and studying her. "You people? Do you mean immigrants or single men or some other group that I'm unaware of being part of?"

Just then, Nero emerged from the bedroom. He smiled and winked at Mary as he sauntered over, draping an arm over Jensen's shoulders. Jensen smiled and leaned his head on Nero's shoulder. Mary's eyes looked about ready to pop out of their sockets as she stared at the two men.

"Hi there, beautiful," Nero said to Mary. "I must apologize for his behavior. Just a little lover's quarrel, you understand. We'll keep it down, although you are quite the screamer in bed, right honey?"

"You never used to complain about it before, sweetheart," Jensen responded.

"Oh, you're a naughty one aren't you?"

Nero dropped his arm and gave Jensen's butt a little spank. Jensen looked back at Mary expectantly. She fumed as she turned and left. Jensen chuckled as he closed the door.

"You realize I'm going to have a reputation now," he mentioned as he sat down on the recliner facing the couch. Nero laughed, entertained.

"Speaking of women, Danielle thinks I'm God," Nero said as he rested his hands on his flat stomach. "That was all I heard last night in bed. 'Oh God, oh God, oh God Nero, yes, yes. You're the best I ever had!'"

Jensen raised an eyebrow at his friend. "Are you still doing the fake accent?"

"It's called a brogue," Nero protested, slipping into the Irish accent that seemed to come and go. "And it's not fake!"

"Of course it's not. It just takes days off," Jensen humored him.

"So, you and Isis," Nero said as he watched his friend. "Somehow I knew the two of you would wind up together. The two of you are *way* too alike not to."

Jensen put one foot up on the coffee table, resting his head against his hand. "I'm not going to get involved with Isis. What happened last night was a one-night occurrence. I won't put her in the line of fire."

"Guardians have mercy, not this shit *again*," Nero moaned as he dropped back on the couch. "How many times do we have to tell you this? Nat and Bryn, their deaths weren't your fault. You are *not* cursed. Just because you're the last Aldridge doesn't mean you have to take a vow of celibacy. Most shape shifters wouldn't even think of messing with you. The parties responsible for the slaughter of your family are long dead. We saw to that, remember?"

"We can't be sure we got every last one and my track record suggests that we didn't," Jensen shook his head. "Orion was close to me. Nat and Bryn were both close to me. Look at what happened to them."

"Okay, Roan killed Orion so that had nothing to do with you. Nothing happened to my brothers and I and we've been around you longer than anyone. You've slept with plenty of people and none of them died. You interact with people on a regular basis and they don't expire when you walk away. You're doing that thing you always do: brooding. It may work on some people, but it doesn't work on me."

Jensen made a noncommittal noise in response. Nero leaned forward, looking at his friend until Jensen looked up.

"Jensen, I love you like a brother, but you need to *lighten* the fuck up," Nero said. Not many saw Jensen's grim side. He was only serious around people he really trusted.

"If only it were that easy," Jensen replied, shaking his head and dropping his hand again. Nero groaned and threw his legs up on the couch, stretching out across the cushions. Jensen looked over at the youngest Deverell.

"What are you doing here anyway?"

Nero waved his hand. "There was nothing for me to do at the mansion, so I decided to drop in on you. Oh, by the way, Isis told me to tell you that she borrowed your car."

"Wonderful," Jensen couldn't help but laugh at Nero. The amusement quickly drained from his face as he realized what Nero had said.

"Wait, she took my car?"

~~*~*~*

Isis was speeding toward the mansion. Jensen's Jaguar handled like a dream, which didn't surprise Isis at all. She had never seen a car so well cared for. *Typical guy,* she thought with a laugh as the winter gray scenery blurred by the immaculate windows. Her cell phone started buzzing again.

"Well there's a nice little how do you do," Isis chuckled when she felt her phone vibrate against her thigh. She reached into her pocket and retrieved the phone, glancing at the number on the clear screen. It was an unfamiliar number. Isis pressed the screen to answer it when she blinked and suddenly she was in a house, her stomach lurching.

Isis dropped to her knees and vomited on the dusty floor. When she was done, she blinked a few more times and then closed her eyes, opening them again. Rising to her feet, Isis rubbed her head, feeling disoriented and a little dizzy.

"What the hell?" she muttered under her breath, turning around in a circle as she tried to figure out where she was. The sound of a thump somewhere below her made Isis jump. She looked around again, paying closer attention to her surroundings. There were cobwebs everywhere and the air had a stale smell to it. Dust was piled on the ground and grime obscured the view outside. The pointed ceiling indicated she was in an attic, but how had she gotten there? Isis hadn't Appeared. There hadn't been a light or noise. She also felt warm after she Appeared, not cold.

Isis swallowed and felt around for her phone, which she couldn't find. She shivered and rubbed her arms. The attic was freezing and she wanted to get out of it as soon as possible. Isis looked around for a door, wishing she had a weapon on her. She was not in a good situation.

The shadows seemed to deepen around her as she made her way to the end of the attic where she spotted a door. She pushed herself against the wall and tested the knob, which turned easily in her hand. Isis pulled the door open, allowing more light into her gloomy surroundings.

There was a narrow staircase in front of her leading down to what she assumed was the first floor. Isis put her foot on the first step, wincing when it creaked. She kept herself pressed against the wall and moved down the steps. At the bottom, Isis found the body of one of the non-descript men in gray suits. She instinctively took a step back, her entire body tensing, but the man remained motionless. He was lying in a strange way, face down with one foot on the bottom step, as if he had collapsed while descending.

Isis hesitantly approached him again, nudging him with her foot. He didn't move. She craned her neck to see his face, which was slack. Isis very carefully crouched next to the strange man, reaching for his throat with two shaking fingers. She felt around for a pulse, but found none. She suppressed a tremor as she next pried open one of his eyelids. The pupil didn't react to the light, indicating the man was dead. Isis swallowed and dug through his pockets, hoping to find anything she could use as a weapon. Or perhaps a phone to call for back-up. Alas, the strange man's pockets were empty.

Isis suddenly noticed how familiar her surroundings were. She recognized the small kitchen she was standing in. She straightened up as she looked around. It was Cara's house, the woman Jet and Lilly had sent the Four to check on. She turned to the back door, testing the knob. It was locked. Isis crossed the kitchen, moving to the various drawers and cabinets, opening all of them in the hopes of finding a knife or something sharp. All she found was more dust. Isis ran a hand through her hair, closing her eyes briefly. She was in trouble.

Isis walked over toward the entrance that lead to the front room, hoping she would have better luck with the front door. She paused at the doorway, listening for any sounds. Isis could have sworn she heard a soft swishing noise.

She only saw a flash of silver before the blade buried itself in her chest. Isis heard herself let out a soft gasp and she looked down to see a knife buried up to the hilt in the center of her chest. It felt as though she were drowning as it became more and more difficult to breathe. The pain was excruciating and her vision swam. She tasted the blood starting to fill the back of her mouth.

"That's blood filling your lungs, baby protector," a familiar voice stated. Isis looked down the arm that still held the knife into Onyx's yellow eyes. The assassin smirked in triumph, but it melted into a look of shock when Isis grabbed one of the throwing blades Onyx kept in her belt and buried it deeply in the assassin's side. Onyx twisted the knife in Isis' chest before yanking it out, causing Isis to crumple.

"The fucking bitch stabbed me! *She stabbed me*!" Isis distantly heard Onyx yell. She could see a pool of blood starting to form on the kitchen floor. Too much, she was losing too much blood. Her vision began to darken and Isis realized she was dying. Terror began to engulf her as her breath slowly ran out.

"That's what you get for bringing too many weapons and wearing them so openly," a familiar masculine voice stated, laughing. It was Blackjack.

"Draw the symbol on the wall," he said. "I'll text her."

~~*~*~*

At Steve's house, Tracy smiled to herself as she tapped the phone against her hand. She was waiting for a text. It had been easy to get the hybrid into the trap, using one of the reconnaissance teams. They could move fast, though the taxation on the system did eventually kill them. There had only been three left after the club and she had wasted two on that damn assassin. It was the end of that line, but it had been worth it. They had served their purpose.

Tracy rose from where she sat at the kitchen table, glancing toward the couch where Steve was in a drugged slumber. She had slipped a powerful sedative in his food last night. In another hour, he'd wake up with Tracy asleep next to him. *In the spoons position, how sweet,* she thought with skin-crawling distaste. Her phone buzzed and she looked at it again, smiling widely.

It's done.

Tracy let out a breath of relief and forwarded the message to the recovery team. She then messaged the assassin back, telling him to wait for the team to pick up the body. Punching another number in, Tracy raised the phone to her delicate ear and waited for the man on the other end to answer.

"Hello, my dear," a soft voice crooned. Tracy smiled in delight. He was in a good mood, and she was going to make it better.

"She'll be yours tonight, sir," she told him in a respectful tone. "Everything went according to plan and the recovery team just has to retrieve the body."

"Spectacular. I knew you wouldn't let me down," the voice on the other end stated. "My dear, you are going to be richly rewarded for this."

"Thank you sir, but working for you is all the reward I require," she replied. There was a deep chuckle on the other line.

"I'll tell Mr. Carding to expect you back by the end of the week then," he said. "Goodbye Tracy."

"Goodbye, sir."

Tracy hung up the phone, feeling a sense of satisfaction in a job well done. Squaring her shoulders, she walked over to where her jacket was draped over a chair. Dropping the cell phone in the jacket pocket, Tracy then hurried over to where Steve still lay on the couch. She maneuvered her petite body into his arms, easily fitting into him. She closed her eyes and feigned sleep, a smile of contentment dancing across her features.

Victory was hers. No, victory was theirs.

~~*~*~*

"I can't believe she took my car."

Nero glanced at Jensen. He had been griping about Isis borrowing his car since they left for the mansion.

"How long are you going to go on about the car? Guardians, you're going to the same place. You'll be reunited with your precious car in a little while. Give it a rest, my friend. God, you dwell on *everything*."

"Nero, stop. Stop the car."

"What? Why?"

"Stop the damn car!"

Nero pulled over to the side of the road, staring when his friend jumped out of the car almost before it fully stopped. He glanced up in the rearview mirror and swore as he got out of the car, running to catch up with Jensen.

Sitting abandoned on the side of the road was Jensen's car. The driver's side door was open and the engine was off. It hadn't crashed into anything. It looked as though someone had just pulled over to the side of the road, got out of the car, and forgot about it. Jensen reached the car first. He slipped and fell in the snow in his rush, but scrambled to his feet and looked inside the car.

"She's not here," he called over to Nero. "But her stuff is."

"Is there any blood or anything to indicate she was hurt?" Nero asked as he skidded to a stop next to the car. The road was icier than he had expected and he had to catch himself on the side of Jensen's car. Nero examined Jensen's abandoned car, searching for any sign of blood. He was almost overcome with relief when he could find none.

"There are footprints," Jensen pointed at the ground, following them for a couple feet. "They stop here."

Jensen hurried back to the car and grabbed the abandoned cell phone. He opened it and scrolled through the contacts. Pressing the one he wanted, Jensen pressed send and held the phone against his ear, listening to it ring. Nero listened as Jensen called Shae and explained the situation. He went back to his car and waited, playing with his fingers, his breath fogging out in front of him. Jensen hung up and returned to Nero's car.

"It's unlikely, but Shae mentioned Cara's house is nearby," Jensen explained. "She'd never go there on her own, not willingly. Not without backup."

Nero looked pointedly at the abandoned car. "If Isis were taken against her will, don't you think there would be evidence of a struggle?"

Jensen was quiet for a moment, his eyes traveling back to the car behind them. "The whole scene is really peculiar. I don't know where else to look for her."

The phone buzzed and Jensen looked at it. He showed it to Nero.

"The address."

"I'll follow you," Nero said. He watched in the rearview mirror as Jensen went back to the silver Jaguar, sinking into the driver's seat. Nero frowned as he watched his friend press things in the car. Even from a distance, he could see the confusion in Jensen's expression. After a minute, he got out of the car and made his way back to Nero's car, looking over his shoulder a couple times.

"It won't start," Jensen explained, looking back at the car again. "That … shouldn't be."

"We'll call for a tow after we check out this address," Nero said, shifting into drive and turning back onto the road.

When they finally reached Cara's house, they knew instantly something was wrong. Two squad cars were parked on the street along with a large ambulance. Had the two men not been so worried about Isis, they would've noticed how bizarre the scene was — the absence of police tape and the missing letters on the ambulance. But they were too concerned with locating Isis.

Jensen leapt out of the car almost before it came to a complete stop, ignoring Nero cursing him out as he followed close on his heels. They tore across the street right as a stretcher with a body bag was being wheeled out. A tall, imposing looking officer grabbed Jensen before he could run into the crime scene. Jensen began to struggle and the scene would have gotten a lot uglier had Nero not intervened.

"Jensen! Settle the hell down!" Nero shouted at his

friend as he pulled him away from the cop. "Settle down!"

Once Nero was sure Jensen was as calm as he was going to get, he turned back to the officer who regarded him with cold gray eyes.

"Officer, what hap—?"

"Nero!?" a high-pitched feminine squeal interrupted Nero's question. "Lindsey, look, it's Nero and Jensen!"

Both Jensen and Nero glanced up and recognized the two perky blonde sisters they had dinner with the previous night. They were wheeling the stretcher toward the ambulance. The two men exchanged a mystified look.

"Did you know they were paramedics?" Jensen asked.

"No."

"You slept with her last night and you didn't know what she did for a living?"

"I don't require a job resume from the people I sleep with, Jensen," Nero responded, waving at the eager sister. "Is it just me or is this a little weird?"

"A little?"

"Officer Brown, it's okay, we know them," Lindsey called over to the cop. He glared at them one last time, and the two men could've sworn they heard the large man growl before stepping aside. Jensen immediately ran to the body bag, his hands shaking as they reached for the zipper.

"Um, we're not really supposed to let you open the bag," Lindsey said, gazing at him with her bright blue-gray eyes. "But I guess if you're feeling kinda kinky …"

The invitation in her eyes turned Jensen's stomach and he wondered why he had agreed to the dinner in the first place. He glanced over at Nero, who also looked disgusted at the invitation. A frigid wind violently swept through the scene, throwing a fine mist of snow over everything. The frozen landscape was sapped of almost all color, leaving only muted dark colors and white.

"Danielle, this might be someone we know," Nero explained, his eyes never moving from the body bag.

"Oh God, I am so sorry," Lindsey said, one of her

hands fluttering to her chest. Jensen didn't pay attention to her as he slowly unzipped the bag. He pulled back the top and felt his stomach start churning, vomit creeping up the back of his throat.

Isis lay in the bag, pale as the snow and dead. There was a large amount of coagulating blood from a hole in her chest where she had been stabbed. There was dried blood around her mouth. Her eyes were closed, and that much was a blessing.

Jensen stumbled away from the stretcher, lurching almost drunkenly. He dropped to his knees on the curb and heaved, emptying all the contents of his stomach. Nero swallowed the bile that rose up in his own throat as he turned his eyes back to the two sisters. They stood there, looking vacant as ever.

"It's her," he murmured, scrubbing a hand over his face.

"Oh, well, you can pick the body up at the St. Francis morgue in town," Danielle said in her perky voice. "I think they gotta do an autopsy or something."

"Yeah," Nero replied as he watched them load his young niece's body into the ambulance. He watched as it sped away, followed closely by the two squad cars with sirens blaring, gradually fading into the distance. Soon, the only sound was Jensen's retching.

Nero couldn't move; he didn't know what to do. Snow started to drift down again, clinging to everything it touched. Distantly, he heard his cell phone ring. Nero remembered he had left the driver's door open but he couldn't make his body respond to any commands.

Finally, when Jensen finished retching, Nero was able to make his neck turn so he could look over at his friend. Jensen spit one more time and got to his feet, walking away in the direction they had come from.

"Where are you going?" Nero called after him. Jensen turned around, tears glistening in his eyes as he gestured vaguely behind him. He looked broken. The wind rushed over him, tossing his brown hair about, but he didn't seem to notice.

"I have to … go. I have to go home."

Nero watched as Jensen walked in the direction of his apartment. He sighed and went to his car. Nero picked up his cell phone and dialed his oldest brother's number. Ajax answered after the second ring, sounding concerned.

"Ajax?" Nero managed to choke out.

"Nero? Are you all right? What's wrong?"

"She's dead, Ajax. She was stabbed and they have her at the morgue in town," Nero said, his words almost blending together. "Someone needs to go down to I.D. the body."

"Nero, slow down," Ajax said, his voice calm and steady, though still tinged with concern. "Whose body? What happened?"

"Isis," Nero replied before hanging up. He started his car and headed back toward the mansion, swiping at the tears in his eyes.

CHAPTER TWELVE

The morgue was never a crowded place, but there were always bodies behind the large red doors. There always would be bodies in the morgue. At night, it was particularly quiet. The sickly pale green glow of florescent lights illuminated the clean tiled floor. The lights flickered occasionally, their buzz the only sound in the morgue.

A single woman sat behind the desk at the entrance. She had shoulder length hair, which was tied back in a neat ponytail. Her skeletal fingers flipped idly through a book her gray eyes were fixed on. The lines on her face spoke of too much stress. She might have once been youthful, but the years had not been kind and now she always looked tired. Her bright eyes were still sharp, however, and could pick up the smallest movement. She had only started working at the morgue that night, but no one would know it. The woman would be gone as soon as the sun rose.

The woman glanced up when two men entered the morgue. She closed her book — she had been expecting them. One stood back a few feet by the door as the other approached the desk.

"Can I help you gentlemen?" she asked in a pleasant tone, smiling.

Jet laid his hands on the desk. "I'm here to I.D. a body. Detective Loman faxed over the necessary paperwork earlier this evening."

"I'm sorry, but I can't allow that," the woman responded. Jet frowned and glanced over his shoulder, exchanging a puzzled look with Remington. It was one of the first times he had seen the loyal trainer look somewhat baffled.

"I'm sorry, didn't the paperwork come through? Should I call Detective Loman?" Jet asked politely but wearily. He was so tired and could only think of his best friend. When he had left the mansion, Passion had been weeping in Lilly's arms, inconsolable. Lilly had offered to stay with the guardian while Jet and Remington retrieved the body.

"Oh no. The paperwork came through a couple hours ago. Everything was in place," the woman answered, playing with her necklace. Hearing a quiet shuffle behind him, Jet turned his eyes back to Remington, who had straightened up and was now studying the woman. Jet swallowed and turned his eyes back to the receptionist. The hair on the back of his neck was starting to stand up. Jet studied the gold charm on the thin gold chain. It looked a little familiar but he had no idea from where.

"Then what's the problem?" Jet asked.

The woman shrugged, still smiling. Jet stared at her, glancing back at Remington again. He wasn't sure what the issue was. He licked his lips and turned back to the woman, looking at her nametag.

"Ms. Green," he began.

"Jet," she said. At first, the protector was a little startled to hear her say his name. Then he remembered her saying the paperwork had come through. She smiled at him and there was something almost predatory about the expression.

"I cleared this with the detective and if the paperwork came through, I don't understand what the problem is,"

Jet tried again. "Could I please use your phone?"

"I'm sorry, Jet. The phone is for morgue business only," Ms. Green responded.

"Okay, ma'am, it has been a *very* long, *very* bad day," Jet began, his patience thinning. "I just want to claim the body of my friend."

"Is that a Chi Rho?"

Jet looked over his shoulder when he heard Remington's strange question. The trainer took a step forward and nodded at the woman's charm. Jet turned his eyes back to the woman, studying the charm a little closer. Her eyes narrowed for a split second before her pleasant expression slipped back into place.

"It is. What good eyes you have, Remington."

That got Jet's attention. He understood how the woman knew his name, but she couldn't possibly know Remington's.

"Who are you?" Jet asked, turning his attention fully on her.

The woman picked up the phone. "Officer White, could you please come down here?" She then turned back to Jet. "I'm going to have to ask you gentlemen to leave now."

Suddenly, as if out of thin air, a large security guard came up on the right side of the desk. He was in full uniform, including a hat atop his head and a vicious-looking firearm on his hip, which Jet didn't recognize as the standard issued weapon of the local police force. The holster was unsnapped and his hand rested on the butt. The guard's brown eyes were calm but cold as he glared at the trio.

"Is there a problem here?" he asked, his voice a rumbling growl. Jet straightened his posture, meeting the guard's glare with one of his own. Out of the corner of his eye, he noticed Remington shift his weight.

"Yes, there is. I'm here to claim a body, I have the proper paperwork, and Ms. Green won't let me enter the morgue," Jet explained.

"Jet's making unfounded accusations. I believe he's a threat to my personal safety," Ms. Green spoke with chilling calmness.

"Okay, what the hell is going on here?" Jet demanded. Remington suddenly stepped in front of him, putting himself between Jet and the guard.

"Jet, I really think we should leave," he murmured under his breath.

"I can't just—"

"The man just drew his gun."

Jet immediately looked over at the guard, noticing he had taken out his gun and now held it loosely at his side. Why this officer was drawing on an obviously unarmed man, Jet had no clue. He held up his hands, indicating he wasn't armed, turning his eyes back to Remington.

"Remington, I can't. I can't just leave her here," Jet whispered, feeling tears creep into his eyes. Remington turned his attention back to Jet.

"We have already lost too much, my friend. Please do not make me bring news back to Lilly and Passion that you have fallen as well," Remington replied. Jet closed his eyes and dropped his head.

"I suggest you both go on your way," the guard warned in his intimidating voice. Jet looked up again, turned his eyes back to the guard, and nodded.

As quickly and as cautiously as he could, Jet turned and made his way for the door. He heard Remington follow close behind him, keeping himself between Jet and the strange people in the morgue.

The protectors stepped out into the frigid night and Jet let out the breath he didn't realize he had been holding. He looked at Remington, disturbed, and Jet could tell Remington felt the same.

"Something is rotten in the state of Denmark," Remington quipped, sticking his hands in his pockets.

"What was that question about the Chi Rho?" Jet asked

as they made their way toward the car. Remington lifted his shoulders, rubbing the bottom of his chin with one hand.

"Haven't seen one in quite some time — it's a very old Christian symbol. Practically a relic," Remington explained. "As a symbol, it was mostly stamped on coins or written in books. I have never seen one worn, certainly not in the modern day. Modern Christians typically wear a crucifix or a pendant of a patron saint as symbols of their faith. Although, I must admit I have never seen such a complex and corrupted Chi Rho with those designs on the stem. Usually it's just plain lines."

Jet looked back at the morgue, which looked darker.

"I can't be certain, not with the fumes in there," Jet began, hesitating before turning his eyes back to Remington. "But I could have sworn that neither of them had a scent."

Remington had a grave look on his face. "I noticed it too."

~~*~*~*

Between the sobbing and the accusations, the mansion had fallen into utter chaos.

"You promised me, you promised me you'd protect her! You said you'd protect her with your dying breath! Well she's dead, not you!" Passion spat at Jet. She was sitting on the floor and Lilly knelt beside her, holding the grieving guardian tightly, offering her what little comfort she could. Jet opened his mouth to respond only to be cut off by her again. The only silent ones in the room were Adonia, Artemis, and Electra. Adonia and Artemis stood in the thick of things while Electra remained off to the side. She brushed a strand of hair out of her eyes. She had cried herself out hours ago and now just felt numb. Emotions swirled up inside of her, not all of which she was familiar with, and it left her feeling drained.

"You can't even get her damn body!" Passion continued before burying her face in Lilly's shoulder again, a loud wail escaping her lips. Lilly continued to stroke Passion's soft hair, whispering words of comfort to her. Electra glanced around at the people in the room: the remaining members of the Four, Steve, Remington, the Deverells, and …

Electra frowned when she realized someone was missing. Where the hell was Jensen? Happy to be able to focus on something else, Electra slipped out of the room and away from the commotion. She didn't want to hear any more — she couldn't. Let them sort all this shit out. Right now, Electra wanted to know where Jensen was. And she wasn't going to stop until she found him. After she found him, she'd find another asinine thing to focus on and then another and another.

Electra leaned against a wall, putting her head back with a thunk.

"I don't want to Appear," she groaned to herself. It was unavoidable though. She closed her eyes and felt her temperature rise a little as she disappeared from the mansion and Appeared in the dark hallway of Jensen's apartment. Electra knew she'd be in trouble later for Appearing in such a public place, but she really didn't care. She would be in even more trouble for venturing out without a chaperone, which Electra was also unconcerned about.

The young guardian started down the dark quiet hallway. It was very late at night and most people were asleep. She stopped in front of Jensen's door, having remembered it from back in the day when Nat and Bryn were thought to be part of the Four. She knocked on the door, glancing down the dimly lit hallway to the window at the end. The night seemed ominous, tainting everything it touched. It was darker than it normally was in the winter. Electra suppressed a shudder as she knocked on the door again.

"Jensen?" she called out as she tested the knob, surprised to find it unlocked. She pushed the door open and stepped inside. Electra looked down when she heard glass crunching under her boots. The entire apartment was shrouded in blackness. The only light was a muted blue glow creeping through the large windows across from her, casting shadows of the frames on the floor.

Electra closed the door behind her and crouched down to examine the glass shards littering the floor in front of the door. A sudden movement a few feet in front of her caused her head to jerk up.

"Oh great, it's the other one," Jensen slurred as he stumbled out from the short hall leading to his bedroom. His clothes were in disarray and he looked as disheveled as Electra had ever seen him. A powerful handgun was gripped tightly in his right hand while his left held a half empty bottle of some clear liquid. Electra guessed it was alcohol, most likely vodka.

"Um, there's a meeting at the mansion," Electra said, watching as Jensen flipped the safety back on the gun. "What's with the glass?"

Jensen gave her a sarcastic little smile before hurling the half-full bottle at her. Electra couldn't prevent the startled gasp that escaped from her lips as she ducked, narrowly avoiding getting hit in the face with the bottle. It hit the door and shattered, raining small shards of glass and cold liquid on Electra's back.

"Alarm system," Jensen responded as he made his way over to the darkened kitchen, placing his gun on the counter as he made his way to the fridge. Electra straightened up, fury burning in her chest.

"Have you completely lost your mind!?" Electra hissed at him. He snorted humorlessly.

"No, but I'm getting there," Jensen replied as he opened the fridge. The dull light of the fridge illuminated his face as he retrieved another bottle of alcohol. The amber liquid told Electra it was most likely whiskey. Jensen held the bottle out to her — an offering. She grimaced in disgust and looked away from him. He shrugged and unscrewed the top of the bottle, slapping the fancy square top on the counter next to his gun before taking a deep swig. He unsteadily made his way over to the couch, Electra right on his heels.

"Listen, you drunken ass," she snapped at him. "My sister was … there's a mandatory meeting so we can try to figure out what's going on. Give me one good reason why you're not there!"

"Cause I'm gettin' drunk," Jensen replied, making a face as though the answer were obvious and turned his attention back to the whiskey bottle, taking a long swig from it. Electra closed her eyes, attempting to regain her composure.

"You can grieve however you want after you tell Jet and Lilly exactly what you saw, so we can catch whomever—"

"You'll never catch them, but you want my report? Fine, I saw your sister's body with a big gaping hole in her chest," Jensen paused and swallowed, looking up at Electra. "From a knife. There was blood around her mouth, meaning she most likely drowned in her own blood. Because it filled her lungs, you see. It would have painful, excruciatingly so, and she probably died terrified. Satisfied? Now get the hell out."

Electra felt as if someone had just punched her in the chest. She stumbled back, away from Jensen, who took another swig of whiskey.

"Aw, what's the matter, sweetie? Too graphic for you?" Jensen asked in a condescending tone.

"You are despicable," Electra spoke shakily.

"Well those shoes make your ankles look fat, but I'm too much of a gentleman to say anything," he shot back.

Electra turned away from him. "I hope you drink yourself to death!"

"That makes two of us!" Jensen yelled just before she

disappeared. He turned his attention back to the whiskey, tossing the full bottle over his shoulder with a frustrated scowl. He heard the bottle shatter against the hardwood floor with an echoing crash. The whole room seemed to be spinning as the alcohol he had already consumed snuck up on him. Before he knew it, Jensen flopped on his side on the couch. He was soon in a deep sleep, lost to the world. The protector had always been a heavy sleeper, even when he wasn't blackout drunk. Jensen was oblivious to everything around him, including the windows, one of which slowly slid up as a shadow entered the apartment.

Coop's feet touched the hardwood floor, his sharp glowing eyes scanning the apartment to make sure it was empty. He carefully made his way over to the sleeping man, pausing when Jensen mumbled nonsense in his sleep. Coop tilted his head, making note of Jensen's breathing pattern. His heightened senses told Coop the protector was fast asleep and unlikely to wake up any time soon. He made his way over to the glass coffee table, reaching into one of his pockets to retrieve an item.

A jolt of electricity shot through his body causing Coop to gasp in pain. The charge was so high it would've killed an ordinary shape shifter on the spot. Coop crumpled to the ground, twitching and writhing as he panted for breath. Jensen muttered in his sleep and turned over onto his other side.

"Too much time in the outside world has made you rusty, Coop," a familiar taunting voice stated from somewhere just outside his line of vision. Coop tried to crawl away from his attacker. The shadow loomed over him, barely distinguishable in the murky night.

"You're an asshole, Dane," Coop snarled, frowning at the way his words slurred. *Great, I'm not going to be able to walk straight for at least twenty-four hours,* he thought grimly.

Above him, Dane shrugged. "Maybe, but I'm an asshole with a taser."

Coop stopped crawling and launched himself to his

knees. In a movement faster than the eye could see, he snatched a lamp from the nearby table and hurled it at Dane. Dane, also moving with a supernatural speed not even shape shifters were able to match, dodged out of the way. Coop had anticipated this and so had thrown the lamp at a slight angle. When Dane ducked out of the way, the lamp still struck his shoulder, shattering and causing the man to curse out loud and drop the taser.

Coop wasted no time, moving as fast as he was able to in the direction of the kitchen in the hopes of grabbing a knife or some other weapon. A charge that high would mess with his shape shifting abilities, but he could still put up a good fight. Dane launched himself at the other man, tackling him around the middle and sending them both careening to the floor in an undignified tangle of limbs. The two of them struggled to untangle themselves while also trying to land punches. Dane managed to punch Coop in the face, snapping his head back so that it bounced off the side of the cabinet. Coop easily shook off the dazed feeling, deflected the second punch and lashed out with his foot, catching Dane on the side of the head and knocking him backward. The two men struggled to their feet, breathing heavily, their eyes never moving from each other.

"Why are you doing this?" Coop asked.

"The Corporation is tired of your meddling," Dane answered in his nonchalant way. "And I was feeling rather bored, needed some practice."

"The Corporation is now into taser manufacturing?"

"Whatever gets the job done. Inanimate weapons do have their uses."

Suddenly, Coop ran for the front room where Jensen still slept in peaceful oblivion. He dove for the taser, which lay forgotten near the shards of the lamp. Dane reached it first, kicking it away and following through by striking Coop in the mouth with his heel. Coop winced, but maneuvered out of the way to avoid getting kicked in the face again. He spun his body around, lashing out with one leg and catching Dane in the back of the knees. Dane swore as he hit the hardwood floor.

"You still got it, Coop. I'll be damned," he laughed.

Coop saw a brief shadow of movement and grabbed the glass coffee table, raising it up like a shield. Dane's powerful roundhouse kick shattered it. Coop quickly turned his face away from the shards, shielding his eyes from the sharp projectiles. When he turned back, Dane had grabbed the frame of the coffee table. Before Coop had a chance to react, he found himself hurled backward into the screen of the television set, shattering it. Coop fell down in a rain of dark glass, dazed. He grabbed one of the larger shards, wrapping his fingers around the sharp edge, which cut into his skin, then struggled to his feet again. He saw a flash of silver come up a few feet away from him. Dane had a combat knife trained on him.

The two stood in silence for a moment, locked in a silent battle of wills. Each mirrored the other's position: weapon held at the ready, one hand slightly lower to deflect any strikes. Granted, Coop's position was not as steady as Dane's, but he was still a dangerous enough opponent that Dane wouldn't take his glowing brown eyes off him. Had Jensen awoken, all he would've seen were two sets of unnaturally luminous eyes in the dark. He remained lost in a dreamless sleep.

"Dane," Coop began, unable to keep the pleading tone out of his voice.

"For christsakes," Dane grumbled, rolling his eyes. "You know, Coop, if there's one thing more annoying than your wide-eyed idealism … no, there's nothing. That is by far the *most* irritating thing about you."

"For once, would you just listen to me?" Coop snapped. "The Corporation murdered my entire family. My wife, my daughter, my granddaughter — they're all gone now."

Dane raised an eyebrow. "You didn't expect that to

happen? Hell, Grenich kills hundreds of shape shifters in a week and most of those have had billions invested in them."

"Yes, and now I'm going to help destroy the whole cursed place. The experiments will be free and we will stop the higher ups. You just have to turn around and walk away."

Dane let out a bark of laughter and shook his head, sheathing his combat knife again. He knew Coop had a strange sense of honor now and wouldn't stab him unless in self-defense.

"You are a fucking idiot, Coop. I don't tell you that enough," Dane scoffed bitterly before returning to his normal emotionless demeanor. "We don't want to be free. We can't be."

"What are you talking about?" Coop asked, lowering his weapon. He was surprised Dane had put his knife away.

"Just because it worked for you doesn't mean that it would work for all of us," Dane responded. "You had a life before the Corporation and you had the doctor once you got out, but that's not true for all experiments. That place is all we know. In your little revenge temper tantrum, you would just be releasing us into a whole other prison."

"That's not true," Coop protested.

"Do you even remember your family or your life as Mark Waterson before Grenich?"

Coop hesitated. "A little, enough to know that I was loved and I loved—"

"Right, so in other words, no. Even if you did, do you honestly think it would be the same for all of us? You really think we'd just be accepted into the world? That those of us with families would be welcomed back with open arms? Look at us Coop, we're freaks. Monsters. Killers. And we're the *successful* experimentations. None of us fit into this world, not really. Oh sure, we can blend in, but we will never entirely fit in."

Coop shook his head. "Don't you see, Dane? That's what they want you to think, what he wants you to think."

"Really? Okay, if that's not the truth, why do you wear sunglasses almost round the clock? What about the contact lenses that the good doctor whips up especially for you?"

"That's different—"

"Is it, Coop? Is it really? You keep saying that we live in a prison, but the way I see it, you live in one too. And yours is just as bad, whether or not you're willing to admit it."

"At least I have freedom," Coop said after a pause. "Dane, I really don't give a shit how you view the outside world. What they're doing in the laboratory and training fields and simulations is wrong. What they're doing to this world is wrong. It has to stop. Kill me if you want, but someone will just take my place."

"Oh my god," Dane laughed bitterly and rubbed his eyes, shaking his head. Coop swallowed, watching the other experiment. He wished he could give Dane hope, something to show him the world was not a lost cause.

"You've already lost this war. Why don't you see that? Are you really that delusional?" Dane said dully, glancing at his watch. "I have another hour before I have to go back to the barracks. Is there any other nauseating argument about there being goodness in the world that you would like to make?"

"I haven't lost yet," Coop whispered, though some part of him wondered if there might be some truth to Dane's pessimistic words. He had already lost so much in the endless war and Coop could feel his hope waver a little.

"You're a multi-billion dollar weapon off the assembly line, just like me. You can't possibly take on the Grenich higher ups, even with the help of the doctor and whomever else you've recruited to your cause."

"I can't," Coop admitted. "But someone can, and I can help them."

"Who?"

Coop chewed his lower lip, hesitating. "I can't tell you, not unless you come with me."

Dane chuckled at the response. "Afraid I'll spill the beans to Big Brother?"

Coop didn't respond but shifted his weight uncomfortably.

"Yeah, I don't blame you. No telling what I might say under the influence during the daily interrogations. Hell, I don't even remember what I say half the time," Dane said with a grin as he began to move toward the windows they had entered through. "Damn, Coop. I never thought I'd say this, but you almost fit in with the normals."

"Where are you going?" Coop asked, confused. Dane paused with one leg on the window sill and shrugged.

"We worked together in the Corporation, which I guess makes you the closest thing I have to a friend," he said in that almost carefree tone of his. "Besides, I was only supposed to prevent you from interfering and I did, even if only temporarily. After this, we're even. You're on your own because I sure as hell won't stick my neck out for you. If you get caught, that's your own damn fault."

With that, Dane dropped out of the window, disappearing into the night. Coop sighed and scrubbed a hand over his face, glancing toward the still sleeping Jensen. He placed an envelope among the shards of glass. His body had already healed most of the damage done by Dane.

Coop made his way to the windows, shutting the open one. He crossed the apartment and moved to the front door, opening it. Softly shutting the door behind him, Coop put his finger against the deadbolt, letting the finger change into the proper key shape. He locked the deadbolt, withdrew his finger, and turned away, walking down the hall.

~~*~*~*

Tracy smiled as she walked around Steve's home, cracking her ancient knuckles. The plan had gone off without a hitch, although she would've chosen a less messy way to kill off the hybrid. Stabbing, what the hell was that assassin thinking? You could tell them a thousand times and assassins still wouldn't listen, wretched forms of life that they were.

The team, of course, had dispersed in order to avoid detection. Come morning they would be richer than they had ever imagined. The Grenich higher ups had been pleased beyond belief at how smoothly their plan had gone. Tracy herself was sticking around to tie up a few loose ends, namely Steve. All she had to do was get him in bed, which wouldn't be so difficult. She fingered the small glass ball in her hands, filled with powder. It was brown and resembled cinnamon although it was a bit lighter in color. It was her backup plan. Should her spell over Steve not work, the powder would erase his memory of her. She'd be gone before the protectors even had a chance to start looking for her.

She glanced to her right when she heard footsteps in the hallway, heavier than usual. Tracy smirked and put the ball on the kitchen counter before moving into the hallway to greet her boyfriend. She put on her innocent face, which she had a millennia's practice to perfect. It was a look that made people fall in love with her and desire her. She was just an innocent school girl who couldn't harm a fly. Tracy had to prevent herself from smiling at that thought. The locks on the door began turning and she sat on a chair near the door, patiently waiting.

He came in through the door, looking like a little boy whose puppy had just been smashed by a truck. It was disgusting, but Tracy maintained her innocent persona.

"Steven?" she asked as she stood up. "What's wrong?"

He leapt about a foot in the air when he realized he wasn't alone. "Tracy? What are you—?"

"You missed our date last night," she said. "I was worried about you, so I came here. I hope you don't mind, but I used your emergency key to let myself in."

Another lie, she had used her mind to open the door. It was another power gifted to her by her masters.

"Oh," Steve said, running a hand through his soft black hair. "Yeah, I'm sorry."

"Steven?" She approached him, running her hands over his chest. "What's wrong? You look upset."

"I – um," he swallowed thickly, tears springing to his eyes. "It's Isis. She's – uh – she's … dead."

He choked on a sob and she was the perfect portrait of horrified disbelief.

"Guardians have mercy," she breathed as she wrapped her arms around him, allowing him to sob on her shoulder. "What happened?"

Steve sniffled and embraced her, tears flowing freely down his face. Tracy whispered soothing words to him, reassuring him it would be all right, her voice beginning to take on a hypnotic quality. Suddenly, his body relaxed and Tracy had to fight not to smile. She had him. She slowly pushed him back, catching his eyes with her own.

"Steven, I want to take away your pain. Will you let me?" Tracy murmured, maintaining the hypnotic quality in her voice. He nodded, his brown eyes blank as he remained lost in a trance. She grinned and took his hand, leading him toward his bedroom.

It was almost too easy, but then again, Tracy had millennia of experience under her belt.

CHAPTER THIRTEEN

Jensen jerked awake from a dreamless sleep. For a moment, he was disoriented. Then it felt like someone hit him in the head with a sack of bricks. He winced and raised a hand to his head, swearing out loud. The hangover hit him without warning or mercy and Jensen soon found himself stumbling toward the bathroom. He cursed even louder when he stepped on something sharp. The nausea that swept over him prevented Jensen from looking around. At the moment, all he could think about was making it to the bathroom before he projectile vomited all over his apartment.

He made it to the bathroom just in time. Once he was through puking out whatever was left in his stomach, Jensen reached over and turned on the shower, attempting to get into some semblance of his usual morning routine. He refused to let thoughts of the past twenty-four hours, whatever foggy ones remained, enter his mind. At the moment, he was going to take a shower, like he did every day. Jensen scrunched his nose at the sickly sweet smell of vomit and reached over to flush the toilet. Once he did that, he noticed the amount of blood that he had tracked into the bathroom.

"Fucking hell," he grumbled as he looked at his wounded right foot. There was a sharp shard of glass sticking to the bottom of it, blood oozing out around it. Jensen winced, saying every colorful word he knew, and pulled it out of his foot before tossing it into the nearby wastebasket. He got up, balancing on his uninjured foot and hopped into the shower.

Jensen thoroughly cleaned himself, making sure to use up every last drop of steaming hot water. He stepped out of the shower and reached over to the mirror cabinet above the sink, retrieving a first aid kit. Grabbing a roll of gauze out of the small kit, Jensen wrapped his still bleeding foot. Once he was satisfied with that, he wrapped a towel around his waist and retrieved his razor. He shaved his face, making sure to get rid of every last trace of stubble. There wasn't much, but he preferred feeling freshly shaved in the morning. Jensen dabbed away the few remaining traces of shaving cream with a hand towel and turned his attention to the closed bathroom door. Letting out a heavy sigh and squaring his shoulders, Jensen prepared himself to face the day. When he was ready, he left the bathroom and headed for his bedroom. Jensen went immediately to the closet and grabbed some fresh clothing. Once he had changed and put on his shoes, he left his room and stepped out into the main part of the apartment. Jensen had only taken a couple steps when he froze in shock.

"What the hell?"

He felt his jaw drop open when he saw the destruction that lay before him. His TV was shattered, as was his coffee table. There had obviously been some kind of fight in his home. Jensen ran a hand through his damp short hair, confusion dancing across his face. How drunk had he been last night? *Did I really trash my place?* Jensen wondered as he tried to recall the previous night. He vaguely remembered fighting with Electra, but everything after that was blank.

"Fuck me," was all he could think to say. Jensen

squinted, slowly making his way back to the couch. He made sure to avoid the glass strewn across the floor, which proved to be difficult. There, among the shards surrounding what had once been his coffee table, was a plain envelope. He picked it up and twisted it in his fingers, examining it with keen eyes. After a moment, Jensen ripped off the side of it, blew into the envelope, and looked inside. He cupped his hand and turned it over, allowing the contents to spill out into his waiting palm.

It was a shamrock necklace, engraved on the back with a date and the word "luck." Jensen recognized it from somewhere, but his mind was still too hazy to place exactly from where. A small white card, the size of a business card, also fell into his waiting palm. Hastily written across the front, in plain black pen, were two names: Coop and Mark Waterson. Jensen placed the empty envelope on his couch and flipped the card over. On the back was a symbol that caused Jensen to gasp in horror and drop the small card, unconsciously taking a step back. It was a symbol he had seen once before, one he hoped to never see again. It brought back the memory of flames, of the bodies of his parents in the main room of their house, Nat screaming …

Jensen swallowed and quelled the tremors that raced through his lean frame. He approached the card again, bending down and picking it up. He quickly stuffed it into his jacket's inner pocket without looking at it again.

He turned his attention back to the necklace still clutched in his hand and examined it closer, frustrated at his inability to place where he'd seen it. When it hit him, Jensen swallowed the pain that welled up in his chest. He quickly put the necklace in the pocket of his jacket. There were some questions he needed answered, and he knew whom he had to ask. Although, he wasn't sure she would be willing to speak to him.

~~*~*~*

Jet moved through Sly's forest, lost in grief and self-loathing. Passion had locked herself in her room in the Meadows and steadfastly refused to come out. The only one whom she would allow in and would speak to was Lilly, who was currently with her. Jet knew Passion blamed him for what had happened. Hell, he blamed himself. Though he knew there was no way he could've done anything to prevent Isis' death, Jet still felt guilty. He didn't know what to do and was at the end of his rope, which was why he decided to try and speak with Sly. He had searched the forest for about an hour and still could find no trace of his sometime informant.

"Sly, please!" he called out. The only response he received was the sound of the winter winds rustling the branches of the taller trees. It made a sound similar to bones rattling together. He pressed his back against the nearest tree and slid down into a sitting position, closing his eyes. He needed a quiet moment in solitude to sort out his thoughts. A rumbling growl made Jet open his eyes again.

In front of him sat a large tigress. She blended in with her surroundings, her piercing emerald eyes made even more vivid by the surrounding winter's frost. Jet tilted his head as he looked at her, laughing without a hint of mirth.

"I look for you for about an hour and the second I want solitude, here you are," he commented. The tigress' muscles began to change form as she melted into her usual human appearance. Muscles expanded and contracted, fur disappeared, and the tigress' snout shrank and smoothly formed a human face. The enigmatic Sly soon sat before him.

"Do you want me to leave?" she asked, raising an eyebrow as she took in his appearance. Jet shook his head in response. It was one of the first times he had ever heard her sound … serious.

"I need your advice and your help," he explained softly, looking to her with grief-filled eyes. Sly rested her elbows on her knees, her chin supported by her hands which were folded on top of each other. She studied his face.

"I captured Onyx when the Deverells and the Four tried to find the strange men at the Lair. Didn't have a chance to question her though. I blinked and I was suddenly out in my forest and it was the afternoon, with the body of a scentless man next to me," Sly told him. "I didn't black out and I didn't Appear, so whatever we're dealing with has the ability to affect time and perception. The body of the man disappeared shortly afterward, as I had expected it would."

"How is that even possible?"

Sly shrugged as she reclined on her elbows. "Got me. So what's got you all gloom-and-doom now?"

"Sly, it's Isis," he managed to choke out. That got Sly's attention and she immediately sat up straight, a stunned expression on her face. Jet dropped his eyes, not able to hold her gaze anymore. He knew that she had read the grief in his eyes and deduced what had happened. Sly had always been perceptive, frighteningly so.

"I don't know what to say," she stated. Jet glanced over to her, his blue-green eyes teary. Had it been any other time, Sly most likely would've taunted him mercilessly. Now she just looked at him with something that could almost be construed as sympathy or compassion. Sly got to her feet, moving over to Jet's side, and sat down next to him. She leaned back so she was resting against the same tree. For a moment, they sat in silence and Jet was reminded of years long past, when they had been friends. Sly curved one leg so that she could rest her wrist on her knee

"If you want my help, you have to listen to me," Sly began after a moment, pinching her fingers together. "And follow my every instruction down to the letter."

Jet nodded. "I know."

"First, you need to tell me exactly what happened. If you weren't there, tell me who was and who gave the account," Sly instructed. "Have you heard from the High Council yet?"

Jet let out another bark of laughter. "About an hour before I came to find you. They approved our request."

"Figures," Sly responded. "Then we're going to meet with an old acquaintance. The sooner the better. I recommend calling your better half to join us. Lilly has always been talented at parsing out roundabout answers."

~~*~*~*

Electra was determined not to cry. She stood in her sister's room, rubbing her upper arms against the chill that seemed to invade the once warm space. She was looking around for something, though she wasn't sure what exactly. A clue, a memento, a sign maybe. It was her current asinine task, something to keep her away from the heart-wrenching sobs from behind her mother's door.

Electra moved over to the nightstand, swallowing the lump that rose in her throat. She closed her eyes briefly and then reached out to the drawer. Sinking to her knees, Electra pulled open the small drawer. When she opened her light green eyes — a sob catching in her throat — something caught her attention. She noticed an open spiral; its pages covered with random notes. Electra pulled the spiral out of the drawer, leafing through the pages, her brow creasing. She sat back on her heels as she studied it. It was all about Coop, what little information the protectors had found out about him. Electra turned another page and frowned at the strange symbol drawn in pen.

A shadow fell over her. Without a moment of hesitation, Electra dropped the spiral and spun around, lashing out with her fist. Jensen let out a yelp of pain and crumpled to the floor as Electra's solid punch came into contact with his gut. It felt like her fist was made of granite.

"Dammit!" he managed to cough.

When Electra realized whom she had hit, her eyes narrowed. The young guardian opened her mouth to make a sarcastic comment when she noticed something glistening on the floor near Jensen's head. Her eyes widened when she realized what it was.

"Where did you get this?" Electra demanded as she reached out and snatched the necklace that was identical to her own. She held the small charm in her hand, running her index finger over the smooth cool gem.

"Ow," Jensen moaned, turning onto his side and trying to get his breath back.

"Oh quit being a baby. I didn't hit you that hard," Electra growled as she stood up, holding the necklace up to the dull light of the winter sun. It glistened and sparkled, even in the gray light. It was Isis' — she was sure of it. There were only two like it and she was wearing the other one. Jensen gave her a venomous look as he pushed himself into a sitting position.

"I found it." Jensen paused to clear his throat, reaching into his inner pocket. "I found it with this."

He produced the small business card he found in the envelope along with Isis' necklace. Electra snatched it out of his hand, her hand moving like a cobra striking its prey. Jensen looked irritated as he got to his feet, but she was too busy examining both objects to care. She glanced around the room and her eyes fell on the spiral. Electra picked it up from the floor and put it on the bed.

"What were you looking for? What did you find?" Electra said to herself as she looked at the spiral. The wind rattled against the panes of glass. She glanced to the side when lamp light fell across the bed, better illuminating the hastily scribbled notes. Jensen pulled his hand back from the lamp, his attention focused on the spiral. The color drained from his face and he took a step back, looking nothing short of terrified.

"Jensen? What's wrong?" Electra asked. Jensen pointed at the spiral with a shaking finger.

"That-that symbol, what is it? Why did she draw that?" he stammered, his wide eyes never moving from the open page. Electra glanced at it again before looking back to Jensen.

"Have you seen it before?" she asked. Jensen swallowed, his hands trembling. He stepped forward again, forcing himself to look at the page.

"Flip over the business card," he said, running a hand over his mouth. Electra did and her eyes widened a little.

"It's the same one," she observed, glancing up at Jensen again.

"I've seen it before. The night my family was murdered, our house burned to the ground. My sister and I managed to escape, barely. When we were leaving, I happened to catch a glimpse of the main hall, where the bodies of our parents had fallen. On the wall, in flames, was this exact same symbol," he explained, swallowing again. He looked as though he would be sick.

"Are you sure?" Electra asked, looking back to the symbol.

"I'll never be able to forget it. I've looked for it everywhere: history books, anthropology studies, various mythologies, anywhere else I could think of. I've found similar symbols in history, parts of it, but never this exact combination," Jensen answered. "Why did she draw it? Where did she see it?"

"When we first found my sister, she had photographed Bryn's body. This symbol was painted in her blood on the wall near where she fell," Electra said, her voice going quiet. Jensen looked over at her. Electra met his gaze, before turning her attention back to the spiral. She knew his story. Though the Aldridges had all been wiped out long before she was born, every guardian knew about them. They had always been loyal to the guardians, fighting bravely when called upon to do so. Their praises were sung in many ancient guardian ballads. When Jensen's parents had been murdered, along with the rest of his family, the guardians observed a period of mourning.

"Tell me about Coop," Jensen requested, drawing Electra's attention back to him.

"You've heard what little we know about him," she replied, noticing how the protector was avoiding looking at the picture in the spiral. She turned the page and flipped it over.

"I've heard the official story from Jet and I know they were looking into his possible connection with this Mark Waterson. Now I want the real story behind this guy," Jensen clarified.

Electra turned around, sitting on her sister's bed, running her fingers through her hair. "Coop was a man Isis met in a dance club in town. From what she told me, he was a nice guy, if a bit strange. She thought he might have survived some kind of trauma. Whether it was from his mannerisms or just a feeling she had, I don't know. I only met him briefly, when he was being held in the dungeons. He was … different. He was able to punch through guardian glass and didn't even damage his hand. Coop also showed signs of having superior speed, agility, and senses. The Four were researching old stories of the rebels about similar mysterious shape shifters. I really don't know how far they got."

Electra leaned back a little, studying the protector. Jensen had an expression of intense concentration on his face as he started pacing, rubbing his palms together. His brows knitted together and Electra could tell he was disturbed.

Electra tilted her head as she looked at Jensen. "Something wrong?"

Jensen shook his head. "This whole thing was set up."

"Pardon?"

"Jet was right," Jensen said as though to himself. "Everything is connected somehow, going back to Coop, maybe even further. Dammit! I didn't see it!"

"See what?" Electra got to her feet. "Jensen? See what?"

"That whole scene, it was too perfect," Jensen continued, still pacing about in front of her. "The cop cars, the ambulance, the two sisters Nero and I went out with the night before. This whole thing was a ploy to kill your sister. I know it sounds completely mad, but I know plots when I see them. Trust me."

Jensen adjusted one of his sleeves, checking the button to make sure it wasn't loose. His fine clothing was perfectly ironed and fit him like a glove. Gone was the disheveled grieving protector and in his place was the normal confident man.

"How does Coop factor into this?" Electra asked. She wasn't following his train of thought at all, but she was curious about it.

"I'm still trying to work that out." Jensen massaged the knuckles of his hand. "Maybe because of what he is or where he came from. Look, I woke up today and my apartment had been trashed. I think someone left those things in the hopes that I would pick up where Isis left off. There's a puzzle here and we only have a few of the pieces. We need to arrange them."

Electra stared at Jensen, her expression reflecting disbelief. She was disturbed by everything that had taken place, but there was one thing in particular that was bothering her.

"Jensen, why would they take her body?" she asked softly. Jensen stopped his pacing and looked back at her. She dropped her eyes to the floor, twisting her fingers.

"I don't know," he admitted.

Jensen seemed to be onto something and Electra would be damned if she let him go at it alone. Isis was her sister, and she wanted to avenge her.

"I need to find out what that symbol means," Jensen's quiet voice brought Electra out of her thoughts. "It's important. It has turned up in too many places not to be."

"I'll see if I can find anything in the Meadows library," Electra offered. She stood up and disappeared in a flash of bright silver light. Jensen looked to the bed. Without thinking about it, he grabbed the spiral and left the room.

~~*~*~*

Roan paced around his cell in an almost neurotic way, as he had been doing ever since Astrea told him of his daughter's demise. *Damn fool, I told him, I* told *him not to play this game with her life, but did he listen to me? No! If I ever see the bastard again, I'll throttle the life out of him,* he thought, fury coursing through his veins. Still, Roan knew he was to blame as much as his associate. He had agreed to go along with the plan — it seemed like their best bet at the time. Roan stopped pacing, looking up at the ceiling. This was just one more thing he'd have to live with for the rest of his days.

When he noticed movement out of the corner of his eye, Roan glanced to the side. There, leaning against the wall across from the glass, was an old acquaintance. She hadn't aged a day, which wasn't unusual among shape shifters. Her sleek black hair was still short, barely touching her elegant neck. Her intelligent green eyes were still expressive and bright, though not betraying a single emotion or feeling. She was the epitome of the term *femme fatale*, a woman as dangerous as she was beautiful. The mysterious Sly.

Jet stood next to her, stone-faced. He was wearing jeans and a long-sleeved shirt. Like Sly, he also hadn't aged a day. His hair was dark as ever and his blue-green eyes were still bright. He showed a few more signs of age than Sly and still looked as though he held the weight of the world on his shoulders.

Standing a few feet in front of Jet was the protector's lovely wife, Lilly. Her golden hair was done up in a messy bun rather than the usual braid and her dark blue eyes were red-rimmed from crying. Like Sly, her expression was unreadable, but there was a softness to her features. It gave her a very feminine appearance, common to most guardian women. The protectors had learned early on that underestimating Lilly was something they did at their own risk. She was a capable leader and had frequently proved it over the many years she ruled with Jet. Lilly stood framed in the sunlight that poured through the windows. Her long green dress glistened a little in the light.

"Roan." Sly nodded her head in greeting, drawing the assassin's attention back to her. He approached the glass, smirking.

"Of all the people I expected to see, *you* certainly weren't one," he stated. She mirrored his smirk as she looked up at him, raising an eyebrow.

"And why is that?"

"Because you've never been concerned with the affairs of other shape shifters, especially not the protectors," Roan replied, a thin smile dancing across his features. "You were one of the only shape shifters who never feared me, and that's why I've always respected you."

Sly leaned her shoulder against the glass, her eyes never leaving his. "Talk is cheap, Roan, and certainly not worth my valuable time. If you truly are here for some sort of redemption, tell me what you know about the people who were hunting Isis. We both know that you're keeping something close to your chest. It's time to show your hand."

Roan looked between the three on the other side of the glass. "I take it the High Council finally granted your request to see me. Guardians, always too little too late, right?"

Jet's eyes narrowed briefly. Like the rest of his family,

Jet had never liked the assassin, and after everything that had happened, the sentiment wasn't going to change in the foreseeable future. Lilly's expression remained neutral as she continued watching Roan.

"I can't tell you exactly who was hunting her, because even I'm not entirely sure," he began, pulling the chair in his cell up to the glass. "However, I can offer advice as to what your next move should be and why. I doubt you'll listen—"

"Roan, whatever little patience I had has long since expired," Jet warned. "No more riddles, tell us what you know."

Roan crossed his arms over his chest, looking over at Jet, unimpressed with the attempt at toughness. The dungeons were quiet and still around them.

"Can I finish now, or would you like to vaguely threaten me some more?" he asked coolly. Lilly's eyebrow raised a little and she crossed her arms over her chest.

"Boys, boys," Sly interrupted, raising both hands to prevent any further bickering. "We can drop our pants and compare sizes later. Right now, we have much more pressing matters at hand."

Roan sighed and sank down into the small chair in his cell, tilting it back. "If I do tell you what I know, there will be no going back."

"Go on," Lilly spoke without hesitation. Roan turned his eyes to her and then to Jet, nodding once.

"Very well, but don't say I didn't warn you," he responded, pausing before beginning his story. "As we all know, since the beginning of time there has been a struggle between good and evil, in a manner of speaking. It has been widely accepted that the difference between good and evil is one of choice and perspective, and to a certain extent, that's true. *But*, what if the origins of evil could be traced back to one source?"

"Impossible," Jet scoffed. "If that were true, the guardians would've seen it long ago. The amount of power required for that theory to be true would undoubtedly make an impact on the world, which the guardians keep in working order."

Roan glanced at Lilly and Sly. The other protector leader looked unsure and Sly appeared to be intrigued.

"Zealotry, racism, bigotry, intolerance, hatred, war," Roan listed as he turned his eyes back to Jet. "There has never been a guardian to watch over these things or keep them in check. They came from somewhere, Jet."

"We're imperfect people living in an imperfect world," the leader of the protectors was quick to reply.

Roan shook his head. "We had to have gotten them from somewhere. Everyone is capable of both good and evil and every shade of gray in between, but that's not the point. These intolerances, they have been planted in the minds of humans and shape shifters and all supernatural species alike by someone or something."

Jet opened his mouth to respond, but closed it again. He exchanged a look with his wife, who still seemed unsure. Sly glanced back to him before looking at Roan again.

"That's how this source would hide," he continued. "Through these mediums of evil, using simple human nature to conceal its presence. It's quite ingenious when you really think about it. Using fear and in turn hatred to hide, because when is there not intolerance in the world?"

"So what does this have to with what happened to Isis and why you're here?" Lilly asked.

Roan let out a bark of laughter. "Oh everything. When I was an assassin, I was employed by an organization known as the Grenich Corporation. On the outside, they mostly appeared to be a highly covert government laboratory doing research on tissue regeneration. Their purpose, or so they claimed, was to find a way to make skin heal itself quicker. You know, you get wounded and the tissue automatically removes the foreign body while also healing the damage. Very sci-fi, in my opinion. This purpose was only a miniscule part of what they were actually doing, as I would later find out."

Roan leaned forward, clasping his hands in his lap as he looked up to Sly and the Monroes. "What is the one thing almost everyone on the planet has craved since the beginning of time?"

"Power," Sly answered without hesitation.

Roan nodded. "And how does one normally go about trying to attain power?"

There was a momentary pause as Lilly and Jet exchanged a look. Lilly's brow furrowed and Jet held out a hand, shrugging. Sly bit the inside of her cheek and Roan knew she probably guessed what he was getting at. He stood up from the chair.

"Through war, survival of the fittest," he said, answering his own question. "It's a simple equation: the side with the better weapons, more resources, and usually greater numbers wins. That is what the Grenich Corporation is about. Making the fastest, smartest, deadliest weapon."

"Weapons manufacturing? I don't understand."

"They don't manufacture nuclear arms or missiles or even guns," Roan replied. "They make living, breathing weapons … through experimentation on shape shifters."

"Guardians have mercy," Lilly breathed in disbelief, her eyes widening a little. A similar look of horror crossed Jet's face.

"The rebels have stories," Sly began, putting her hands behind her back. She was doing an admirable job of keeping a neutral expression, but Roan could tell she was unnerved.

"Of strange shape shifters, called the glowing-eyes, I believe," Roan finished, then nodded. "Yes, those are modified shape shifters from Grenich. I know you've already met one, his name is Coop."

That made all three of them stare at the assassin. Jet stepped forward and opened his mouth as if to say something, a denial more likely than not, but closed it again when Lilly placed a hand on his arm. The former guardian turned her dark blue eyes back to Roan.

"They capture or buy some shape shifters. Others are bred inside their facilities," Roan continued. "They all end up the same: a living weapon, the likes of which the world has never seen before. They are perfect; faster and smarter than the average shape shifter, and more lethal than even the most dangerous assassin. Grenich has been experimenting since before humans even discovered what genetics were, before they had even mastered electricity. Each series of experiments has been better than the previous one."

Roan paused and let out a bitter laugh, shaking his head. "Torture for profit, sometimes it seems like the world runs on the practice. Anything to make the strong stronger and the rich richer."

"How is it possible that this goes on without anyone knowing about it?" Jet asked, his expression reflecting horrified disgust. Roan looked at him.

"Have you heard a word I've said?" he asked. "The Grenich Corporation has been doing this longer than any of us has been alive, probably longer than most current guardians have been around. It's their trade and they know it well. They know how to hide, even in plain sight.

"When I was a young up and coming assassin, I was approached by one of the higher-ups in the Corporation. He offered me a job: use fear, intimidation, and, if warranted, force to keep employees in line. If one got a bit too problematic, I was to … get rid of him or her. The pay was good, the powerful contacts valuable, so I accepted the offer," Roan replied. "Orion worked as a doctor in the Corporation, as did his wife. They became the heads of the medical department."

"Orion never would have worked for a place like the one you're describing," Jet stated vehemently. Roan couldn't help the grim smile that danced across his face.

Jet was right about that. His elder brother had been a loyal protector and dedicated his life to relieving suffering.

"You're right. Orion would never have knowingly caused pain, bleeding heart that he always was. He wouldn't have accepted the position if he knew what the Corporation was really doing. But you have to understand, Jet, this place makes cover-ups an art form. They know how to hide their true purpose and how to cover their tracks. Many of their lower level employees are convinced they're working for a bank. I'm sure a small bank has opened up in your town under the Corporation's name, right?"

Sly and Lilly exchanged a look. Jet scratched the back of his head, confirming what the assassin already knew. Roan nodded.

"Yeah, those tend to pop up every now and again, usually when there's something the Corporation needs in a town."

"Is that why you killed Orion? He found out what was going on?" Jet demanded. Roan looked at him and nodded once.

"When he and Cheryl, his wife, discovered what the Corporation was really doing, they began a resistance in the hopes of destroying it from the inside. My brother was always idealistic to the point of being hopelessly naïve." Roan shook his head. "The head of the Corporation found out and one of his right hand men, Carding, ordered me to eliminate both of them. So I did."

Jet closed his eyes and looked away from Roan, making the assassin raise an eyebrow. The protector leader was disgusted by how cavalierly the man spoke of murder, but protectors tended to be oblivious to the way the world worked. Roan's eyes traveled to Lilly, who was regarding him with something akin to puzzlement. He knew she was thinking about every word out of his mouth and it made Roan a little uneasy. He was a man of many secrets and Lilly was one of the very few who could probably catch any minor slip he made. It was a skill that made the former guardian a great leader and it was why Roan respected her.

"You still haven't explained what any of this has to do with your return or Coop or the Key," Lilly pointed out in her gentle voice. Sly was leaning against the glass wall of the cell, a half-smile playing on her lips. Jet was standing stiffly in the middle of the hall, his hands clasped behind his back. Roan rubbed the back of his neck as he stepped closer to the glass wall of his cell, resting a hand against it.

"Coop is an early prototype of a long abandoned series, which was called the Lock Series or L-series for short. He's an experiment, recruited from the outside as payment for a debt his grandfather owed to the Corporation. He escaped from a main laboratory in the first great escape. When I 'died,' I woke up in one of the Corporation's larger laboratories. I had no interest in becoming a lab rat or a corpse, as employees tend to do once they outlive their usefulness, so I did the only thing I could think of. I snuck into the power center of the place, flipped the switch that set off the alarms in the laboratory to signal evacuation and then opened the cages of the experimentations. Some of them escaped; most of them didn't. Coop was one of the few lucky ones. I slipped out in the chaos," Roan explained, closing his eyes and letting out a breath. He ran his hands over his face before opening his eyes and looking back at the three people in front of him. Jet still seemed skeptical, but Lilly and Sly appeared to be nervous.

"So what about the Key?" Sly asked. "How does that figure into all of this?"

"The head of the Corporation believes it is his destiny to find the true Key. He follows a prophecy that foretells of a key, which will give its wielder power over the guardians, shape shifters, and all the worlds, including Earth and the Meadows. The main purpose of the Corporation and the experimentations is to find this being, the one I told you about when I turned myself in. The flashdrive was created in the hopes that it would throw the protectors off the trail, keep them in the dark. He also needed Jet and Lilly to gather the Four, but he hoped they would remain oblivious to what the Key was. He obviously hadn't counted on me evading capture or turning myself in to the protectors and guardians.

"After Orion's death, I met Passion and decided to change my ways. Whether you believe it or not, I do love and care about her. I joined up with a small group who helped organize the first Grenich Resistance in the hopes we could destroy the Corporation, a goal that's looking less and less attainable. I came here and turned myself in, hoping that I could do some good as your informant. The more people who know about this, the less advantages the Corporation has. At least, that's what we hope."

"I still don't understand how humans can know this much and still keep it secret," Jet stated, skepticism clear in his voice. Roan went quiet and looked over at Sly.

"It's not run by humans, is it?" Lilly's soft question sounded more like a statement. Jet turned his attention to her. Roan shook his head, tapping his fingers on the glass.

"You're not going to believe what I tell you next," Roan began.

"You're assuming we believe most of what you've told us so far," Jet countered. Roan looked at him as he moved back over to the chair, folding his tall form into it. Long ago, he might have given a snarky retort. That time was long past and Roan was too tired to verbally spar with Jet. He leaned back in his chair, tilting it on two legs.

"I assume you got my message in the book, about the War of the Meadows?"

"Yes, we already know the story. Chaos attempted to take the Meadows and was vanquished," Lilly replied, moving over to Jet. "It is an important legend to both shape shifters and guardians; one we're told in our youth."

Roan leaned forward, the two legs of the chair resting back on the floor, pointing at them.

"Ah, there's an interesting word: vanquished. Much like

humans, shape shifters and guardians assume it has the same definition as 'killed.' It does not. Nowhere in the definition of vanquished is there a mention of death. Chaos did not die in the war. He and his lover, Pyra, slunk off with their tails between their legs. They went back to Earth and bided their time, building up power but keeping a low profile. Chaos eventually became the first necromancer and remains the most powerful."

"Do you honestly expect us to believe a guardian is behind this Grenich Corporation?" Jet asked, skepticism clear in his calm tone. Lilly wrapped an arm around his elbow, concern reflected in her expression. She believed the assassin, Roan could tell. Sly remained leaning against the glass, ever the silent observer. Roan leaned back in his chair.

"Oh, there's *nothing* guardian about him anymore. He's pure necromancer, through and through," Roan said, shaking his head. "He rules Grenich from afar, never getting his hands dirty. His revenants are in charge of running the Corporation — mindless servants that retain just enough humanity to pass as normal. He feeds on the pain and suffering churned out by that place, growing stronger every day. He will not be sated until the world is in a state of anarchy. He wants to wipe out the shape shifters and the guardians."

Roan leaned forward again, pressing his palms together as his eyes went to Sly. "When he became a necromancer, he left the name of Chaos behind. He chose the name Set."

"Guardians have mercy," Jet shook his head and rubbed the back of his neck. Sly glanced at the Monroes and then looked back to Roan.

"Set, as in the Egyptian god?" Lilly asked.

"The coincidence wasn't lost on me either. Set is cunning and no member of the resistance was ever able to figure out the identities of all his allies or even of all the aliases he uses. I tried and could get nowhere. When I found out what he was, I swore then and there that I would destroy him or die trying. That was the night I got in a fight with Draco and well, you know how that turned out."

Roan leaned forward, his green eyes becoming even more intense. "Passion asked me why I came back. That's why. I'm a man of my word. The Grenich Corporation needs to be destroyed and I will do anything to make sure that happens."

Roan leaned back in the chair again, watching the Monroes and Sly. Sly looked over at Jet, who continued watching Roan. Lilly crossed her arms over her chest again, biting her lower lip. Her expression reflected how disturbed she was by Roan's story.

"You have a rogue former guardian on your hands, the first necromancer. He's cunning and smart, as is his wife, Pyra, who still retains all the abilities she had as a fire guardian. This is something that has not been encountered for a very, very long time. Neither of you have ever gone toe-to-toe with a necromancer. Neither have I and I'd venture to guess not many current protectors have either. We're all out of our depth."

Jet was quiet for a moment before glancing at Lilly. Her lips were set in a tight straight line and she met Jet's eyes, raising her chin a little. Jet turned his eyes back to the assassin.

"Where's this Corporation located?" Jet asked, pinching the bridge of his nose.

Roan shook his head. "Grenich doesn't have just one location, it has multiple locations all over the globe. But you shouldn't try targeting their facilities, not yet anyway. There are more important matters you must attend to. Going gung-ho would be unwise. First, you need to complete the Four again. You'll need them for what's coming."

Jet glared at the man, opening his mouth to say something. Lilly placed a calming hand on his arm.

"That's impossible. Isis is dead. The Four is no longer—" Sly started.

"Orion had a daughter," Roan interrupted.

Sly and the Monroes stared at him with varying degrees of skepticism.

"Ace — she was raised by the rebels, according to my sources. My elder brother was always infuriatingly clever and wise when it came to friendships. I have tried finding Ace in the past, but Orion had some kind of agreement with them, because any rebel I spoke with became tight-lipped when it came to the subject of Orion's family."

"Maybe it was your winning personality and stellar reputation," Sly mentioned in a dry tone. "Assassins are welcome in rebel Lairs, but that doesn't mean the rebels are overly fond of you lot."

Roan smiled despite himself and turned his eyes back to the Monroes.

"I know it's probably not likely the protectors will have more success than I, but perhaps you can put aside whatever petty quarrels you have with the rebels. Because this is much more important than personal slights or disagreements. You find Ace and you complete the Four again," Roan explained. "Believe me. If you're going to tangle with Grenich, you are definitely going to need the Four."

Jet stepped up to the glass. "We'll look into your information. If it turns out to be factual, I want you to know that by withholding it, you have caused your own daughter's death. I'd mention the countless other shape shifters that we could have saved, but I highly doubt you have the empathy required to care about any of that."

Jet turned away from the cell and left without so much as a glance back. Lilly turned and followed her husband, soon disappearing from Roan's sight. Sly glanced at Roan one last time and he could tell she agreed with Jet's statement. Once they had left, Roan stood from his chair and walked toward his cot. He turned around at the last minute and kicked at the chair. It clattered against the glass wall, the bang echoing through the empty corridor. Roan sat on the cot and dropped his face to his hands, wondering if the plan had just gone completely to hell.

CHAPTER FOURTEEN

Steve woke up feeling a lot groggier than normal. The room was dark, but a little light fell through the drawn blinds. He frowned and glanced toward his bathroom where he could hear the shower running. *Tracy must be up already,* he thought. Steve groaned as he tried to sort out his foggy thoughts. He yawned and stretched out on the bed, cringing when he felt the frigid temperature on the other side of the bed. Steve briefly considered hopping in the shower with his lover and surprising her. He snickered as he opened his eyes and glanced over to the dresser, noticing her small silver cell phone sitting on the smooth surface. *Odd,* Steve thought as he ran a hand over his face. Tracy always kept her phone in her jacket pocket. He couldn't remember the last time he had seen it just laying out in the open.

They were supposed to have lunch with a couple of her friends over the weekend, but he couldn't remember their names. They would definitely be in her phone. She wouldn't mind if he just took a quick peek.

Steve got out of bed and retrieved his boxers, pulling them on as he moved toward the dresser. He glanced over toward the washroom door, which was opened a crack. Soft light spilled just outside the door and wafts of steam curled out from the room. The shower was still going; she probably wouldn't be out for a bit. Steve picked up the cell phone, shivering at the icy cold feel of it, and turned the device around a few times in his hand, his brown eyes studying it. He debated whether or not to open it. On the one hand, he didn't want to betray his girlfriend's trust. On the other hand, it was just to jog his memory and Tracy wouldn't mind such a small thing. It was just an instinct, but Steve always listened to his instincts. He was similar to Isis in that way. *Isis* …

~~*~*~*

Shae sat in a dark blue car in front of the house where her cousin had met her untimely demise. She sipped her coffee as she studied the house. There were a number of things wrong with the scene before her. There was no police tape and the house still looked abandoned. It was as if nothing had happened there.

Shae was startled by a knocking on the window. She groaned when the individual moved around the car, opened the passenger door, and sank into the seat.

"Dammit, Jade," Shae grumbled as she sipped her coffee again. Jade shut the door behind her and rubbed her hands together as she sat back in the seat, regarding Shae.

"You want to tell me what the hell you're doing out here?" she asked before blowing into her cold hands. Temperatures had been reaching record lows all week. It was predicted to continue on for a few days yet. Shape shifters had a higher cold tolerance than humans, but they still felt frigid temperatures.

"None of your damn business, that's what I'm doing," Shae replied as she put her coffee in the cupholder. Jade grabbed her arm in an iron-tight grasp and jerked her around so that she was facing her. Jade's dark brown eyes were blazing with fury and something else … grief?

"You're not the only one grieving, Shae," Jade warned, her tone causing a shiver to go down Shae's spine. She released the younger protector's arm after a moment, her eyes going back to the house. An uncomfortable silence fell over them for a few moments.

"If you start sneaking out, Jet and Lilly are going to be pissed," Jade muttered. "And they won't be the only ones."

"Uh huh, how did you convince Alex to cover your ass?" Shae inquired, already knowing their teammate would probably be the one offering their alibi. Poor girl. Shae reached toward the dashboard, cranking the heat up another few degrees. The frigid temperature was starting to seep into the car, even with the heat on.

"I didn't, she offered," Jade responded, noticing Shae's skeptical look. "We all grieve differently. Alex is keeping busy at the mansion and she didn't feel like running out to retrieve you. She never did care for cooler climes. I believe you're the only one who actually enjoys this sort of weather."

Shae looked back to the small suburban home outside her window. The cookie cutter houses and equally fake people who lived in them were just a bit too creepy for her tastes. It was all just neutral colors with the occasional bland child scribbling with equally bland chalk or making a snow fort. The streets were bare. A bad snowstorm had been forecast that day and everyone had locked themselves up in their warm and cozy homes. The wind was already starting to pick up and snow was beginning to fall. The windshield wipers would sweep across the glass in front of them every now and again.

"Where's the police tape?" Jade asked, squinting as she looked at the house.

Shae shrugged and shook her head. "I was wondering

the same when you came along. The longer I look at it the more I realize this scene doesn't make any sense."

Shae suddenly got out of the car, followed closely by Jade. Their boots crunched in the snow. Judging from the thick layer of snow, the sidewalks hadn't been shoveled yet. They started moving toward the house, stopped only by the sound of a door closing nearby. Shae's hand drifted toward the Beretta she had brought with her. Jade smacked her arm and shook her head, a look of exasperation on her face. The last thing they needed was an accidental shooting of an unarmed civilian.

An older man in a winter coat with matching hat and mittens started to make his way down the steps of his porch at the house next door. He noticed Shae and Jade standing in front of the neighboring house and waved at them.

"Can I help you ladies?" he asked in a friendly voice.

"Um, what happened to the people who lived here?" Jade asked as she approached the man. The man looked at her as if he didn't understand her question.

"Nobody's lived in that old place for a good twenty years," the man answered. "Of course, after what happened a few nights ago, I doubt anyone will live in it for another twenty."

"What happened?" Shae asked, curious about the man's version. A frigid wind whipped up their hair and knifed through their coats and boots.

"There was some kind of break in," he responded, scratching his head. "Or at least, that's what the police said happened, I think. It's rather fuzzy."

"Who called the police?" Jade asked, as Shae looked back at the house.

"Oh, um, nice girl who lives a couple blocks over. She heard something in the house while she was on her daily jog," the man said, squinting slightly. "It was odd though. I live right next door and I didn't hear a thing. The wife must be right. I'm going deaf as a post."

"Does this girl have a name?" Jade asked.

"Yes, ma'am. Her name is Tracy Reynolds. We saw her when we came out on the porch, after hearing the sirens. She was the one who told us about the break in," the man answered. Shae whipped around, her mouth dropping open. She pulled her phone out of her pocket and began scrolling through it. Jade glanced over at her, giving her a questioning look that Shae ignored. She had a bad feeling in the pit of her stomach. *Please don't let me be right,* she thought as she frantically moved her fingers.

"She's moving out, going back to live with her folks I think. At least, that's what she told us that night."

Shae clicked on a photo to enlarge it and thrust her phone at the man.

"Just out of curiosity, is that Tracy Reynolds?" Shae asked. Jade stared at her, obviously confused. The man removed thick glasses from his pocket and placed them on his nose, holding the phone further from his face. After a moment, the man nodded.

"Yeah," he confirmed, which made Shae's blood run cold. "Yeah, that's her. Pretty little thing, isn't she? Face of an angel, that one."

~~*~*~*

Steve opened Tracy's phone, glancing once more at the shower. The screen showed her contacts. He noticed Isis' number and swallowed the lump in his throat, running a hand through his hair. Steve could already feel tears burning his eyes and he blinked rapidly, swiping at his eyes with his free hand. His thumb slipped on the phone and he hit the text message symbol. Before he had a chance to close it, he noticed a text from Blackjack: *It's done.*

"What the fuck?" Steve whispered to himself.

"Ahem," a soft feminine voice came from the doorway. Steve jerked around, stunned to see a fully clothed and dry Tracy standing in the doorway. She had a powerful-looking pistol trained on him, complete with a specially made silencer. The blonde woman clicked her tongue and shook her head.

"Steven, darling, didn't mommy ever tell you that it's incredibly impolite to snoop through a lady's things?" she asked, a strange lilt to her words. "This makes me question whether I can trust you at all. I think we need to seriously consider counseling."

~~*~*~*

Jade thanked the old man and then chased after Shae, who dove back into the car. After the man had identified the woman on Shae's phone as Tracy Reynolds, Shae had made a beeline for the car, muttering every swear word there was.

"Shae, what's going on?" Jade asked as she got into the passenger seat. She barely had time to close the door before Shae floored the accelerator, spinning the car out of the parking spot. She tore down the street and Jade chose not to look at the speedometer.

"Tracy Reynolds — it's Steve's girlfriend," Shae explained, flipping on the turn signal.

"What? How did you come to that conclusion? Why did you even suspect that?"

"I remember she said she lived in this area, so I had a hunch," Shae answered, swerving around a turn. Shae could only pray they would get to Steve's place in time. She couldn't lose another friend.

~~*~*~*

"You killed her, didn't you?" Steve demanded, fury burning beneath his skin. Tracy smirked and shook her head once.

"Steven, what do you take me for? A common

assassin? No, nothing so crude. I merely arranged the pieces," Tracy replied. "Your little friend got herself killed."

"You won't get away with this," Steve warned, trying his best to sound threatening. It was difficult since he was unarmed and wearing nothing but his boxers. Tracy smiled even wider.

"Oh love, I already have," she stated with sympathy. Steve glanced toward the nightstand where he kept a knife. It wasn't much, but it was better than nothing.

"Don't even think about it!" Tracy warned sharply, causing Steve to jolt. "Keep your hands where I can see them and move into the bathroom."

Steve raised his hands. Getting himself killed wouldn't help matters. He had to tell Jet and Lilly about this woman, whoever or whatever she was.

Tracy laughed, a delicate tinkling sound. "By the time you tell the Monroes anything, I will be long gone. They will never be able to find me."

Steve's eyes widened. "You're a telepath."

Tracy nodded, running her tongue over her teeth. "That's just one of my abilities, love. One of the lesser ones, at that."

Suddenly, she ripped out another pistol from her other shoulder holster. The gun was identical to the one she already had on Steve.

"One more step and I color the wall with his brains!" she snapped. Steve knew she could easily do it. Probably didn't even have to look, judging by how steadily she held the gun. Steve watched her taut form, still not quite comprehending how he could've been so deceived. She kept looking out of the room, but the gun pointed at him never wavered. Steve found himself wondering if perhaps he could grab it …

"Acting rashly would be unwise, Steven. I'd be forced to kill our unexpected guest and then you," she growled at him, without looking in his direction. *Dammit,* Steve thought. She was a very skilled mind-reader from what he had witnessed so far. Telepathy was a gift usually only the guardians possessed, and not even many of them had it. Steve wasn't even sure if any of the current guardians possessed it.

"Come in here, very slowly, and keep your hands where I can see them," Tracy commanded, moving further into Steve's bedroom. "When you get into the room, put your hands against the wall. Try anything and I will kill him. Same goes for you, Steven."

Tracy backed further into the room, one gun still on Steve while the other pointed at the doorway. Soon, Shae stepped into the bedroom with her hands held up. She looked at Steve and closed her eyes for a moment, shaking her head.

"Goddammit, Steve," she mumbled. Steve spread his hands helplessly.

"Don't blame the poor boy," Tracy chimed in. "I'm irresistible, especially when I choose to be. Believe me, he didn't stand a chance."

Shae looked at Tracy, confused by the cryptic statement. Tracy gestured with her gun for Shae to turn around and put her hands on the wall, which she did. Steve let out a breath of relief. He had already lost one friend and couldn't handle losing another one so soon.

"She's a telepath, Shae," Steve muttered, rubbing his eyes.

"Great," Shae commented dryly, unable to keep the concern out of her green eyes as she looked over at Steve.

Tracy quickly but cautiously approached Shae. She put one of her firearms in its holster and frisked the protector, removing a gun and a throwing knife. She buried the throwing knife up to the hilt in the wall right next to Shae's face, causing the other woman to flinch. Tracy smiled again and stepped back.

"Honestly, you really are quite a pathetic species. How natural selection hasn't caught up with the lot of you, I will never know," Tracy commented. "Both of you, in the bathroom, now."

Steve entered the small washroom first, followed closely by Shae. They both noticed what looked like a small version of a caulking gun on the sink. They exchanged a look as Tracy reached into the room and retrieved it.

"Luckily for the two of you, I'm under strict orders not to kill either one of you unless absolutely necessary," she commented almost to herself. "But I cannot risk you following me."

She sprayed a translucent pink gel around the door frame, starting up at the top and going around the entire door. The gel stayed in place as if it were part of the door. Tracy put the small caulking gun in a holster at her waist. She smiled at them one last time and nodded once.

"Well kiddies, I'm afraid the time has come for me to bid you adieu. Don't worry. We'll meet again."

She closed the door. There was a strange foaming sound and suddenly, the door melted into the wall. Steve couldn't believe his eyes as he opened his mouth to say something but closed it again.

"What the fuck?" Shae shouted, slamming her hand against the wall where the door had been. "Are you kidding me!?"

She began to punch the wall, while Steve shut off the shower. The noise had been driving him crazy. The steam from the shower added humidity to the room that made it difficult to breathe. Sweat had already begun to bead on the two shape shifters trapped inside. Steve figured the situation didn't need to be any more unpleasant than it already was. Turning his attention back to where Shae was still beating the hell out of the door, Steve carefully reached out and gently grabbed her wrists.

"Hey, Shae. What good is breaking every bone in your hand going to do?" he asked, noticing that her knuckles had already split wide open.

"Don't even try that goddamn bullshit on me, Steve!" Shae snapped, turning back to the door. She punched the wall one last time, swearing at the pain it caused her split knuckles. Smears of blood decorated the wall as she withdrew her fist.

"The next time you decide to get laid when Justin is away, do me a gigantic favor and make sure he or she isn't a psycho," Shae snapped at her friend. Steve swallowed and looked at his feet for a moment. He knew she wasn't really angry at him, but he was the closest one to her. Shae needed to vent and he was willing to let her. Steve looked up at her, guilt swimming in the depths of his dark brown eyes.

"I'm sorry," he whispered. Shae scrubbed her hands over her face, glancing back at the wall and letting out a long breath.

"What the hell did she use?" Shae asked, examining where the door frame had once been. "What the hell even was she?"

"I don't know," Steve replied. "And . . . I don't know."

He approached the wall and ran his hand over it, not finding any trace of a door. Glancing to the side when Shae slumped against the wall and slid down to sit on the floor, Steve ran his hand over the smooth wall one last time. He moved to sit next to his friend, draping an arm around her shoulders. Shae leaned against him.

"Jade came with me," she mentioned and Steve nodded. At least that was something. They just had to wait for a bit.

"Steve?" Shae's voice trembled a little. Steve turned his attention back to her and Shae crossed her arms tightly over her chest, curling into a ball against her friend.

"I really miss her," Shae whispered, swiping at the tears that had begun to roll down her cheeks. Steve was quiet for a moment, sniffling a little.

"Me too," he agreed, feeling the ache deep in his chest.

~~*~*~*

Jade circled Steve's apartment building, looking for a sign from Shae. She closed her eyes when another gust of wind blew snow into her face. The protector was hoping there wasn't going to be a whiteout. The storm had grown steadily worse since they arrived at Steve's place and Jade wasn't a huge fan of driving in blizzards.

Jade was patrolling the outside of the building to ensure Tracy wouldn't be able to escape. Shae had insisted on this particular course of action. *If that bitch gets past me, kill her,* she had ordered Jade before going into the apartment. Jade glanced at her watch, the wind howling in her ears. The five minutes she had allowed Shae had just run out. That was it, something was wrong and it was time to go in.

Jade moved back to the front of the building just as an older, hunched over woman was exiting. She had a colorful floral scarf wrapped about her head, which fluttered wildly in the violent winds. Jade smiled politely and held the door open for the woman, then entered through the front door. She reached behind her back where a Beretta was tucked into her pants. As she made her way to the stairs, Jade scrubbed the snow out of her dark hair. She jogged up the stairs to the second floor, where Steve's apartment was. Hurrying down the hall, Jade pulled out the gun as she got close to his door.

When she reached his apartment, Jade pressed herself against the wall and reached out to knock on the door. As soon as her knuckles met the wood, the door swung open. Jade immediately pointed the gun in front of her, her eyes scanning the immediate area. Then she cautiously stepped inside the apartment and kicked the door shut behind her. She moved through the front room and then started creeping back to the bedroom.

Jade was debating whether or not to call out when she suddenly heard a strange thumping sound. She entered the small hall, which led to the bedroom. The room was dark, all the curtains had been drawn, but it was completely empty. There was a faint chill in the air and Jade shivered as it seeped into her flesh.

"Dammit! It can't be drywall. It's tougher than solid steel!" a muffled voice came from the wall. Jade turned in that direction, frowning in confusion. She recognized Steve's voice, though she was surprised to hear his frustration. In the short amount of time she had known him, Jade had never even heard him raise his voice. He was quiet and patient — which was why he had been assigned to Isis. Steve's quiet personality complimented Isis' fiery one.

"Steve?" she called out.

There was silence for a moment and then he shouted her name. "*Jade*!"

"Jade! Thank the guardians!" Shae's voice came shortly after.

"Shae? Where are you guys?"

"In the bathroom," Shae responded. "It's in the bedroom. Or it was."

"I'm in the bedroom and I don't see a bathroom. You're behind a wall?" Jade couldn't keep the confusion out of her voice as she ran her hands over the smooth wall. She couldn't find any trace of a door.

"Tracy did something to it. She made the door disappear somehow, with some kind of . . . pink gunk or something," Steve explained. Jade tilted her head as she continued to examine the smooth wall. The only thing she could think of that even resembled what Steve was explaining was alchemy. But that was impossible. Alchemy hadn't been practiced since the eighteenth century. Jade herself had never encountered alchemy. She had only read about it in shape shifter and guardian lore. What the hell was this woman? The afternoon sun filtered in through the drawn blinds, casting everything in shadows.

"Jade, please tell me you caught the bitch." Shae's sudden statement brought Jade out of her thoughts. She tucked the gun back in her pants.

"I didn't see her," Jade responded. There was quiet for a moment and Jade could practically hear Shae's ire rising. Jade was curious how Tracy managed to escape unnoticed. When she took the stairs, there had been no one in the elevators and when she reached the second story, none of the elevators had been called up.

"Jade, there's a chainsaw in the tool shed in the small garage around back. Think you could maybe saw a hole in the wall so we could get out?" Steve asked, exasperation clear in his tone.

"Yeah, give me a minute," Jade said, shaking her head as she moved out of the room and back down the stairs. Something strange was going on.

~~*~*~*

An hour and a half later, Shae and Steve were still in the bathroom. After the chainsaw failed to even make a dent in the wall, Jade had decided to call Jet and Lilly, who in turn told them to hold tight while they informed the guardians about the situation. The High Council wanted a sample of whatever Tracy had used, so they were sending Silver, the blacksmith of the guardian women. She made everything from the few weapons in the Meadows — which were mainly for decorative purposes — to the eating utensils and dishes.

"So, do you two want to play a game or something while we wait?" Jade asked. She sat near the wall that had once been a door. Jade had pulled up all the blinds, allowing the natural light to pierce through the shadows. The light also seemed to chase away the lingering cold in the room.

"Yeah, that's a great idea!" Shae said with gusto. Jade hadn't expected that response.

"It is?" she asked suspiciously. *Maybe she has finally lost her sanity,* Jade thought as she continued to play with her fingers.

"Yes, I love games," Shae continued eagerly. "I already know what I want to play. I'll start listing everything I'm going to use on that psychotic blonde demon when we find her and we'll laugh and laugh."

"The cramped quarters have robbed you of your sanity," Jade commented.

"I'm going to start with a chainsaw," Shae grumbled, a lot less eagerly. Jade closed her eyes and put her head against the wall behind her. She had a feeling Shae was going to be a handful. The older protector could already hear the dark desire for revenge under the anger and that was a road they couldn't afford to go down. They had lost too much already.

"Jade?" She heard Lilly's melodic voice out in the main part of the apartment.

"Finally," Jade muttered under her breath before calling out, "We're back here, in the bedroom."

Lilly soon entered the bedroom, followed closely by Artemis and Silver. Silver had a nymph-like appearance. She had brown eyes, long flowing silver hair, and slender limbs. The guardian blacksmith wore a short gray dress that was tattered and burned around the edges, though it still looked lovely. The guardian had tied her hair back in a messy bun and there were goggles on her forehead, which glistened in the light.

"Where was the door?" Silver asked. Her voice was high-pitched, but not annoyingly so. It was girlish in a way, though Silver herself was one of the oldest guardians in the Meadows.

Jade jerked her thumb toward the wall next to her. "Right there."

Silver put the goggles over her eyes and moved over to the wall, drawing a long broad sword from the sheath she wore around her waist. The steel glimmered in the light, casting dancing light patterns on the wall. The pommel was decorated with small stones from different gem guardians. Silver ran a hand over the wall, studying it. She shook her head after a minute, glancing back at Artemis and Lilly.

"This is ancient alchemy. I can barely see where the door was, even with these," she said, pointing at her goggles. "It's certainly not any kind that was practiced by humans or shape shifters."

"Can you cut through it?" Artemis asked, toying with a small silver charm she wore about her neck. Silver smiled and lifted her sword.

"This can cut through anything, ancient magic or not."

She turned her attention back to the wall.

"Everyone on the other side, stand back," she ordered. Jade took a few steps back, moving to stand with Lilly and Artemis. All three watched as the small guardian forced the sleek blade through the wall. Sparks shot out from where the sword met the wall. It took some effort, but Silver's weapon finally got through. Once it had, there was a strange crackling sound, almost like flames, and small orange sparks continued pouring out from where the sword and wall met. Silver pushed the weapon down and then withdrew it. The blade glowed and smoked as though it were white-hot. She continued to work on the area that had once been a door until she had finally cut an oval shape, large enough for Shae and Steve to step through. Steve blushed bright red when he saw Lilly, Silver, and Artemis and put his hands over himself as if he were completely nude. He quickly grabbed some sweatpants and yanked them on. Both Jade and Shae stared at him, amused at his attempt at modesty.

Artemis stepped forward to where Silver was examining the wall. They conversed quietly as they searched for any sign of the substance that Tracy had used to meld the door and wall together. After a moment, Silver shook her head and disappeared in a flash of silver light. Artemis turned and approached the others.

"Whatever it was, it somehow became part of the door

and wall," Artemis explained. "It could be alchemy, but it's not any sort I've ever seen before."

A heavy silence fell over the small group, each of them lost in their own thoughts.

~~*~*~*

Jensen sat at his kitchen table, examining the envelope and the two objects that had been in it. He was sipping expensive scotch from an old-fashioned glass, occasionally grimacing when the liquor hit his throat. The sound of glass being swept into a dustpan drew him briefly from his thoughts and he glanced to the side. Behind him, the Deverell brothers were cleaning up the apartment. Nero looked up from sweeping as Jensen turned back to observing the objects on the table.

"Seeing as how this is your place, the least you can do is help a little," he commented. Jensen made a noncommittal noise in response, which had become his trademark answer, and finished his scotch in one gulp. He wiped his mouth with the back of his hand and grabbed a pencil he had put on the table earlier, lightly shading the envelope. Nero approached and dumped a dustpan full of glass into the garbage, making a racket. Jensen's attention remained focused on the envelope in front of him. His hand moved swiftly as he shaded over the paper.

A week had passed since Isis had died. No questions had been answered, no body had been recovered, and grief still hung heavy in the air. Ajax had gone to check on Jensen that morning and found him at the table in the apartment, studying three objects laid out in front of him. His apartment was still in shambles. Jensen was normally insistent on cleanliness, but he had other things on his mind. Ajax, being a neat freak, ordered his brothers to help him clean up Jensen's place.

Jensen didn't notice them when they dropped by. His attention was focused solely on the objects, which he knew were important. He had become obsessively relentless in his study of them. He barely ate or drank, and it showed. His already lean physique had begun to slim down to the point where he looked sick.

"What are you looking for?" Nero asked. Jensen gave him a look that clearly told Nero to back off and leave him alone. Nero had been on the receiving end of that look before — he hadn't cared then and he didn't care now. Jensen twisted in his seat, looking up at his friend.

"You're not the slightest bit curious about this Grenich Corporation Roan talked about?" Jensen asked. "You don't care about this Coop guy and his possible connection to Isis?"

"I do care," Nero argued. "But I'm also taking the time to grieve. Take a couple days off, okay?"

Jensen shook his head and turned back to the envelope. "I will … after I get answers or a good lead. Or at least when I'm sure I'm on the right path — Hello."

He got up and moved over into the kitchen, holding the envelope to the light. When he stared at the sketch, Jensen felt ill. He had a feeling that was what he would find.

There was the impression of a symbol, nearly invisible, on the envelope. The same symbol Isis had drawn in her spiral. The same symbol that had burned in the wall of his home, all those years ago. The same symbol that was on the back of the business card.

"What are you?" Jensen asked under his breath. He had to find out the importance of the symbol. He knew it would lead him to the people responsible for Isis' death. Jensen just had to figure out where to start looking.

CHAPTER FIFTEEN

Sunrise bathed the mansion in a healthy warm glow. The frost on the ground glistened like diamonds. There were no signs of spring in the forecast, but that wasn't surprising. All the occupants of the mansion were asleep — there wasn't much to do during the early hours of the morning. One shape shifter, however, was awake and he stood in the garage.

Jensen pulled into the garage an hour after the sun rose. In the back of his Jaguar, two dark green duffle bags sat on the seat. He turned off the ignition and got out of the car. He was dressed in his normal fine clothing: jacket, vest, shirt, and trousers with a nice pair of shoes. He made his way down the row of cars and hurried into the mansion, bouncing his keys in his hand. Jensen strode down the silent halls, toward the Monroes' study. He didn't have to worry about any confrontations, as he was sure everyone was still asleep.

On the way to the study, Jensen pocketed his car keys and paused in front of a particular tapestry. Selene in battle, the stunning guardian of night whose bravery was unsurpassed. Jensen gazed up at her, memories of Isis causing his eyes to well. Gently laying a hand on the soft fabric, the protector said a silent prayer to the guardian: *Selene, please help me in my search for answers and justice.* It was a bedtime story shape shifter parents told their children: the spirit of Selene would always watch over them, especially if they were ever afraid. Being orphaned at a fairly early age in a traumatic event, Jensen didn't remember his parents telling him the story. It had been Orion who had told Jensen the legend, shortly before he had been murdered. The story had always stuck with Jensen, especially in his darkest hours.

The protector dropped his hand and continued on his way, feeling a small amount of inner peace for the first time in a long while. Once he reached the study, Jensen withdrew a business-sized envelope from the inner pocket of his jacket and laid it on the large desk where he knew the Monroes would see it. Tapping it once with his finger, Jensen thought about Jet and Lilly. They had saved him and his sister, taken them in when they had nowhere to go, protected them and made them part of their family. Jensen owed them a great debt, one he could never repay. He knew they would understand why he had to leave. Hopefully whatever answers he managed to find could help them as well.

Jensen hurried out of the room and jogged to the main stairway, leaping up two stairs at a time. Navigating the halls he knew like the back of his hand, Jensen reached the door he was heading for and took a deep breath before knocking softly. When he received no answer, Jensen pressed down on the handle and entered the room. The curtains were drawn and everything was bathed in thin shadows, including the figure curled up on the bed, her back to the door. She was wearing a silky raspberry sorbet-colored nightgown. Her messy auburn hair haloed about her head and her slender limbs were held tightly against her body.

Jensen approached the bed, hoping to be in and out of the room before she woke up. He laid a small note on the nightstand, just under the lamp, so she would see it. Turning, he started to make his way back to the open door, his footsteps silent.

"Jensen?" asked a groggy voice, thick with sleep. Jensen grimaced, mentally swearing. He turned to the woman in the bed who had twisted around partway to look over her shoulder. She uncurled herself to sit up on the bed, running a hand through her messy hair.

"Shae, I'm sorry, I didn't mean to wake you," he apologized. She rubbed her eyes, shaking her head with a dismissive wave of her hand. Judging from how red and puffy her eyes were, she had been crying.

"You didn't," she lied, stretching her arms above her head. "What's up?"

"Go back to sleep. It's nothing that can't wait till morning," Jensen replied. Shae looked him up and down, squinting as she scrutinized him.

"You're leaving, aren't you?" she asked. Jensen's shoulders slumped a little and he approached the bed again, sitting lightly on the edge. He tapped his fingertips together as he considered his words.

"Shae, I was a thief for a short time before the Deverells and Monroes brought me to the mansion. I had to be in order for Nat and me to survive. I gave it up when Jet and Lilly were able to smuggle us out of Europe, but I still have connections. I have channels I can go through to get answers, but most of them are quite shady. I can do better on my—"

"You really liked her, didn't you?" Shae asked bluntly, smiling a little when Jensen looked over at her. "I see it in your eyes, just like I saw it in hers."

Jensen went quiet for a moment. "Those responsible, they're not going to get away with what they did. I don't care if I have to hunt them to the ends of the Earth. I will find them and they will answer for what they did."

Shae studied his face, nodding once. "I know. Good luck."

Jensen stood up. "It's all in the note. I'll call when I have a chance. And I'll keep you updated on whatever I find."

He made his way to the open door and shut it behind him, leaving Shae to her sleep.

Jensen next made his way to the kitchen. He grabbed a paper bag from under one of the sinks and moved over to the pantry. He borrowed some food, already falling back into his thief habits. Moving over to the fridge, Jensen opened the door and grabbed a couple bottles of water, then left the kitchen. It was eerie how still the mansion was in the early morning hours, but it made things quite a bit easier.

Jensen picked up his pace as he headed toward the garage again.

"Leaving so soon, Jensen?"

"Guardians have mercy!" Jensen jumped, so badly startled that he almost dropped the bag. Remington was stretched out on the couch in the front room, reading a book. Shakespeare, Jensen could see on the spine. The ancient trainer's position gave him a perfect view of the garage door and Jensen was certain the trainer had seen him enter. Remington cocked a dark eyebrow as he marked his place with his index finger and looked over to Jensen, waiting for an explanation.

"Dammit, Remington. You scared the living hell out of me," Jensen breathed, leaning back against the nearest wall. He dropped his head back with a thump, still staring at the trainer. The lamp next to the couch was on, bathing the room in a brighter glow than the winter sun could.

"My apologies," Remington replied in his soft voice. Jensen wondered if Remington ever slept. He was sure he did … most likely hanging upside down from a beam in the attic.

"I left a note," Jensen protested. Remington nodded and turned his attention back to his book.

"You're a grown man, free to come and go as you like,"

he replied, his attention never moving from the book. "I hope you find what you're looking for."

Jensen nodded. "Me too."

He turned and opened the door that led into the garage. The hinges in the mansion never squeaked, something Jensen had always marveled at. He was glad his short trek through the garage was uninterrupted. Shivering at the winter chill that invaded the large space, Jensen fished his keys out of his pocket and opened the trunk, laying the bag inside. He didn't anticipate getting hungry for quite some time and decided food in the front seat would just be a distraction. Slamming the trunk closed, Jensen began to make his way to the front of the car again when he thought he saw a ghost to his left, making him freeze in his tracks.

Electra was dressed casually, in jeans and a nice purple blouse. She had a plain gray bag slung over her left shoulder. Her soft brown hair was pulled back, held in place by a sparkling green hair tie. She looked so much like her sister that it was almost painful.

Jensen gave her a questioning look. "Does your mother know you're here?"

She shrugged. "Thought you could use some help."

"Well, I don't," Jensen replied flatly as he made his way to the driver's side. Electra approached him, blocking the door with her slender body, pinning him with her bright green eyes. She opened her mouth to say something, closed it again, and looked down for a moment. Jensen waited for her to speak, though he was anxious to get moving.

"Jensen, she was my sister, my twin. I had just found her," Electra said, pausing. "Please. I can't stay up in the Meadows doing nothing. I just . . . I can't."

Jensen hesitated, studying her. She must have had to swallow an enormous amount of pride to approach him. He knew he wasn't her favorite person. And she had just as much right to get answers as he did. Besides, knowing

Electra, she would find some way to follow him. Based on what Jet and Lilly had told him, once the young guardian had set her mind on a task, it was nearly impossible to dissuade her from accomplishing it.

"You do realize how much trouble you're going to be in?" Jensen asked, leaning against the car next to her. "Electra, I'm going to be doing some dodgy things that aren't exactly in the protector's code. I'm going to be a thief on this search. You understand what that means?"

Electra rolled her eyes, resting her hip against the Jaguar. "I am Passion's daughter. I know a thing or two about bending rules … and outright breaking them if the situation calls for it."

Jensen stared at her for another moment, and then with a resigned sigh he grabbed her bag. He nearly stumbled from the weight. *Guardians have mercy, what the hell is she packing? Bricks?* Jensen couldn't help but wonder as he shoved her bag next to his in the back seat of the Jaguar.

"Hop in," he muttered. "I'm driving."

Electra strode around the car and opened the passenger's door, sinking into the dark interior of the car. She buckled her seatbelt and then stared ahead. Jensen did the same on the driver's side. They were both silent as he drove out of the garage. It was one of the first times the silence was comfortable between the two. They were both lost in grief, but somehow being with someone who felt the same made it more bearable.

The Jaguar drove quickly down the long, winding driveway until they reached the large gate at the end of the mansion's property. Jensen briefly put the car in park and got out, his nice shoes crunching in the snow. He didn't notice the frigid cold or the bitter winds on his trek to the security box. Opening the cover, Jensen placed his hand on the scanner and waited patiently as the light went from blue to green before the gate swung open. He returned to the car, sinking back in the driver's seat and drove through the opened gate, glancing in the rearview mirror to make sure the gate swung shut and locked behind them.

Jensen kept his eyes forward on the winding hidden path before them, forcing himself not to look back. The mansion had always felt like home to him and leaving it pained him. He pressed on the brakes when they were halfway through the hidden path. Electra glanced over at him, her expression reflecting puzzlement. Jensen tightly gripped the steering wheel, watching his breath fog in front of him. After a moment, his hands relaxed on the wheel and he turned his eyes to the young guardian.

"Ready?" Jensen asked and Electra nodded. He shifted into drive and the Jaguar drove out of the hidden path and onto the street, disappearing around a corner.

~~*~*~*

Later that morning, Jet and Lilly entered the study. Jet rubbed the lingering sleep from his stinging eyes. He hadn't been able to get much sleep and now he had a long day ahead of him, one he was not looking forward to. Thankfully, he had Lilly by his side to help share the heavy burden of leadership. Sly was also at the mansion working with them, which took some of the burden off their shoulders. She was still being a pain in the ass, insisting on doing things her way and critiquing everything they did or had done up to that point.

"Jet." Lilly picked up an envelope from his desk.

"What's that?" he asked, frowning as he sank into the chair behind the desk.

"I don't know. That's Jensen's handwriting, isn't it?" Lilly replied, studying the envelope. Jet nodded, recognizing Jensen's flawless handwriting across the front in neat script letters. Jensen had always had immaculate penmanship, likely taught to him by his late mother, who had been an accomplished author. Jet groaned as he thought of all the possible things that envelope could contain. Lilly lifted a letter opener from the desk and slid the sharp edge through the top.

"What has that damn reckless Aldridge done now?" Jet grumbled, his mood sour from lack of sleep. Lilly raised an eyebrow at him, smiling and clicking her tongue in a playful manner, before turning her attention back to the envelope she held. Jet smiled despite himself, reaching out and running his hand over Lilly's knee. Even in the most trying of times, the two leaders could always get a smile out of each other.

"Oh dear," Lilly said as her eyes traveled over the letter.

"What?" Jet asked and Lilly handed him the letter, which he took and read.

Dear Jet and Lilly,

You and the Deverells are the closest people I have to family, so I felt I needed to inform you of my leaving. By the time you read this, I'll be gone. I've gone off to get answers, which we all need. I will be using my own channels, which you won't want to be a part of. Please tell the Deverells not to worry about me.

I don't know when, or if, I'll be back. I'll let you know if I find anything useful.

Sincerely,
Jensen

Jet tossed the paper to the desk and rested his elbows on the surface, running his hands over his face. Lilly glanced at the paper before standing from where she sat on the desk and moving to sit on the arm of the chair. After a moment, she laid her head atop her husband's.

"I worry about him too, my darling. But he will return," she reassured him. "Jensen is grieving now, as we all are, but eventually the grief will not be as great."

"The last Aldridge and the only shape shifter guardian hybrid on Earth," Jet let out a soft laugh as he intertwined his fingers with his wife's. "One of the stranger pairings we've seen."

They sat in silence, finding comfort in the nearness of one another. Jet stared at the bookshelves, becoming lost in thought. *Well Jensen, I hope you find what you're looking for. For all our sakes,* Jet thought.

~~*~*~*

Alpha watched the doctor pack up the few belongings he had in his small living space. The temperature was still quite cold in the room, but they both ignored it. He secured the latch on his last bag and looked over at her.

"It's morning. No one will see you slip out," Alpha answered the question she read in his eyes, dropping her hands so she could hook her thumbs in the pockets of her tight black jeans. "No one who doesn't already know you're here, anyway."

"Thank you," the doctor said, retrieving his hat from the empty desk. He put it on his head and buttoned up his long coat. Alpha considered asking him where he was going, but decided against it. He wouldn't tell her and she didn't really care. She ran a hand through her messy black hair.

"Jet will probably contact you about finding a rebel by the name of Ace. You should help him," the doctor said.

"I've met Ace before," Alpha replied, nodding. She looked around the empty room. She didn't know how he was able to stand being in such a dark cramped space. Alpha tended to prefer the night, but even she needed the natural light of the sun at times. There were no windows in the room and the doctor only used a single lamp for light. It gave the entire space a gloomy atmosphere, which seemed to suit him. The doctor was pulling on his gloves, preparing to leave.

"It's all gone wrong, hasn't it?" Alpha asked softly after a moment. The doctor sighed and nodded once.

"Yes, I'm afraid it has," he answered, pausing. "Alpha . . . I don't think I can fix it this time. And if what's coming is what I suspect, I fear for us all."

"So what should I do? What should the rebels do?"

The doctor slung a bag over his left shoulder and lifted the two small suitcases that contained most of his worldly possessions.

"If things get really bad, and you'll know if they do, get out. You gather your people and get as far away from civilization and society as you can," he answered without hesitation. Alpha stared at him, lifting her chin defiantly.

"Rebels never run," she reminded him. An expression of sadness crossed his normally grim face and he nodded.

"Then the only thing you or any of us can do is hope," the doctor responded. "Hope for some kind of miracle, because barring that, I don't see how we can possibly win this fight."

He gave her a thin smile and then strode to the door, opening it and disappearing down the hallway. Alpha turned her head slightly, listening to his footsteps fade as he got further down the hall. The rebel leader looked around the empty room once more before turning to leave. She reached out and switched the light off as she left.

~~*~*~*

"It took us a year to break 7-299. Strong-willed that one was, though women are usually harder to break. We don't know exactly why."

Set stood in front of a large window, gazing down at five large human men. They held powerful looking semi-automatic weapons. They were surrounded on all sides by brush. They stood back-to-back in a tight circle, a decent strategy.

"As you requested, we've kept her participation in simulations to a minimum. But I knew you wanted to check on her progress, so I had this arranged."

In the observation room above, a scientist in a white

lab coat stood beside Set. The scientist was humanoid in appearance, except for his gray iridescent skin. Set was dressed in a tailored caramel-colored suit. He was wearing his more youthful appearance, with dark hair and darker eyes. Set was on the shorter side, which surprised the people he interacted with. Even when he had been a guardian, he had been one of the shortest people in the Meadows. He held one hand in a fist beneath his chin, occasionally moving his fingers in a methodical motion.

"It's going to take at least another year and a half to train her fully, preferably two if you want to unlock her full potential," the scientist continued, noisily turning a page on his clipboard. A tree rustled in the pseudo-forest below them and one of the men responded with a barrage of bullets, causing Set to roll his eyes. *Humans, so predictable,* he thought with a shake of his head.

There was a sudden blur of motion and blood splattered across the window. The scientist jumped back with a small yelp, but Set merely smiled. He was very pleased at what he saw. Very pleased indeed.

"What is she using?" he asked, watching as the other men tried to tighten the circle. A few shots took out two more. She had grabbed the first victim's weapon. A barrage of bullets hit the bushes where the shots had come from.

"A bladed weapon," the scientist answered. "A combat knife, I believe."

Set leaned forward, watching as she attacked the final two. They had unwisely used up their bullets shooting at shadows. A slender form jumped out of the bushes behind them, stabbing one in the back of the neck and severing his spinal cord. She then leapt at the other one, tackling him to the ground and stabbing him repeatedly.

"When will we know which of the three is the Key?" Set asked softly. He was very quiet by nature, only speaking when absolutely necessary. Even when he did speak, it was rarely above a whisper. Yet he always spoke with conviction and confidence, which reminded the few individuals he spoke with of his power. He was always in control.

"Ah, Carding has us working around the clock on that. It could be some time though, possibly four or five years if you want to be sure," the scientist answered. Set clasped his hands behind his back, taking a step closer to the glass and peering down through the blood. There she stood. Even coated in blood, she was stunning. The perfect killing machine. She looked up at him, her green eyes unnaturally luminescent. She stood at attention, splattered with blood and viscera. Her dark hair was extremely short to ensure no enemy could grab it in battle. Her body was sleek for maximum speed and agility. None would expect the strength contained in that wiry frame. *The guardians will never see her coming,* Set thought, his smile growing.

"I am patient. Take all the time you need," he told the scientist. "Give me daily updates about her progress and the progress of the other two as well. And make sure she knows how to kill cleanly. Can't have her going on a bloody rampage just yet."

"It's always the women," the scientist mentioned, shaking his head. "They're so brutal and aggressive. I don't know why."

"It's because they're constantly underestimated. Makes people assume they can be taken advantage of," Set responded before turning and making his way out of the viewing deck. He made his way down the long flight of metal stairs to the main hall. A woman in a red dress and heels waited for him at the bottom of the stairs. She had curly blonde hair and light brown eyes. Her nails and lips were painted the same shade of fiery red as her dress. A ball of golden flame floated just above her hand. When she saw him coming, she clenched her hand in a fist and the flame extinguished with just a trace of smoke.

"Pyra, my love, you missed quite a show," Set mentioned.

"It went well then?" she asked, following him as he made his way down the hall.

"Oh yes. She's a perfect killing machine. Perhaps our best weapon to date."

"Is she the Key?"

"Possibly."

"Then what are we waiting for? Let's take the Meadows and be done with it."

"Patience, my darling. She's not fully trained yet and neither is 7-295," Set responded firmly. "And I suspect that 7-082 is sneaking out again. I still need to make contact with the wereanimals and there are a few demon clans that have yet to respond to my calls."

"We have thousands—"

"Hundreds, dear. Please don't be overdramatic."

"Fine. We have *hundreds* of perfect weapons at our disposal, we'll definitely surpass a thousand by year's end. We should strike now while the protectors are still grieving. They're vulnerable."

"I don't care whether or not they're vulnerable. I want them to see how futile it is to fight against me. I want them to feel every last moment of slaughter when it finally comes. I want to see the fear in their eyes as their blood is spilled," Set stated, chuckling at the thought. "I want to have *fun*. And that's exactly what this is going to be."

"You'll never win when they're at full strength."

"Have you forgotten the prophecy? The one who wields the Key shall destroy all who stand against him. They will scream in anguish as they are cut down and strewn at his feet. To wield the Key is to be invincible. The guardians and their protectors have already lost the war. They just don't realize it yet."

"So what are we supposed to do in the meantime?" the woman asked, creating another fireball over her hand.

"We keep growing our army, keep them fighting fit. Send them out regularly to hone their skills, allowing them to do what they do best: kill. We will use them to start picking off the shape shifters. Not enough to raise attention, just enough to start a few rumors. We're also going to start targeting the other supernatural races who might ally with the protectors and guardians," he said, turning to look through another window. "Any demon that doesn't bend a knee, we're going to wipe out."

Pyra also turned to look through the window, clenching her fist and extinguishing the golden ball of flame. She watched as 7-299 was brought into the shower room and sprayed down. The woman didn't even flinch when hit with a powerful jet of water, tan uniform and all. Blood colored the water that rolled off her. The fire guardian smiled. The 7-series did look promising, the perfect monster.

"Once we have confirmed which one is the Key, then we take our legions and we wipe out the protectors first. After we have conquered the Earth, the Meadows will easily fall. I will take the Key, destroy the guardians, and then I shall reign with you as my queen. Our thrones shall be made from the bones of our enemies and we shall drink their blood with our victory feast."

The woman shivered in pleasure, smiling as she looked over at Set. A smile grew on his face and he offered his elbow.

"Now, let's get out of this dreary place. It's time to make a little chaos."

She wrapped her arm around his elbow and they strode out of the sterile white halls.

To Be Continued…

ACKNOWLEDGMENTS

Thank you so much to my friends and family, who are continually supportive of me. Thank you to my parents for their endless patience, love, and support. Thank you to my brother, Michael, and Mom for being great proofreaders. Thank you to my amazing godmother, Leandra Torres (Aunt Punkey), a woman who I very much admire and who is always there with an encouraging word.

Thank you to my amazing editor, Rose Anne Roper. Thank you to my cover artist, Najla Qamber. Thank you to my always awesome beta reader, Taia Hartman.

Thank you so much to Crimson Fox/Snowy Wings Publishing for helping me achieve a dream and providing support, as well as helping immensely with marketing. I must give a very special thank you to my good friend, Lyssa Chiavari, who invited me to join Snowy Wings and for being one of the absolute best people in the world. It is truly an honor to know you and call you a friend.

Thank you so much to all the wonderful professors in my life, who have taught me and continue to teach me to this day. Thank you so much, Alex and Jess Hall for your continued knowledge of all things concerning mythology. It is an honor to know you both. Thank you, Marco Benassi and Alexander Bolyanatz, for never giving up on me and providing advice when needed. Thank you Ángela Rebellón (the best ASL teacher there is). Thank you to all the professors and teachers who I've thanked in previous novels. If you enjoyed this novel, it is thanks to them. Any success I've experienced is thanks in large part to the dedicated professors and teachers I've had the privilege to learn from.

Thank you so much to all the incredible asexual artists who I have met through Asexual Artists. Thank you to my dear friends, Joel Cornah, Darcie Little Badger, and T. Hueston. You put such beautiful art into the world and it inspires me so very much. I love you all.

Thank you so much to my family and friends for providing me with the support I need to continue on the rocky path that is writing. Thank you, Billy Payne, for coming to my first reading and making the experience a lot less terrifying. Thank you Robyn Byrd, Emily Kittell-Queller (extra special thanks to you and your housemates for being a safe haven on the holidays), Julie Denninger-Greensly, Ryan Prior, Leigh Hellman, and anyone else who I'm forgetting (and will undoubtedly feel just awful about later). Your love, kind words, encouragement, and support make a world of difference in my life.

A special thank you to Becca (who gave me the most wonderful compliment a writer can ever hope to hear) and Susan Sandahl, who continue to be active on my author page and are some of the most awesome people I've ever had the pleasure of meeting. You're both my favorite readers and I apologize for the ridiculously long wait.

Again, I must thank all my readers. Thank you for your kind words and gestures. Thank you for getting lost in the crazy world I created. Thank you for continuing to be so generous with your time. I cannot begin to express my gratitude to you all. You continue to humble me and I hope this book lived up to your expectations. Thank you all, so very, very much.

ABOUT THE AUTHOR

Lauren Jankowski, an openly aromantic asexual feminist activist and author from Illinois, has been an avid reader and a genre feminist for most of her life. She holds a degree in Women and Genders Studies from Beloit College. In 2015, she founded "Asexual Artists," a Tumblr and WordPress site dedicated to highlighting the contributions of asexual identifying individuals to the arts.

She has been writing fiction since high school, when she noticed a lack of strong women in the popular genre books. When she's not writing or researching, she enjoys reading (particularly anything relating to ancient myths) or playing with her pets. She participates in activism for asexual visibility and feminist causes. She hopes to bring more strong heroines to literature, including badass asexual women.

Her ongoing fantasy series is *The Shape Shifter Chronicles*, which is published through Crimson Fox Publishing.